WHERE TIME IS ROUND AND RAVENS RIDE THE WIND

A Novel

Margret Berendes

AmErica House
Baltimore

First printing

ISBN: 1-58851-076-X
PUBLISHED BY AMERICA HOUSE BOOK PUBLISHERS
www.publishamerica.com
Baltimore

Printed in the United States of America

For Cecilia

Acknowledgements

For three years I lived in the bush of Western Alaska and the intensity and contrast of my experiences affected me deeply. My exposure to the warmth of the Yup'ik people, their efficiency and sense of humor, but also their immense suffering, touched me and will never be forgotten. It was a time of compassion and adventure, set in an archaic landscape of stark beauty.

In writing this book I followed my heartfelt desire to create against this authentic background a fictional story that would capture the emotions of the Yup'ik Eskimos and myself during this time of great tragedy, when eight young natives of the same village took their lives. I owe thanks to many people who helped me in this endeavor.

Bruce Merrell, Alaska Bibliographer of the Z.J. Loussac Public Library, Anchorage, and Deree Brand of the Wilkinson Public Library of Telluride, CO. were untiring in their efforts to get any book I needed for my research and were always available for advice. My thanks also to the entire staff of the Wilkinson library. Steven A. Jacobson, Asst. Prof. of Yup'ik, and Eliza Orr of the Alaska Native Language Center at the Univ. of Alaska in Fairbanks, assisted me with translations of the Yup'ik language. CPT Mike Haller of Fort Richardson, Alaska, provided me with information regarding the participation of Yup'ik Eskimo in the Air force in WWII. Mary Ellen Baker was knowledgeable with the details of the city of Anchorage. Christoph Berendes offered help as a consultant at any time. Dagmar and Peter Schroeder in Washington, D.C.and Mary Burns in Missoula read the early manuscript with constructive critique. In Telluride I further have to thank Sid Pope and Al Lewis for their expert knowledge as pilots and Kevin Hurtley, who helped me deal with the idiosyncrasies of my computer. Last but not least, my gratitude to Laura Zuckermann for her labor of love to thoroughly go over the whole manuscript For the interesting photograph on the cover of the book I am indebted to Jerrie Uelsmann in Gainesville, Florida. Special thanks to an anonymous poet for two lines of a poem which I rearranged and used.

December 24, 1981

The single turbo prop Cessna Caravan was ready to take off from the short runway of St. Mary's, an Eskimo village in the Delta on the Bering Sea. A Yup'ik Eskimo man, his young son and a woman physician were the only passengers returning to Bethel on the Kuskokwim River, the only town in the bush of western Alaska. A fierce winter storm had raged the night before and the tundra was heavily covered with new snow on this day before Christmas.

The young bush pilot had only recently started to fly the Super Caravan, a plane ideally suited for landing on the tundra, that accommodated twelve rather than six passengers. A few days ago, for the first time in her career, she had caused a minor accident while landing on the narrow tundra airstrip of Napakiak. She hadn't let the gears down in time and badly scraped the lower surface of the plane. This morning, after a serious disagreement with her husband, a bush pilot as well, she found herself in an irritable mood.

Before take off she mechanically checked all the flight instruments but her mind was still entangled in the screaming match with her husband at breakfast. Taxiing into the wind, the plane roared forward and the wheels lifted off the ground. When she raised the flaps she checked the fuel selector and was gripped by panic: the fuel selector was in the off position. With only the fuel lines filled, the plane suffered fuel starvation. Rather than gliding down to a landing dead stick without power, she hastily opened the valve and frantically jerked the stick back. A short, steep climb and the engine died. The plane abruptly nose dived and crashed on the tundra several miles away from the village. The emergency locator transmitter did not go off and nobody saw the plane come down.

Two hours later, when the wreckage was discovered, the severely injured man, his son and the woman pilot miraculously were still alive; the physician seemed to have been killed immediately on impact. Not a single one of the twelve eggs in a carton found in the duffel bag of the surviving Eskimo was broken or cracked.

But the physician's knapsack had been torn and a small book had fallen out with an inscription on the first page, handwritten in Yup'ik.

Next to it, a white little feather was glued, with the word *'qaumaneq'* written underneath in a different penmanship.

YUKON KUSKOKWIM DELTA 1980

1

Where time is round and ravens ride the wind, where the tundra reaches the icy waters of the Bering Sea and expands in all direction endlessly into the horizon, where biting winds at times blow even in the summer, thousands of thaw lakes and hundreds of rivers subdivide the land and tuck away into isolation some sixty Yup'ik Eskimo villages. And it was here where Apaiyak Takutak grew up, the youth known only as Roxy to the white men.

This tundra, mysterious in its thousandfold moods, but always serenely detached, was equally capable of leisurely unfolding its nostalgic beauty or cruelly swallowing an innocent victim with its vastness. For the Yup'ik people, this tundra was a timeless woman. The mother who cradled them, she gave them shelter and was their home.

Fifteen years ago a woman shaman had predicted disaster for the young people of this generation, so impatient to wait for their own time. They had fallen for the glitter without soul of the intruder and were rapidly losing their roots. Only the sacrifice of a human heart belonging to an outsider could atone the curse and undo the deadly spell which had been cast. The inua, the soul of the tundra, had ceased to sing and was mourning in despair.

* * *

It was early in the morning on a spring day in May and the arctic land was still frozen. High winds had caused the temperature to plummet to forty below and the Twin Otter, circling down from a clear sky, came safely to a stop on the narrow and rough landing strip near the village.

Roxy stepped down from the plane. For a year he had been in college in Anchorage, away from the village on the Bering Sea. He genuinely had enjoyed the stimulation of new knowledge, but during the last semester he became unsure about his real goal in life.

As he watched a magnificent fireball slowly rising from behind the skyline, he became aware of how much he had missed the wide open tundra, which now abruptly came to life. The horizon was bleeding into the snow and ghostlike streaks of purple shadows danced over the white surface, kindling thousands of blue, sparkling diamonds.

This celebration of light announced the beginning of a new day; it filled his heart with happiness and there was no room left for all the nagging self-doubts. He was home, and being home felt like promise and hope again.

Roxy, the only passenger, walks slowly over the tundra toward the dirt road of the village of Emomeguk. He needs time to prepare himself mentally for the transition from his college life in a big city to rejoining his relatives and friends in the village. He has been gone for two semesters and his visit is meant to be a surprise.

First, he is going to see the grandparents who raised him. In his exhilarated mood he glorifies the one and only joyful experience of his childhood, being taught by his grandfather how to hunt geese and ducks in the tundra. He represses the memories of physical abuse he endured over the years by this violent man. Roxy, so willing to forgive, is trying to convince himself that his success at college will make his grandfather proud of him.

He also can hardly wait to meet Ayuluk, one of the elders in the village, whom he admires for his knowledge and wisdom. Whenever Roxy had needed emotional support he would visit him and listen to Ayuluk's stories about his own lonely and unhappy childhood without a mother. Ayuluk had never failed in encouraging Roxy to develop his own inborn strength as a proud Yup'ik Eskimo .

Then he will visit his mother. After all, he loves her even though she gave him and his brother away when they were very young and drank heavily as long as he can remember.

While he is walking down the dirt road he tries to convince himself that she has become sober during his absence. Everything seems possible on this beautiful morning.

Most of all, he looks forward to being with his older brother, Ronnie, who has always envied him for going to college. He is sure that Ronnie has outgrown that attitude by now and is determined to help him get more education too.

And there is his girlfriend, Eva, who never wanted him to leave and grieved so bitterly when he did. And all his close friends, Dennis, Demian, Simon, and Gregory. His first visit back to the village is going to be exciting.

By now, he has come to the end of the dirt road, which stretches for several miles along the river and lines up all the scattered little houses of the village. He has arrived at his grandparents' house and knocks at the door...

Only seven days have gone by since he first knocked on his grandparents' door and yet this has been time enough to shatter all Roxy's hopes. His visit has been a terrible mistake. Except for his encounter with Ayuluk, who acknowledged his accomplishments at college, the visit had been an unending nightmare.

It began with his grandparents' humiliating response to his sudden appearance. They did not appreciate this kind of surprise. Since he had left a year ago against their will, he was, in their mind, a deserter. Gone forever. He was supposed to stay in the village and take over the daily chores of his aging grandparents. Was this the gratitude he showed for all the years they had put up with him? What a waste to study biology in a big city when there were seal to hunt and fish to catch, when there were skins to stretch and traps to set right here in the tundra. Had he forgotten that he was an Eskimo and that it was cheap, trying to imitate a white man? They showed no interest in his experiences in the big city and that provoked fierce anger in Roxy.

The encounter with his mother was even more painful. She had been so drunk that she did not even recognize him. And how disheveled she looked, sitting at the kitchen table and staring at the bottle. Close to tears of disgust, he had run off to find Eva, hoping for consolation and understanding. What a disappointment. He forgot that this girl, though sweet and loving, had always been naive and never comprehended his ambitious goals.

And yet the greatest blow was his discovery that his brother, Ronnie, and some friends had begun drinking heavily during his absence. They didn't know what to do with their lives and were bored. The village had no playground for children and no swimming pool, there was no field for ball games for teenagers and the community hall was reserved almost exclusively for adults. The rare occasions when young people had access to this place for a dance or a party were frowned upon by the missionaries, who considered music and dance works of the devil, and the elders supported this attitude. Bingo and church, the only available distractions in the village, meant nothing to

13

them. What was left were the three- wheeler races up and down that depressing dirt road with deep potholes in the spring, gigantic mud puddles in the summer, and dangerous plaques of ice in the winter. But how long could anybody pursue this mindless pleasure of noisy speed before this also turned into monotony?...

Tonight Ronnie and his friends are looking for something exciting to do. It spells suspense to break into the village store and not get caught. They want Roxy to participate but he resists all their provocations, even after they call him a teacher's pet and white college boy.

Roxy, disgusted and disappointed with everybody, finds himself back on the dirt road again. The same old depressing road, however, also leads to the airstrip and now takes on the meaning of the umbilical cord to a better world.

Should he take the next plane and return to the city? But this consideration does not feel right, does not bring relief. He would be a coward to run away from the problems in the village. He should stay and prevent the evil plan of his friends.

On his way home to his grandparents' house he runs into Eva. She convinces him that Ronnie and his friends mean no harm. Feeling isolated and extremely lonely, Roxy does not need much persuasion to find himself that evening drinking with all of them. The village is dry like all the others but there are enough bootleggers around to overcome this hurdle.

There is plenty of beer and whiskey and one glass leads to another. His friends now call him their "pal." That pleases him for he wants and needs so desperately to belong. This is his village, these are his peers. He is no longer an outsider, an Eskimo among white college students.

There is more beer and more whiskey to sufficiently drown his conscience. Two hours later they break into the village store and vandalize the place. Roxy is one of the gang.

The next morning, Roxy only dimly remembers the night before but he clearly feels hatred and disgust for himself. He grabs a piece of paper and begins to write a note to his grandparents. They need to understand how he feels. His headache is excruciating and he can't finish what he wanted to say . He needs fresh air, has to get out of the

14

house. He squeezes the letter into a pocket of his down jacket, jumps on his brother's snowmobile and takes off into the white tundra.

Suddenly the sputtering noise of the engine breaks into Roxy's confused thoughts. No more gasoline. This unexpected frustration is too much for him. His body shakes, tears run down his cheeks and he cries hard.

He leaves his snowmobile and like a sleepwalker walks aimlessly further away from the village. There is no one who understands, nobody to talk to. If only the teacher who once supported him so much had not left the village.

Was it only a week ago, upon his arrival on the runway, that he had that overwhelming experience of trust in himself again, that he hoped the link to the village, his roots, would help him succeed in the outside world?

He feels distraught now thinking of the village, so he tries to concentrate on college.

The big city is so far away. He had been willing to cope with those frustrating adjustments to an unfamiliar and threatening environment because of his great love for biology and his secret dream of becoming a teacher. But his trust in himself is shattered, all his enthusiasm is gone and there is no remaining desire to return to college.

The more he dwells on these depressing thoughts, the more humiliated he feels. Why could he never get high marks as easily as the white students? His teachers assured him repeatedly that he was very bright. They blamed his village school for insufficient teaching and recommended remedial classes. He is now convinced more than ever that they had pulled his leg.

By now Roxy has lost all sensation in his feet. He is vaguely aware of the danger and turns around to find his snowmobile and the tracks back to the village. In his physical and emotional numbness, he cannot tell how long he has trekked through the snow, when several snowmobiles are approaching. Eva and his friends are looking for him; he is embarrassed and thrown into a flap, but his guilt-ridden buddies are relieved to have found him.

They drive back to the village and again Roxy finds himself at the door of his grandparents' house. This time, however, he does not

15

knock. He just wants to go to sleep and forget all his misery. But he hears them yelling at each other in the kitchen and is disturbed. Are they mad at him? It does not cross his mind that they might be drinking heavily. Maybe they found out about the burglary. He convinces himself that they know.

Heavy guilt feelings break though his numbness which so mercifully had alleviated his raging anger. It was bad enough that he had deserted his grandparents a year ago when he left for college. And now all the shame about the break-in. He alone is at fault for everything. Did his mother give him away as a child because he was bad from the very beginning and already born as a misfit? But then who determined he had to be a misfit, was that God? Anger flares up at this thought and the pain of being torn between the two powerful emotions of guilt and anger becomes unbearable.

Roxy enters the porch and sees his grandfather's pistol lying on top of some seal skins. He stops and stares. The pistol is waiting for him.. He points the muzzle at his heart. A sensation of seductive warmth slowly fills his body. With relief he is yielding to that dark compulsion and pulls the trigger.

There is one shot and then silence. The grandparents have stopped fighting. Too late, however. It is done.

A storm whipped the tundra that night, a heavy snowfall swallowed the village as if trying to mercifully cover the tragedy. Yet an unfinished letter, found in Roxy's parka the next morning, didn't let the villagers easily forget: "...Don't know why I did it ...am so confused...all I want is to belong and be accepted by my own people... can't live any longer between two worlds... tried my best to keep up...Why did I fail ...why did nobody...."

Several days later, a brief funeral took place and only a few villagers attended. One was his mother and she was not drunk. The tundra was too frozen that day for an excavation and the casket remained on the surface. Following custom, Roxy's mother threw food on the coffin but a gust of wind picked it up and scattered it over the tundra. That was a bad omen and frightened the villagers. It meant the deceased son had rejected his mother's gift. And then a raven shrieked. Or was it the cry of the shaman who had claimed her first victim?

2

Ayuluk was restlessly tossing around in his bed. Ever since Roxy had killed himself and rumors about the curse were spreading through the village, sleep did not come easily at night. He decided to get up and reached for his blue jeans, slipped into his rubber boots and put his windbreaker over a heavy sweater. He noiselessly opened and closed the door again in order not to wake his wife, and carefully walked over the wet tundra behind the house towards the river.

It was shortly after midnight in late May, the sun had just set and lined the horizon with a deep red afterglow. *Cupvik,* the time of breakup, had started. The river was pushing and squeezing huge chunks of ice that crashed with sizzling noises against and on top of each other, a symphony of thunder.

Ayuluk sat down on a large piece of drift log on top of the ice blocks, which were piled up several feet on the riverbank, the remnants of a furious surge. Watching this yearly drama of nature helped him appease his own inner turmoil about Roxy. He always liked this boy, a bright and sensitive teenager who so desperately tried to cope with his alcoholic grandparents and the violent outbreaks of the old man. College had seemed to be the way out. Though he had never openly discouraged Roxy, he also purposely never supported his plans either. College was the way of the white man to educate their young people; Yup'ik teenagers had to learn on the land from their parents, relatives and elders.

Roxy was radiant when he came to see him in March and the sparkle in his eyes almost convinced him that this youth had succeeded in integrating two different lifestyles without any harm. Roxy's suicide a week later, however, told the shattering true story and painfully reminded Ayuluk of his own struggles as a youngster and his emotional devastation at his return from Russia.

Ayuluk's distress was growing. Staring into the fading red of the horizon, his worried thoughts carried him back into his own past. He found himself to be that six year old boy again, who mourned for his deceased mother and later was given into the custody of a stranger, Stefanos Dubrov, who, old and homesick, wanted to return to the country of his ancestors.

In 1932, at the request of his father, Dimitri, this man had taken Ayuluk along on his journey to Russia with the task to deliver him to his grandparents in Moscow. After his wife's death, his Russian father showed no interest any more in raising his own son. A devastating insight for a child. He had traveled with Stefanos by dog sled and bush plane to Seattle, across the continent by train to New York, crossing the Atlantic to Paris and again by train to Moscow. Good old Stefanos had tried to keep him distracted and entertained on this long, exhausting trip and never got tired of telling him colorful stories about his own past. This man had been very proud of being an offspring of the ninety original Russians who lived in St. Michael on the Norton Sound of the Bering Sea, when the Russian flag came down in 1867. But most of all he felt honored to have served Igumen Amphilokhy, the Russian Orthodox priest at the time of the original cathedral.

Equally painful as his departure to Russia, Ayuluk remembered the disappointment of his return to Alaska. Not only did his estranged father, Dimitry, and his new wife receive him with coldness, he also found the villagers of Emomeguk and their way of life very different from what he nostalgically remembered from seven years before.

It must have been similar for Roxy, he thought, that same anguish and not being prepared for it. Ayuluk felt too upset to return home. He walked back from the river, along the four miles of the dirt road to the very end towards the landing strip on the other side of the village. He was ruminating now about his own son, eighteen-year-old Thomas, a late and unexpected surprise in his otherwise childless marriage.

He had to spare Thomas the alienation he once had felt, he had to spare him Roxy's despair. Without local high schools, a boarding school away from home had been a necessity for his son. But under no circumstances would he let Thomas leave the Delta for college. Everything he needed and wanted to learn beyond school could be learned right here. And that would foster in Thomas a strong identity as a self-sufficient Yup'ik Eskimo, who belonged to the land, where he was born.

For many years Ayuluk had struggled with those feelings of being torn between two worlds and his name, Ayuluk Dimitry Zaykov, reminded him to this very day of his dual origin. Ayuluk, his mother's last name, was picked by his father like an afterthought to balance his son's Russian blood with the Eskimo heritage of his mother. He felt whole in his identity now but this had not come easy and years of emotional struggle had taken their toll.

The years with his grandparents, however, he remembered as supportive and most influential, a time to be recalled in gratitude. Again and again his grandfather Anatole had described to him the day when Stefanos Dubrov appeared at his door to deliver not only a letter from his lost son but a bewildered young Eskimo boy as well: he, Ayuluk, his grandson, had arrived in Moscow. Fifty-seven years old and a former high school teacher, Anatole felt suddenly young and motivated again and raised him like a son. He supervised the heavy load of homework, so typical for the school system under the Bolsheviks, he taught him to speak fluently Russian and English and even offered some help in French and German, mandatory at school. He introduced him to Russian literature and showered him with loving dedication he never had experienced from his father.

Those years in Moscow coincided with dangerous political changes in Russia. His grandparents, fortunately both retired, consciously avoided unnecessary outside contact and kept as much as possible to themselves. Their whole life concentrated on him, Ayuluk. This nurturing attention and refined educated atmosphere in those years had become a carapace, protecting him from his sadness and yet, at times intense spells of homesickness ruptured this shell. The constant necessary caution regarding the secret police of the political regime made him feel like a locked-in prisoner and he would wistfully yearn for the harsh but free adventurous life on the Bering Sea.

His grandparents sensed from early on that his identity was rooted immutably on the tundra of Alaska. He remembered with great warmth how grandmother Natalia, a former music teacher, would play pieces by Bach from *The Well Tempered Piano* and let him choose images of the tundra, a fox hunt, a sunset, a storm or whatever he could conjure up. And every day he looked forward to the evening and their game of dream and fantasy.

Sometimes they all three would attend an underground service in a Russian Orthodox Church, always a risky worship because of the unpredictable interference by the anti-religious government. These services had meant something very special to him. He always was taken with awe by the serene atmosphere in candlelight, the smell of incense and the mysterious chanting of the liturgy. He later came to understand his early intuition: this religion drew its strength from the simple piety of common people who accepted hardship and suffering with uttermost humility, a life so familiar to Yup'ik Eskimos as well.

And to this present day he sometimes felt the need to fly to the village of Russian Mission further up on the Yukon River, where he grew up. Here in that little wooden Orthodox chapel with its tin roof, replacing the cathedral from before the century, the religious ceremony would always confirm anew his identity in its unique and undivided entirety. He was neither an Eskimo nor a Russian, he was both in one.

The horizon started to glow again and almost next to where the sun had set a few hours ago, the same sun slowly lifted itself up. And the brief purplish radiance of the tundra magically transformed Ayuluk's mood. He was back in the here and now and totally surrendered himself to the very presence of this moment. He was at peace again and ready to return home....

Back to the village, along the same old muddy dirt road, he returned to the wooden boardwalk which led across the soaking tundra to his log cabin, away from the clustered houses and rickety buildings. His home was his pride and anchor to this land.

Thirty-five years ago, just before he got married, he had started building it with his own hands. The wood came from the forest way up river and there had been a lot of resistance from the local people to support his plan. A log cabin was just not customary along the coast. And then those separate rooms. But strong willed as he was, the public opinion did not affect him. Over the years he even built all the furniture for his home.

The heart is buried where the hand has wrought, Ayuluk reflected with contentment. He stepped up to the deck and walked through the little arctic entrance porch, lined with fishing and hunting equipment to the bedroom behind the kitchen.

His wife Lucy was still asleep. He bent over her and studied the sad expression in her face; she had never been a happy woman. Ever since the miscarriage early in their marriage, she had been depressed, and when she gave birth to Thomas at the age of thirty-five she did not feel emotionally able to be a mother. She nevertheless had tried her best to raise the boy through all these years.

He liked his wife and and did not regret this marriage, though it was a lonely one. This union had blessed him with the fulfillment of his secret wish for a son. And from the first day on Thomas could not have been closer to his heart.

Ayuluk sat down on the bed and continued to look at her. He was aware how loyal she had been to him to this very day. Her loyalty, however, affected him at times more like an obligation and therefore a burden on her side rather than spontaneous affection. But then again, reliability and mutual trust, not love, were the required qualities for a working partnership in this northern land where under the harsh conditions of nature the overcoming of adversities and survival represented the deeper meaning of life. He had examined these facts very seriously in his youth. His grandfather's library had offered him ample opportunity to browse around and find answers to his secret questions. He got familiar with Gorki's optimistic view of life, read many of Dostojewskij's sad novels and loved the lyrics of Pushkin. But Tolstoi's *Anna Karenina* became the most influential book for him at that time; it was not Anna but Constantine Levin who impressed him, he represented exactly what should be his own calling in life: to dedicate himself to work and help others improve their lot.

Anna's love story had left no mark; the notion and importance of love as presented in books seemed either superficial like lovely little flowers or too melodramatic. Either way, there was no place for so-called love in Eskimo life. His very own concept, the demanding request for nothing less than a spiritual union, he had buried long ago as too stern an expectation and not attainable.

It seemed as if the intensity of his thoughts had stirred Lucy's sleep. She woke up and as so many times in his life when he had taken her by surprise looking right into her face Ayuluk wondered about the childlike expression of innocence in her eyes. She had never grown emotionally into a woman.

Being embarrassed that Ayuluk had been up before her, Lucy quickly got dressed to make tea and have pancakes with smoked fish sticks ready for breakfast.

3

Somewhere on the tundra a lonely wooden cross was casting a mute shadow on the ground where Roxy lay buried. Thomas had visited the grave more than once to be granted absolution for his raging anger. How did Roxy dare to take his life when he had everything going for him? A sense of betrayal overwhelmed him. He now had twice the obligation to succeed. Nothing could deter him from the goals he had set for himself.

It was his last and only school year at the new local high school of the village and his mind was constantly preoccupied with making plans for his future. He was determined to go to college and later to an Ivy League university in the States to study languages and possibly astronomy as well. His father had taken him as a child many times at night out on the tundra, explaining the different constellations and arousing in him awe and curiosity about the mysterious cosmos with meteor showers, asteroids, comets and worlds light years away.

His first interest, however, was dedicated to languages. It all had started with a little book his father owned and cherished like a treasure to the present day, a prayer book, written in Yup'ik. The pages were bound in leather which had become brittle and yellowed over the years.

And it was this little book that his father had loaned him during his stay away from home, those six long years at the boarding school of Mt. Edgecombe. He had only been ten years old and feeling already homesick when his father brought him on the ferry from Sitka to one of the Japlonski Islands, where the campus was located.

"No reason to be sad. To learn is a privilege," his father had said, when he gave him the book. "This is special, a reminder of your heritage, the preciousness of our language. Take good care of it."

Thomas respected his father and wanted to become a man just like him. He had admiration not only for his strength of character and universal knowledge but his war experience as well, even though only the superficial facts were known to him. He had served with the Territorial Guard and was later trained at Fort Richardson with the 297th battalion. After his transfer to Fort Lewis in Washington State he got assigned to the 8th Air Force in Europe as a pilot, where, towards the end of the war, he flew air raids from England over Germany. But much to Thomas' regret, he had always avoided talking more personally about his war adventures and emotional involvement.

His father stood out from the rest of the villagers. Though already sixty he appeared younger and looked different from other elders because of his curly black hair, slightly graying already, and the darker areas around his chin drawing up to the temples, which meant he had to shave. He was also the most outspoken elder, willful with high ideals. He did not yield easily, he looked people straight into the eyes-- which was never done in Yup'ik tradition--and cared little what others thought of him. He marched to a different drummer and many villagers felt uncomfortable in his presence.

It just recently had come to Thomas as a shock that his father did not support his college plans at all. It was true, he himself went only to high school in Russia, never attended a college or university and owed his remarkable universality to self-education. But times had changed and, as he would never have the experience of so many different life situations as his father, the university was in his mind the only way to knowledge.

When Thomas joined his parents this morning his father seemed to be in a very special mood. He asked Thomas to walk with him after breakfast to the river and see whether all the ice had been washed out to the Bering Sea. It had to be something serious his father had on his mind, most likely new and persuasive reasons against his college plans.

Yet Thomas was mistaken. While they were putting on their hip waders, prepared for a flooded tundra near the river, Ayuluk unexpectedly said: "I never told you much about my father and that had its reason."

Taken totally by surprise, Thomas felt relief that it wasn't college they would discuss.

They now carefully worked themselves over the uneven marshy tundra, watching out for startled ptarmigans fearfully taking off.

It was true that his father had always seemed reluctant to talk about his own father. Thomas respected his reasons, whatever they were, and never had pushed him. He knew his Russian grandfather Dimitry only from a photo as a young man with a strong body, bushy eyebrows and a stern facial expression. But that was about all.

His father remained silent for a while. Was he trying to make out whether the distant river was still struggling to free itself of the

26

onslaught of ice from upriver, or was he just hesitant to talk about something painful? Thomas wondered.

"We weren't close," Ayuluk slowly started, "and most of my life I resented him for the distance he kept. I never knew what he really felt. Only during the years after his death did I finally began to do justice to his complexity. He only wrote one letter to his parents, and that was twenty-one years after he had disappeared, that letter which Stefanos Dubrov delivered in person. Yes, I read those lines again and again since all I know about this period of his life is contained in this very letter."

Thomas was aware that these memories weren't recalled with ease. After a brief pause his father went on:

"He ran away at fifteen—my grandfather told me—and must have taken the Trans Siberian train to Vladivostok. He mentioned in his letter the Russian ice breaker 'Tamyr' which sailed in 1911 all the way through the Bering Strait around Cape Dezhneva to the mouth of the Kolyma River.

"Cape Wales. You'll remember the long trip with the dog sled last year and how we could clearly see the Siberian peninsula. Yes, he likely had been hired as a cabin boy for this expedition. Why he from there ended up in Nome is guesswork. My grandparents read between the lines that the crew dropped him because of his recalcitrant, insubordinate behavior before the Tamyr headed for the Arctic Ocean.

"I recall that on one of the rare occasions my father did talk to me, he briefly mentioned his employment in Nome. Hired as a shepherd for huge reindeer herds from Siberia and Lapland, he must have worked there for several years before he moved in 1918 to Ikogmiut, as he stubbornly all his life continued to call the village Russian Mission.

"He was a very bright child and from what your great-grandmother told me he already read fluently at the age of five. A mind almost too inquisitive for the teachers at school.

"My grandparents had plans for him to attend the University of Moscow and become a schoolteacher. Dimitry did not share his parents' ambition at all. Yes, your grandfather was strong headed and already willful as a child.

27

"Day and night his mind was preoccupied with imagined adventures. He skipped school a lot and preferred to read on his own all he could find about Russian history, the exploration of Siberia and particularly the founding of Russian America. By the age of fourteen he had already consumed bibliographies of those early adventurers like the energetic Cossack Semeon Dezhnev, the daring Captain Vitus Bering and the ambitious Grigori Shelikhof, but it was Alexander Baranov who became his true hero. This man, who as a young boy poor and illiterate, ran away from his home in Western Russia, got self-educated in Moscow and later explored Alaska..." his father paused for a second, "and...the Yup'ik Eskimos."

Ayuluk put his arm around Thomas and added with a smile: "And thus it comes, my son, that both of us are living here on the Alaskan tundra."

Without any talk they continued to walk behind each other, now dragging their boots through the bog until they reached the river. The breakup was over; not even small chunks of ice were floating on the surface any longer. Instead of a solid frozen highway, as it had been not that long ago, water was peacefully flowing toward the Bering Sea.

They were throwing pebbles and dead branches into the current and his father reminisced:

"He loved to watch the breakup. He was quite good in living the presence. However, there was never any mention of his past adventures; he never bragged nor did he ever complain. Yet he must have felt isolated and lonely toward the end. After renouncing his own country, my mother upheld the link to this land and our people. She helped him, this full-blooded Russian, to live like an Eskimo and speak fluently Yup'ik. But when she died his self-created world must have fallen apart and his second marriage did not restore it as he must have hoped. Life in Emomeguk did not appeal to him any longer. So he left his young wife and moved back to Russian Mission. I often wondered why he grew a full beard during his last years. As he was not an Eskimo, only lived like one, he perhaps found more peace in being a Russian toward the end."

Ayuluk and Thomas found some driftwood to sit on. Whole trees, torn out somewhere up river, had made the trip down with the ice last night. Even though it was almost June it was still chilly at this time of the year and their sweatshirts and parkas served them well. They sat next to each other, their knees pulled up, following with their eyes the current of the Yukon River. Thomas waited for his father to continue.

"I am not the most talkative man, I know that," Ayuluk said, "but I don't want us ever to get distant like it was with my father and me."

He paused again, seemingly absorbed by particularly painful memories, then deliberately went on:

"I only vaguely remember my mother. 'The most beautiful girl of the Delta,' as my father always used to refer to her and then routinely would add, 'I met her quite accidentally in Ikogmiut.'

"After she had died in 1926 in Russian Mission my father moved with me to Emomeguk because my mother's brother lived there. But I did not care. I missed my mother, I was homesick for Russian Mission and its people, the cathedral and Vastly Changsak, the Yup'ik priest, whom I loved as I wanted to love my father."

Thomas was listening without interrupting. His father was rarely so emotional that he talked openly about his own feelings. But today he seemed to be carried away.

"At that time only five families lived in that village, my father and I included, just twenty-seven people all together. I felt terribly lonely. My uncle Agapick, however, unmarried and childless, took a liking to me. He let me go seal hunting and fishing with him, took me moose hunting on the tundra and talked to me about strange, fascinating things. People whispered to me that he was a shaman and had to be respected. Thanks to this unusual man I became real proud to be a tough Eskimo boy and was truly happy."

Thomas was aware that his father had switched to talking about himself. He moved closer and leaned against him. His father went on:

"And then my grandparents...well, I shared with you a lot about my time with them, but I never spoke of the devastating years after my return to Emomeguk."

Thomas indeed knew all the details of his father's seven years in Russia, had learned about the dangerous political situation with the conspiracy trials and repeated purges, and was most impressed by the grandparents' ability to get his father out of Russia before the beginning of WWII, with enough money for the long journey home.

His father, however, was right—and Thomas had never given it thought—there *was* a blank in his father's' background.

With a whimsical little smile slipping over his face, his father pulled him closer and said with great warmth:

"I have no right to omit anything, son, do I? Well, those years were hard and it's not easy for me to talk about my weaknesses.

"My father had moved back to Russian Mission, Uncle Agapick had died, and the villagers, who did not know me anymore, did not truly welcome me. I was a stranger, a complete stranger to them. They did not understand me and I did not understand them. I felt lost and did not fit. And I heavily blamed my father for not having raised me here, where I belonged.

"It was confusing to me, the destructive influence of another culture infiltrating the Delta, and our people slowly losing their roots. But I was not mature enough at nineteen to create my own center. I desperately needed structure and meaning in my own life.

"Amidst all this inner turmoil there came my encounter with a man, called by his nickname: Major *Muktuk.*

Thomas chuckled: " Major *Whale Blubber?* "

"Kind of an honor. Our people loved him. A man with a great sense of humor. Had lived part of his life among them and founded the Tundra Army on St. Lawrence Island. Indeed, an American army major. Like my own father, he left his parents at the age of fifteen and ended up in Nome as well."

Thomas knew nothing about the Tundra Army and had never heard about a major Muktuk. His father had become restless and stood up. It seemed to be difficult for him to go on.

"It wasn't patriotism, Thomas, no, it was personal despair that caused me to travel to meet him on a float plane on the Kuskokwim river."

He paused again before he continued: "Right from the river he was enlisting men for the Territorial Guard. But I am not an American. I am a Yup'ik Eskimo and Major Marston was aware of my feelings. He lured me by saying, I will never forget his words: Young man, it's not for America, it is your own country here on the Bering Sea, which you are going to protect against the Japanese.' Yes, he helped me to feel motivated and have concrete goals again."

In the past Thomas had heard his father mention Major Marston here and there but he had never revealed these details and the tremendous importance of his meeting with him. Whatever the reasons, through all these years his curiosity about his father's war experiences had never been quenched. But today his father seemed to be in the mood to open up and share. Instead he only added:

"The rest of this story, well... a long and gruesome detour of four years before I was back in Emomeguk again."

This final statement came with an abruptness that disappointed Thomas. "How can you declare adventures as a detour?" He was puzzled.

He felt touched by his father's admission of alienation, loneliness and the military as an escape but didn't know what to do with the meaning of a detour in life. He sensed an unspoken message and felt uneasy, not understanding what was expected of him. His father—and that was typical for him— had obviously planned it this way. They got up to stretch their legs, ready to walk home. Slowly making their way through the muddy tundra, Ayuluk engaged Thomas in details about the running of the king salmon next month and the fish camp at Black River near Cape Romanov. And there were no more references to his father's early life and the emotional impact of his past experiences.

4

Her little red house was surrounded by wide open tundra and completely encircled by an unbroken horizon except for one minute irregularity, a little hill that was a *pingo*.

The geological secret of this innocent-looking hill had attracted her the very first time she walked up to it. Once an ancient lake, dying, and pushed up by permafrost, this dome of ice had been covered by soil and plants over hundreds of years. And tonight after supper she again would visit her favorite spot.

It was early August. Vren stepped out on the deck, climbed over the railing and jumped down into a green carpet, dotted with blueberries. In minutes her bowl was filled. She went inside, fixed herself something to eat with the berries and sat down at the kitchen table. While looking through the window over an endless field of white puffs, the delicate tassels of arctic cotton, she couldn't help but reminisce about her new life and the circumstances which had brought her here.

Two years ago, right after her divorce, she had traveled on her own throughout Alaska, trying to heal emotionally and get a new perspective on life. It had become a journey into herself and, ever since, she was aware of a strange yearning to return. It seemed impossible to explain to her grown children or anybody else what was drawing her to the subarctic tundra on the Bering Sea. She was known to love adventures, but to give up her full-time psychiatric practice in Washington D.C. for a place in the middle of nowhere seemed unrealistic and foolish to her friends, particularly at the age of fifty-five.

Her wish finally came true when the Yup'ik Eskimo Health Corporation offered her a position in Bethel, the only little town in the bush of the Delta and the center of about sixty Yup'ik Eskimo villages.

A month had already passed since her move to the new home on the tundra of western Alaska. She mailed a few photos of her house in this setting to friends and ever since—according to their point of view—she lived in a "little red barrack in Siberia," which, to be precise, was still three hundred miles away, as the crow flies across the Bering Strait.

Her friends in the east were also wrong about her "red barrack", which was indeed a very cozy rambler and offered all the comfort of city living. Yet she didn't have to struggle from the 10th floor in the apartment building down the elevator to the second underground level, with keys fumbling to open several security locks of metal doors to finally drive her car up to street level and merge with heavy traffic.

Here she just would step down on the subarctic tundra, drive in her small Subaru over to the landing strip and fly a few minutes later with a bush pilot to villages on the Bering Sea, with thousands of lakes and rivers sliding away under the wings of the plane.

Her wooden house, painted in rusty red, was built like a dock on stilts in deep water. Pillars, more than twenty feet deep, reached into the permafrost for anchorage and were covered by a wooden apron all around. A narrow built-up driveway connected it to a dead-end dirt road, a berm consisting of several layers of gravel and sand on top of the tundra.

With a central utility room, containing a huge water tank, pipes, switches, motors, hoses, gauges, electrical cords, thermostats and reset buttons, she indeed had her independent support system. Water was going to be delivered by truck every two weeks; the oil drum, gas tank and sewer were tucked behind the house and protected with polyurethane foam against the coming cold of the winter.

Ready for her evening walk on the tundra, she put on her rubber boots and set out toward the pingo, abandoning herself to the free range of her memories. She gratefully acknowledged that her sense of adventure and the totally new lifestyle in the bush of Alaska would help her overcome the past.

Vren's marriage had been functional and in certain ways quite satisfactory. But what she had hoped for, the development of a deeper bond with more meaning than the everyday maintenance of a partnership, never happened.

Right after WWII she had returned from Berlin to Munich, the place of her childhood, gotten married and come with her husband to America. Their relationship, however, did not resemble in the least her earlier deep emotional involvement with Achim, the young physician and mountain climber, whose premonition of an early death had spiritually intensified the meaning of their encounter. On his first furlough from Russia he fell to death, climbing a mountain ironically named Death Chapel.

In later years she came to understand that first loves are infatuations and should not be used for comparison and that life was not about attaining happiness—a worn-out word and banal goal. Instead life meant striving for completion as a human being. They raised two children, traveled a lot and as physicians had full professional lives. But the empty part in her heart had grown over the years and her deep love for the arts, the active and willful pursuit of projects, could not compensate for what was missing...

Vren had reached the hill and sat down on the sandy ground, her back against the trunk of a stunted birch no taller than herself. On either side a little spruce tree sheltered the sedge grass underneath and whispered its song into the wind. She looked back at the distance she had walked and now it was her solitary little red house that stood out against the perfect circle of the horizon.

From the top of the hill she could see forever. Countless blue thaw lakes dotted the open plane, and green ridges reached into the far distance. She watched nearby frolicking ptarmigans and detected between the tussocks a shy little fox. Her eyes followed a formation of geese, already leaving for the winter, and she adopted the pingo as her very own, an outpost to the slumbering arctic plains beyond.

It was shortly after ten o'clock when the sun started to sink into the tundra and the white clouds slowly turned into dark purple. Time to turn around: tomorrow would be a busy clinic day and she would have to deal with the challenging problems of her patients.

They would drive for hours on three wheelers cutting through the tundra; they came by boat on the river and by plane from the coast. Whatever the transportation, it was always the tundra which had to be conquered and overcome, regardless of weather and season. And without highways or even roads, miles on the tundra magically measured twice as long.

Life circumstances here were very different, and off hand she had little to offer except for her heart. There was so much she had to experience and learn first. The encounter with death was almost a daily event. People drowned in the river, got lost in the tundra, crashed in planes, killed or got killed and committed suicide. Not only the tundra but everyday life itself seemed to touch eternity all the time.

Preoccupied with her thoughts, Vren leisurely strolled back. All the colors of the spectrum still lingered along the horizon, painting the tundra in an eerie pink. She stopped walking to look around and clear her mind, when suddenly the wind began to stir the grasses around her and a black menacing cloud like a claw pushed itself across the sky. The glowing tundra, which, moments before, had enchanted her, appeared alien and hostile, and inexplicable anguish gripped her heart. Overcome by the powerful presence of something unknown, she rushed home and, entering the house, she was embarrassed to feel relieved.

That night a dark dream haunted her sleep:

She was sitting on the pingo and watched the sunset, when a huge raven flew over her head, shrieking in sudden terror. The two stunted spruce trees next to her began to tremble. Menacing clouds came slowly creeping across the sky and stabbed with ghostlike fingers the sinking sun, which started to bleed and tainted the ground. In horror she tried to get home, but impenetrable darkness had swept the tundra She stumbled and tripped and fell over the moaning tussocks, which were soaked with blood and ensnared her feet until she could not move another step.

With a scream, Vren woke from her nightmare and remembered with awe those singular words by Rilke she always had puzzled about: *"Beauty is only that part of terror we just can bear and we adore it since it serenely disdains to destroy us."*

Tomorrow she had to share her dream with somebody and it would be Cecilia, the eighteen-year-old Yup'ik girl assigned to her as a translator. From the first day on they had liked each other and Vren trusted her. Cecilia's personality reflected a curious mixture of innocence and whimsicality. Her warm and full-sounding voice was spiced with that charming Yup'ik accent. She usually accompanied Vren on her flights to the villages, for the older generation of the natives did not understand English.

They had become a very personal team within the team of her staff of several professionals. Besides the two experienced older local Eskimo health aides there was the young, sensitive woman

36

psychologist from California who could not cope with the many deaths in the Delta, and the tough, versatile older male social worker from New England, who had a hard time getting accustomed to the standard honey buckets in the village clinics. By contrast, for the down- to-earth, red-haired, middle-aged nurse, no situation was ever insurmountable. And so, in spite of all their individual peculiarities, they had already grown into quite a functional group. The vivacious Cecilia with her openness to every issue and sense of humor, however, was special.

In the morning over a cup of coffee Vren described her dream to Cecilia, who showed fear in her face as she whispered:

"Please keep this dream to yourself and don't talk about it to anybody; it's a bad omen. I don't want people to believe in the shaman's curse."

"What curse? Tell me about it," Vren urged.

"Not today. Maybe some other time." With these words Cecilia left the office.

5

Vren had arrived early this morning and was surprised to already find somebody in the waiting room. Patients usually didn't show up before ten o'clock. The young girl from Emomeguk had come by plane the evening before and appeared very anxious.

As she sat down in Vren's office and took off the hood of her parka as well as the earphones of her Walkman, long healthy blond hair fell over her shoulders. She introduced herself as the daughter of a teacher at the local high school. Originally from Chicago, Lisa had already lived in the village for two years. She talked in detail about her present life, her activities at school, how much she liked Eskimos but didn't come to the point. When Vren gently coaxed her she started crying and mumbled:

"I just cannot go through with it. I don't know how to tell my parents. I am pregnant, third month. My boyfriend is so happy about the baby. Dennis is Eskimo and wants to marry me. But my parents would never let me."

"What about you?" Vren asked. "Do you want the baby?"

Hardly audible, Lisa responded: "I am only eighteen and need an abortion. That's why I am here."

Vren decided to say nothing and give the young girl a chance to get it all off her chest. With her request in the open Lisa was promptly composed again, bubbling on:

"I did not tell the truth when I said I liked it in the village. In the beginning, yes, everything was new and exiting, snowmobile rides, fishing trips, all the boys at school who were after me, but now it is not only boring in the village, it has become spooky at times, particularly since that fellow Roxy killed himself. And then the other day when that girl died in the three wheeler accident in front of the community hall, somebody had to exorcise the evil spirit in the building. Worst of all, Dennis is in such a morbid mood since his friend's suicide, he does not flirt with me any more, but constantly has to visit Roxy's grave on the tundra. He even carved a wooden cross for him. People here are so superstitious, really believe in that stupid curse and all that stuff. They don't admit it openly, but constantly whisper about it. Even Dennis thinks it 's not a laughing matter."

Vren did not have to convince herself that this young and very immature girl wasn't going to make it in the village any longer, with or without a baby. It was urgent to involve the parents immediately. The way Lisa presented herself, she indeed wouldn't have the slightest qualms about doing something rash.

Vren offered to talk to her parents and suggested to Lisa she think about it for a few days and then call her back. They would go from there. The girl was agreeable and seemed relieved when she left.

Cecilia had overheard some of Lisa's complaints, when she briefly had to interrupt and get some files from the office.

"Here we go again,' she remarked in returning to Vren's office. "I wish people would stop talking about that so-called curse. Last week my cousin's music box started tinkling and she got frightened for just the same reason. That's pretty superstitious, don't you agree?"

Cecilia was naively unaware that this seemingly innocent question gave away her own ambivalence. Vren would have liked at this moment to ask a lot of questions but she sensed Cecilia's apprehension and decided to talk to some of the physicians at the hospital instead.

A week went by and Lisa did not call back. When Vren tried to reach her, Lisa's father answered the phone. With a cold, detached voice he let Vren know that his daughter had left for Chicago to finish her last year of school there.

Vren was relieved. Lisa must have spoken with her parents and her problem was going to be taken care of in Chicago. And that was best for Dennis as well. Lisa wouldn't have made a good wife for him.

* * *

Dennis had not been himself since Roxy shot himself in spring. He was deeply disturbed and felt somehow responsible for the suicide because he had talked Roxy into breaking into the village store. Dennis had always envied Roxy for everything: his looks, his brain, his opportunity to go to college. Had he taken a kind of emotional revenge to make Roxy feel that he was no better than the rest of them in the village? Dennis couldn't get rid of the idea that all the bad fortune which had haunted him ever since was connected with Roxy's death and was meant to be a punishment.

40

How triumphant and proud he had been last year when Lisa, the daughter of a teacher, responded to his love. She was beautiful, she was bright, and she was white. She represented a status symbol to him and was a boost to his self-esteem.

Early September this year Lisa found out she was carrying Dennis' child and for the first time since Roxy died he felt happy again. This meant more status in the village. If it was a son, his wildest dreams would be fulfilled. His son would equally master the traditional and modern life; he would teach him the skills of a tough Eskimo and would send him to college like Roxy. One culture did not have to die so that another one could live.

What a shock when a few days later Lisa had left the village without an explanation. Her parents would not talk to him. Their only advice was to forget their daughter.

It is already late but Dennis, overwhelmed by emotional turmoil, has to get out of the village and visit the cross on the tundra, where Roxy is buried. He himself carved this cross for his friend in deep remorse and has come to this place many times since spring.

The guilt about Roxy's death seems to alleviate the upcoming demonic anger at Lisa and his terrible fear of an uncontrollable and unexpected outbreak of his feelings.

As Dennis walks back to the village through the silent tundra, glittering in the moonlight, he is able to consider his recent past with some detachment. He is willing to forgive Lisa.

Glad to see the light in the kitchen of his brother's house, he enters, driven by the urgent need to talk to somebody. Alex is still up. He is one of his older brothers and twelve years ahead of him. Their relationship is quite peculiar. Most of the time he resents Alex's fatherly attitude, but today he yearns for it. His brother invites him to have some tea. His wife and children are asleep, which makes it a good time for talking.

Dennis would like to learn a trade like his brother and not sit around anymore doing nothing. They talk all night, yet as soon as Alex starts giving advice, Dennis gets annoyed. It does not make sense since he asked for it, but the presence of Alex, who is mature and successful, reduces Dennis to a nothing. His repressed anger threatens to erupt.

41

His inner peace has been short-lived. He has to leave before his irritation shows.

It's early morning by now and he storms out of Alex's kitchen. He runs home, hoping to find some whisky to drown the emerging anger and confusion about himself. There is none. Yet there is always Lysol in the kitchen and that will do for right now. Lena, his younger sister, is already up eating breakfast and getting ready for school. He ignores her and searches in the shelves.

Lena knows her brother all too well and starts nagging him to behave. As he finds a bottle of Lysol, Lena screams and tries to take it from him. But Dennis is stronger and taller; he holds the bottle over his head and laughs, calling her a plump chicken who is too stupid to understand. He suddenly hates all women. Lena cries hysterically and runs out of the house. As soon as his sister leaves Dennis sits down at the table and cries. He is ashamed and does not like himself.

That afternoon, Lena picks up a small package at the post station, addressed to her brother. Dennis, still moody, unpacks the little parcel with no return address and wonders about its content. A cassette tape. And then he remembers that Lisa liked to correspond by tapes rather than letters.

Dennis rushes out of the house to borrow a cassette player from school. Lena, however, has no illusions and is afraid of whatever Lisa has to say on this tape.

An hour later, Dennis returns, behaving like a madman. He throws the recorder against the wall and screams. In his mind, she purposely killed his child; she paid money to have it murdered in a hospital. An abortion.

Although Lena knows better, she tries to put her arm around Dennis to console him. He pushes her down and curses her. He kicks that human body on the floor, which is no longer Lena but Lisa, or Lena and Lisa, or even Lena, Lisa, and his own mother, whom he has never known; she deserted him, the youngest child, for a job in the city because she had grown tired of raising twelve children.

Before Lena is able to get up, Dennis has already left the house. Swamped by feelings of remorse, he heads for the tundra. Only at Roxy's grave will he find sanity again. Roxy's soul will give him absolution.

Dennis stumbles over the tussocks, unaware that black clouds are darkening the sky. Within a few minutes a storm with thunder and lightening, a rare event at this time of the year, is racing over the tundra, chasing the screeching ravens. The wooden crosses in the cemetery seem to tremble. The next lightning illuminates the sky with a greenish light, Roxy's cross catapults off the ground and is following him like a shadow as he runs back to the village. A lonely raven flaps above his head, its piercing shriek sounds like the eerie cry of the raven at Roxy's funeral.

Dennis storms into the house to get his gun; he must shoot Roxy's ghost or himself. Lena tries to prevent him from grabbing the shells, but he threatens her and she runs to their brother's house next door for help. Dennis loads the gun and follows her.

Alex, aware of the danger, motions Lena, his wife, and the children out of the kitchen. As Dennis enters, Alex ignores his brother's gun and calmly asks him into the kitchen.

How gentle Alex looks as he offers him hot tea, smoked fish, and crackers. Dennis feels suddenly the urge to cry, wanting to be cuddled and comforted like a child who asks for forgiveness. Alex's face is getting blurred and takes on the features of Roxy, smiling at him. Dennis yearns to become one with Roxy, and a sensation of relief overcomes him.

Alex, watching closely, is aware of his brother's fading rigidity and considers this the right moment to seize the gun. But Dennis's dreamlike state bursts like a bubble. Disillusioned and miserable with Alex patronizing him, he jumps up and positions himself against the kitchen door, his legs apart for support and the muzzle of the gun underneath his chin. Alex tries to shuffle the barrel away from Dennis' face but his brother has pulled the trigger a split second before. Dennis' brain splashes all over Alex's face. Overcome by nausea, the floor underneath his feet gives way. Alex has fainted.

Outside, the storm continued throughout the night. The next morning the sun was shining over the tundra, radiant in innocence as if nothing had ever happened. Two suicides within half a year weighed heavily on everyone's conscience. Fear and restlessness, pervading the village and spreading like a disease even beyond, evoked in some old-timers the grueling memory of a powerful woman shaman and her dire prediction for the next generation. The inexorable curse seemed to come true.

6

The telephone in her living room was ringing. A trooper in Bethel asked her to see a young Eskimo man in prison who had arrived with the late plane from Emomeguk and supposedly had been standing for several hours motionless in a catatonic state against a wall in the airport.

"He is definitely not drunk but emotionally disturbed," the trooper explained. "The hospital won't admit him. The excuse, as usual: No facilities for mental patients. The poor devil is now locked up in prison for evaluation and further decisions."

"Do you have any more information?" asked Vren, who had just come home from the clinic.

"Not really. He won't talk."

With the car key still in her hand, Vren hopped in her Subaru again and drove to the prison.

The guard on night call, originally from Illinois and a newcomer to the bush, led her into a small cell without a window. A slim Eskimo man, about thirty years old, with a knitted woolen bandana around his shiny black hair, wearing a Western style parka and traditional seal mukluks, stood motionless between the end of a narrow cot and a toilet seat. His handsome face appeared completely frozen and showed no emotions. Like a sleepwalker he moved a few steps toward Vren and monotonously uttered:

"I cannot sleep. I need a prescription."

"Who is he and what happened to him?" Vren looked at the warden.

The young man shrugged his shoulders. "He won't say. All he wants is to make a phone call, but prisoners are not allowed to do so."

Vren was annoyed: " He is not a prisoner, he is a patient."

"Rules are rules; patient or prisoner, it makes no difference."

How could this frightened young man comprehend why he was locked up in a prison cell? she wondered with compassion. The reasoning behind those hospital regulations had struck her from the first day on as stubborn and inhuman: Patients with emotional problems had to stay in prison for a few days before a trooper would fly with them to a psychiatric hospital in Anchorage.

The Eskimo looked bewildered. His gaze fixed on Vren, he reached into his pocket and handed her a piece of paper with a telephone number. "Kara, my wife. Please call."

Relieved by this request, she gently touched his hand and said: "My name is Vren, what is yours?"

There was a short-lived glimmer in his eyes and hardly audibly he said: Alex.

"Would you like to eat or drink something while I make the call in the front office?"

Alex stood motionless in the middle of the cell and before anybody could have responded, the guard intervened: "Dinner time is over. No food before breakfast tomorrow morning."

As she left, Vren said: "I'll get you something to eat if you are hungry, but let me call your wife first. I'll be back."

The warden banged his keys, quickly locked the cell and accompanied Vren to the office. "Good luck," he grouched. "From what I know, in all Emomeguk there are only two telephones."

When Vren dialed the number a woman's voice answered, but was hard to understand. It seemed to Vren that Alex' wife lived somewhere else in the village and had to be notified to come to the phone. Vren took her chance. She called again twenty minutes later and had Alex' wife on the line. Listening to what an anxious young voice was telling her, a gruesome scene of suicide came vividly to life: Alex is Dennis' brother. Like everybody else she had learned about the gory details and the horror which had taken place in Alex' kitchen two weeks ago. "It stalks him day and night, that scene, his brother's brain all over him. My husband can't sleep, can't eat, can't be with friends, can't be alone. I had to force him to fly to Bethel and get admitted to the hospital. I promised him he would feel safe there." Vren was shaken. No, she wouldn't tell his wife that Alex was locked up in prison. She promised to call in the morning and rushed back to Alex. When she met his eyes, staring in despair at her through the bars of the door, she quickly made up her mind. There was no way that she would let this seriously troubled young man be locked up in a prison cell tonight. Against the advice of the warden and after signing countless forms and papers, she took Alex by his hand, left the prison and drove home with him to her little red house on the tundra. Even though Alex had not said a word in the car and still remained silent while she was fixing the couch in her living room with a pillow and two blankets, he was visibly less rigid and somewhat more at ease. She brought him a cup of hot tea, gently made him take two sleeping pills and urged him to lie down.   As she was leaving the room, Alex suddenly said, "Please, leave the light on." The shock had been broken and Vren felt relieved.   The next morning in the clinic she introduced Alex to Cecilia, who was going to arrange a room for him to stay at Bethel for several days. They were sitting in the waiting room and Vren heard them talking in Yup'ik. When he entered Vren's office the frozen expression in his face had melted and his body moved smoothly again.... Alex remained in Bethel for a week and met with Vren five times in a row for long and painful sessions. Always sitting opposite to her, and Cecilia kneeling on the floor in front of him, holding both his hands, he would allow the memories of horror to mercilessly flood his brain. And when he could not put them into words, he would heavily sob instead, spastically throwing up afterwards   A few days after his return to the village, his wife called to report that Alex now could eat again and even slept without a single nightmare.

* * *

Ayuluk was deep in thought as he was walking home in the evening along the dirt road. Dennis' death had upset him even more than Roxy's suicide. Within a few months two bright youngsters of the village senselessly gone forever. He was struggling with this strange phenomenon of an emotional contagion which had even spread to naive children like six-year- old Linda. A few days after Dennis' death she had pointed with a shiny little water pistol at her temple, pretending with a loud "pow pow" that her brain was splattering all over her new dress . A week later she was found trying to kill herself with a kitchen knife because a voice had told her so.

He understood the curse as a creation of the collective unconscious of the people to have something to blame for these happenings and to avoid the hard work of looking at the true circumstances responsible for these signs of disintegration.

Stuart came to his mind, that young boy who had been sent away by his chronically drunk parents to St. Mary's, but the boarding school there was no cure for his depression and couldn't undo the devastating influence of his home life. He was afraid for him, fragile as he was, this particular youngster, and the thought of him made Ayuluk even more determined to be available for each young person who needed his support. He wanted to prove to each one of them that the curse was man-made.

The honking of a three wheeler driving up behind him interrupted his ruminations. It was Alex. He did not know him personally, only as the brother of Dennis, who had been Thomas' friend.

Several times right after his brother's suicide he had tried to talk to him, but Alex's wife Kara had been very protective of her husband and Ayuluk had to promise her to wait until she considered Alex ready for his visit. He hadn't seen him since and, aware of Alex's painful ordeal three weeks ago, he welcomed this opportunity to invite him over to his house.

Together they entered the kitchen. Alex sat down on the table and without saying anything he watched Ayuluk heating the water and getting some fish sticks and seal oil ready. When Ayuluk joined him he drank his tea slowly and avoided looking into Alex' face. He simply said:

"Haven't seen you for a while. If you want to talk, go ahead, I have all the time in the world."

Alex didn't respond right away. He stirred his tea for a while but finally said:

"Just came back and feel a lot calmer," and after some more silence: "My visit to Bethel helped."

"You went to the clinic?" Ayuluk seemed alarmed.

"Yes," Alex said. "I don't know exactly why I feel less upset, but I do."

"Did a psychiatrist talk to you?"

"Nobody talked to me and I hardly talked either, but she was present and had asked Cecilia from Tununak to be with me," Alex volunteered.

Ayuluk assumed that Alex was referring to the new woman psychiatrist who had been hired by the Corporation, and Cecilia was most likely a Yup'ik health aide. No, he did not approve of this arrangement at all. He was adamantly against all interference from outsiders and could not help expressing his opinion:

"Why would you see an American woman psychiatrist? What does she, can she, know about us here?"

Alex didn't answer. He reached for another fish stick, dipped it into seal oil and then calmly announced: "She is different."

There was something intangible in Alex' statement, only to be picked up by listening with a third ear and Ayuluk was good at that. For some reason it irritated him that he felt curious about this woman, but he did not dwell on it.

Alex did not intend to say any more. He finished his tea and in getting up he asked:

"May I come back some other time? I feel good right now and don't want to stir up my nightmares."

Ayuluk walked with him to the steps on the end of the board walk. He liked Alex and how he carried himself in this most stressful and sad situation. However, with that morbid mood hovering over the village, it was an absolute necessity to get Alex to talk and involve him in dialogue. There should not be a third suicide.

7

The last official barges before the freeze-up had arrived in Bethel and all the merchandise was already distributed by plane to the villages of the Delta. The store in Emomeguk was crowded on this radiant last day in September. Alesia, the owner, an older, heavy-set Eskimo woman with a lined face, was chatting with Ayuluk, who had come to inspect the quantity and quality of the shipment.

"Have you heard about that youngster from Kotlik? Took an overdose, his grandmother's sleeping pills. The health aide had to pump his stomach out." Alesia bent over the counter and whispered into his ear.

"It's all superstition, Alesia, not a curse. There are rational explanations. Don't fall for this rumor." Ayuluk sounded irritated.

He was ready to pay when he noticed Catherine, a fifteen-year-old teenager from the village, debating with her boyfriend, Tony, whether to buy bubble gum or candies. She had heard Ayuluk's remark and confirmed: "That's what I think. Old folks' superstition."

"I am not so sure. How can one know?" Tony hesitantly remarked. "The other day when he was hunting, Roxy's brother did definitely hear a voice over his left shoulder, telling him to kill himself and . . ."

" Sheer nonsense," the girl quickly interrupted. "He is fine, played bingo with us yesterday evening."

"But won't hunt anymore out there. He is too scared," Tony immediately added.

Ayuluk purposely ignored Tony's remark and asked Alesia to show him around in the store and point out the newly arrived goods.

The two teenagers were already gone when Ayuluk finally left the store. He was heading home along the dirt road and his left shoulder and right knee started hurting. It was not the pain that bothered him but the annoyance to be reminded of his old war injuries, acquired not even during but after the war, when, due to engine failure, the B 24 had crashed in landing at the home base in England. His afflictions had symbolically become the epitome of senseless events and the insanity of war.

For his recovery the Air Force had flown him to their convalescence center at the 98th General Army Hospital in Munich, where he had plenty of time to think. In those days an insight had gradually worked itself to the surface of his conscious awareness. His lengthy, painful war experience had been necessary to let him find his own meaningful task in life. Ever since, his heart had been with the young people here on the tundra.

In Ayuluk's mind the occurrence of war was the tragic result of the dark side of patriotism and closely related to the phenomenon of the curse, the realization of a negative prayer which had already led to the senseless death of two young people and the irrational fear in many others.

Caught by his memories he walked along the autumn-yellowed alder bushes that bordered the Emomeguk pass to the Bering Sea. A shrill scream suddenly pierced the air and he saw Catherine coming out of the underbrush, running toward him:

"Help! Fast! Oh my God, he may be dead already!"

Ayuluk followed the girl into the underwood and there was Tony, unconscious, face on the ground, a dirty rope around his neck, fastened to a branch. What ominous power had forced this carefree, gum-bubbling teenager of twenty minutes ago to yield to the dark calling of death? But this was not the time to find out from the girl what happened. He automatically did what had to be done. He reached for his pocket knife in his jacket and cut the rope, turned Tony around and applied mouth-to-mouth resuscitation until he started breathing again and a feeble voice came whimpering through.

Ayuluk lifted him and carried the confused and bewildered boy back to the road, making his way to the house of Tony's mother. Catherine walked behind him, crying and mumbling unfinished sentences. Endless questions raced through his head, finding no answers, and his own helplessness frustrated him. Roxy had taken his life in spring and early this month Dennis' suicide had left Alex with a gruesome aftermath. In a sudden nightmarish fantasy the curse had become for Ayuluk a slimy black octopus, which reached for easy prey, entangling with his tentacles the most vulnerable among the young. Tony, Catherine and Alex—he feared for all three of them.

Alex, however, had been helped, so it appeared, as he remembered the young man's calm and consoling statement after his visit to Bethel: "She is different." For a split second Ayuluk admitted to himself interest in this woman doctor and felt the temptation to meet her in person. Yet he quickly dismissed this straying thought. They had reached Tony's home and he had to deliver a boy with a suspicious ugly mark around his neck to his mother. Then he would bring the young girl to her parents. The burning questions for Catherine and Tony would have to wait until tomorrow.

* * *

It had been two weeks ago that Alex had entered her life. Vren had spent six long and disturbing days with him without escape from gruesome images of a little kitchen, stained forever with tragedy, images which had disturbed her ever since. Last night, however, she had fallen asleep with great ease and without any nightmares.

She woke up the next morning around seven o'clock and it was still dark. As she looked out of the window, the colorful tundra of a few days ago, lingering under an immaculate blue sky and not yet ready for winter, had been covered with a silver-frosted blanket. The reflecting light of a gibbous moon and the whistling song of a gentle wind in the distance completed a miraculous fairy tale mood. It was early October and in one long night autumn had come to an end.

She got dressed and, after breakfast, ready to leave for work, her car, tenaciously crusted with ice, wouldn't start. Rather than being concerned, she marveled at the magic of the scenery and instantly decided to walk across the tundra. She would cut off the bend of the road, which curved toward Bethel, and hitchhike from there. The frozen tundra appeared to be solid, and hiking boots seemed right for this adventure. For the first time she had to reach for a warm jacket with a hood. She packed the contents of her briefcase into a knapsack and took off.

The lights of the town in the far distance would guide her. Though she had never used it, she also remembered a boardwalk further on, which led over part of the tundra directly to town. It was bright enough to see the frozen tussocks clearly, and, like a child, she hopped from one to the other. Concentrating on the uneven ground and planning every step, she missed the accumulation of clouds in the sky. They rapidly grew denser and darkened the moon. The tundra had changed into a shapeless gray expanse without any contrasts. More and more clouds appeared from nowhere and sent the moon permanently into hiding. The fairy tale mood vanished. The air was colder than expected and a pair of gloves in one of the pockets of her jacket came in handy. Vren could not see the lights of the town any more and also had difficulty figuring out the approximate course of the road.

As she turned to the right to reach the boardwalk in the distance, she lost sight of it and decided to turn sharply to the left, assuming she would connect with the road. Her right foot suddenly got stuck in slimy muck. She bent over to remove some heavy clods from her shoe, lost a glove and fell with her face down on the ground. As she clumsily lifted herself up, a mixture of ice crystals and mud were clinging to her blue jeans and jacket and even covered her face.

Vren did not panic easily, but in her deplorable condition, her perception had changed and sinister gloom was lurking in all directions. Those flat little thaw lakes she stumbled between, playful and blue a few days ago, looked black and ominous and threatened to suck her into their spiraling depth. Her hands and feet were ice cold. She was shivering and did not understand why she had not reached the road yet. Had she misjudged the distance? Her progress was painfully slow. Sometimes the frozen surface would hold her and then again one foot or the other would break through to the bog beneath. She now saw white patches all over, which she had not been aware of before. Was that snow, or lichen or parts of Dennis' brain? What a sick association, she told herself, yet she could not stop thinking of what Alex had described to her.

The eerie call of a snow owl scared her. Where did it come from? Or was it an echo? The wind had gotten stronger and was shouting in hysterical spells over the tundra. Something was chasing her from behind. Her heart was racing and short of breath. She no longer doubted the power of the curse, even though she knew it was only her imagination.

But then what was imagination? The hostility of the tundra, her irrational fears, were they not more real at this moment than her little house on Tundra ridge and the clinic with a roomful of patients?

Vren couldn't tell how much time had passed. In spite of the dark clouds the sky had to get much lighter soon and she would be able to make out where to intersect with the road. Her clothes were disheveled and muddy, her face badly scratched from the fall and uncertain of any points of reference, her mind was suspended between two realities.

The noise of an oncoming car should have relieved her, but she was too dazed to give it much significance. She vaguely registered that she had reached the road and that it was Peter Lammert, the town marshal, in his police car. He and his family also lived at Tundra ridge and he was on his way to work. He rolled the window down and exclaimed: " What in the world has happened to you, Dr. Vren?"

"Nothing, absolutely nothing," she said with a limp voice. "Just walked to town and fell, that's all. The car did not start." Finding her in the middle of nowhere, completely tousled and disoriented—what did Peter make of this? she asked herself. His question was written all over his face. She would tell him later. First things first. She needed to warm up and get clean clothes before he could drive her to town....

Vren was late when she arrived at the clinic. As she walked through the waiting room to her office she acknowledged the patients who were all natives and known to her except for a teenage boy with a round face and black straight bangs on his forehead. His eyes were cast down in a shy manner. He was accompanied by a woman, about forty years old and most likely his mother. Cecilia informed her that the two were from Emomeguk, had flown in yesterday, but the plane had been delayed and they hadn't made it in time for the clinic that afternoon.

It wasn't until one o'clock that Vren asked them into her office. The boy unwillingly followed his mother. "I want you to see him alone," she said to Vren. "I only came along to make sure he would see somebody here. I don't know what happened last week and his girlfriend, who was with him, cannot explain it either."

She turned to her son and encouraged him: "Maybe it is easier for you to talk to somebody other than your mother. Trust her, Tony. You do need help. I'll be in the waiting room."

Tony sat down next to Vren's desk and looked most uncomfortable. Remaining silent, head bent and staring at the floor, he restlessly fiddled with his feet.

To help him out Vren started the conversation: "Tony, look me in the face. What do you see?"

The boy lifted his head halfway up, just to comply, and was ready to stare at the floor again, when he became aware of the scratches on her face.

"Let me tell you what happened to me this morning," Vren quickly said. And then she described her early adventure, how she fell and how confused she had been, imagining all kinds of things. Tony visibly relaxed and followed her narration with attention.

"May be you were under the curse as I was," he remarked with some excitement and then spontaneously continued: "I didn't tell, nobody would have believed me anyhow. I was with my girlfriend in the store and some people talked about the curse. When Catherine and I later played hide and seek in the alder bushes, the thing with the curse was still in my head—just couldn't shake it. And then my foot got stuck in something like a dirty rope, sticking out of the ground. I bent down to pull it out, when it started to vibrate and swell. Even though I was scared I couldn't take my eyes off it. My whole body was tingling. It felt good and bad at the same time. It was really strange and I wanted more of it and then I suddenly knew I had to do it and hang myself. But I am real glad now to be alive."

"Who cut you off the rope, Tony?" Vren asked very softly.

"Oh, the Yurodivi!"

"The who?"

"You can't know that," Tony tried to explain. "You see, he is half Russian and last year he gave a talk at school about the time he lived in Moscow with his grandparents and the communists and he told us about old traditions and Yurodivis, who are people who see and hear things others don't."

"And you think that he is a Yurodivi who saved you?"

"How could he otherwise have been right there in time?" Tony paused for a moment and then hesitantly added: "I am not sure, really. All I know is he is different."

Vren did not question the boy further. She made an appointment with him for the following week and promised to explain it all to his mother.

After Tony had left the office she found herself wondering about that unusual elder. Who was that man and what had Tony called him? Oh yes, a Yurodivi. Maybe Cecilia could help her out with this.

8

The barking of a dog woke her up. At first it yelped alone, then was joined by another dog and yet another until hundreds of dogs in the nearby town were howling in a chorus, a strange dialogue with the black ravens, which screeched over the tundra. It was a spooky concert which would keep her awake for some time.

So many impressions, ideas and questions were swirling around in her head since all those flights to different villages during October and early November. She reached for a green spiral notebook on her nightstand, the cover slightly torn and directing in print: 'Personal, do not open.' This morning she had flown to St. Mary's, north of the Yukon River, her first visit for a dark reason to the only boarding school in the Delta. Earlier that week the body of a sixteen-year-old student had been found dangling from the ceiling of the dormitory. The nuns needed to talk. The principal had found a diary in his sleeping bag and wanted Vren to take it along and read it.

Stuart's entries were in longhand, here and there a sentence or just words crossed out and printed over with shaky letters. Starting in January, words were put down only sporadically with empty lined pages in between.

Complaints about his loneliness at school, his drunk parents and homesickness reiterated until October 15, when he referred to the suicide of his friend:

Oct.15
Dennis killed himself, he was my friend, I envy him. Attended his funeral. Poor Alex who couldn't prevent it. Old Jimmy in his shack near the slough said it couldn't have been prevented, because it's a curse. I don't believe that, but what do I really know? Maybe it is the curse. I told elder A. after the funeral how I feel. He will write to me.

Oct.18
This year at school is worse than last year. What am I doing here anyhow? A. was so right, I don't belong here. I don't want to go to this school so far away from home and yet I can't stand it at home either, because I am ashamed of my parents, who drink all the time. Nobody in Emomeguk likes my parents. Everybody wants them to leave. A. tried to help, they don't listen. And also Dennis isn't there anymore.

Oct. 20 Getting up every morning I already feel defeated because I know it is going to be the same every day. I am so ugly and so short and cannot learn like others. At home they all talk about the curse because of the suicide. Maybe it is the curse with me, too ,that I feel so strange every morning, when I wake up and want to kill myself. A. wrote me a note and says I was a Yup'ik Eskimo and therefore I had strength and shouldn't feel sorry for myself. He will talk to my parents about adopting me. He thinks I should have stayed in the village.

Nov. 5 Nobody likes me at school, I am the poorest student of all. My parents don't like A. They are afraid of him, call him a Cossack. They won't let him adopt me.

Nov.10 I am always thinking how to kill myself. On Nov.8 at 2.15 p.m. I slit my wrist, it didn't work, I am a coward. A. sent me a letter and he says that bodies are like houses with a window, small or big, it does not matter, as long as the light of our spirit shines through and I shouldn't worry about my body and he says that my light is needed in the village to help others. But I have to tell him that my light is so little.

Nov.15 Besides me Bobby is the only one from Emomeguk. He told me yesterday that Olly, the little orphan girl, with the teacher, can predict the next suicide. I could really do it now because I have poison in my locker. Maybe I am the next one. I ask myself, are you too chicken to do it? I pray every night that the warm light in A.'s window will protect me.

The dogs and ravens were still chattering with each other when Vren put the notebook back on the nightstand.

The last entry, she thought, yet two days later his body dangling from the ceiling in the dormitory. What happened inside of him in those last hours nobody would ever know. The light through A.'s window had reached him and almost saved him, almost. Tears came to her eyes. She felt for both, for Stuart, for the anonymous A., and in her mind she saw an angel spreading his silent wings over the tundra that night, embracing Stuart's trembling soul and blessing A. for the light in his window.

Her mouth was dry, her chest constricted. She got up to drink some water in the kitchen, her thoughts engrossed in that night Stuart killed himself. She looked through the north window for the nocturnal display of the little white flames, which were dancing on the horizon at this time of the year, but they magically had been stretched to curtains, undulating over the sky in constantly changing colors of purple and green. Or were these the delicate veils of the same angel summoned to appease her as well?

Captivated by this enchantment she got dressed and stepped outside on the deck. The splendor of the light show above her imperceptibly merged with the memory of her first experience of the Northern Light two years ago.

After her divorce she had traveled alone through Alaska and was camping in the foothills of the Brooks Range, north of Fairbanks. Leaning outside against her VW camper, she very consciously had experienced the darkness under the spectacular display as a sacred vessel which held her in the center of its existence and for the first time she accepted her solitude as a precious gift, the key to unexplored spaces in her own heart. It was then that a powerful urge to explore Western Alaska had overtaken her, beckoning her to complete something unfinished like a journey which never had reached its destination. Out of nowhere, two lines of a poem by Robert Service had sprung up, an enigmatic road sign, which two years later had led her to the tundra on the Bering Sea....

The colors in the nightly sky slowly dissolved. Where there had been light, darkness spread and surrounded her with sudden loneliness. She shuddered and went back into the house.

Appeased by the familiarity of things and the warm glow of light through a red lamp shade, she went to bed.

The dogs in town had ceased to bark, no raven screeched and all she could hear, as she fell asleep, was the sound of the night wind. It roamed the tundra and carried a distant melody of great sadness, lamenting the unlived lives of Roxy, Dennis and Stuart.

9

The windblown design on the tundra had not changed for several days. Thousands of identical little hummocks, evenly covered with snow, sparkled in the light of the moon. Vren had stepped out to the deck and felt the bitter cold descending from the sky into the white silence around her. She wistfully remembered the magic promise of this very night as a child in Germany: It was Christmas Eve.

New friends had invited her over for the evening and she looked forward to meeting them. The car was already warmed up. She opened the house door, ready to drive off, when the telephone rang. Would she mind coming to help in an unusual emergency situation? A visiting friend was in an emotional shock since the news about his wife's suicide this morning. Vren was on call tonight. She didn't give this unexpected delay much thought and let her friends know that she would be late.

She drove the several miles along the road which led across the tundra to town. After passing the last house she followed the Kuskokwim River for another mile until she came to the described one-story house, standing all by itself, and surrounded by a beaten-up truck, two snowmobiles and a boat, turned over and covered with snow. Right behind the house a yellow Piper Cub was parked on the bank of the frozen river.

An older American man with a gray beard, in blue jeans and a purple wool sweater, opened the door, his wife, a much younger, pretty Eskimo woman with long black hair, behind him.

"Thank you for coming," the man said. "A terrible tragedy. Lucy found dead in the village, shot herself this morning. Our friend flew in yesterday in his plane to visit us and this afternoon, ready for home, his son called from the village. Hasn't said anything since he learned about his wife's death, sits on the table, the same position without moving."

"I am scared," the wife added. "He does not respond to anything, does not want to eat or drink. An old friend of ours, this is isn't him at all."

"She is right," the husband said. "He usually copes with any situation better than everybody else."

The couple led Vren through the kitchen to a cold, dimly lit room. A little spruce tree was leaning against the wall. The man pushed it over to the floor and shuffled it with one foot toward a wide open door, which framed complete blackness.

"It's a shame, we did not get around to decorate it because, you know..." the man mumbled.

She vaguely could make out a man on a chair, lying with his upper body across a table, both arms stretched out.

"He didn't want to be in the kitchen with us, insisted on staying here," the woman apologetically explained.

"I think we should let you be alone with him," the man said.

His wife brought another chair for Vren and pointed to the open door where the tree was lying: "I'll leave it open for some warmth from the utility room."

The couple had left without introducing her to their friend; his name had not been mentioned either. But what did names matter in this chilly darkness of nameless mourning with one table, two chairs and a stranger whose face she could not see?

Vren moves with her chair close to the table opposite to the man, whose face is buried between his arms. His body does not move, she hardly can hear him breathe. She is reaching out for his hands and as she is holding them, a strangely familiar apprehension takes hold of her. And immediately she knows: it is the same bewildering sensation which had overwhelmed her in a bizarre, never resolved encounter with a red-haired patient some years ago.

Vren wishes she could get up and walk around to ease this mystifying tension and warm up her feet, which are ice cold in spite of her heavy felt-lined boots, but she does not dare to move.

Her eyes are now fully adjusted to the dim light of a little lamp somewhere in the background and she becomes aware of his beautiful parka. Skins of ground squirrels, mink and muskrats are pieced together and decorated with stripes of white caribou hide; the hood, loosely fallen over part of his head, is trimmed with brownish wolverine fur. He appears tall for an Yup'ik Eskimo and she wonders what the face of a man may look like, who flies his own plane and, unlike Eskimos, has curly gray hair.

His silent sadness, filling the empty room, becomes unbearable and something pierces her heart. Yes, she has lived all this before: *a door wide open and not, as typical for a German Christmas Eve, mysteriously locked until last minute; instead a dark room, yawning at her and filled with despair, no splendor of a decorated tree with countless burning candles, only an ordinary spruce, as if knocked over and hurt, helplessly lying on the floor. She is that child again who waits in terror for her mother, for somebody, just for anybody, to explain and make it all go away like a bad dream. But nobody comes. And then there are all of a sudden all these people, huddling around her mother, who is crying.*

"You have to be brave," somebody says, "he is dead." And somebody else: "Yes, it's terrible, he shot himself," but nobody pays attention to her, lost and all by herself helplessly crouching on the floor.

And here is this man, frozen and motionless like she was long ago, overwhelmed by the agony of loss, which he cannot comprehend.

Vren's unease has subsided, she suddenly feels one with him and though she had not seen his face, he is no longer a stranger. She spontaneously acts on what her heart tells her to do. She slowly loosens her hands from his, walks around the table, bends over and gently embraces him. His body starts to tremble and like a thunderstorm he breaks into uncontrollable sobs.

She holds him and the child of long ago silently weeps with him, weeps for her own father, the woman she is now cares and consoles him like a mother.

Time has moved along slowly and there is stillness in the room again. The man awkwardly lifts his upper body from the table, removes Vren's left hand from his shoulder and turns his head towards her. Their eyes meet and, unprotected and vulnerable for a split second, he allows her to look into his innermost self.

She is taken with awe. She only sees his mysterious eyes and senses the complexity of a world of his own making: the Eskimo hunter of an ancient culture on the distant tundra and icy ocean, the modern man with a bush plane, a father and husband, mourning for his dead wife.

But his pride interferes, in his loneliness of this dark hour he rejects her compassion, invisible curtains suddenly veil his eyes and disrupt their intuitive communication of moments before. He wants to ignore her and be ignored, he wants them to be strangers again.

He abruptly stood up: "Please leave." His voice was shaky and rough. He walked away from her to the window on the other side of the room and with his back toward her he said: "Go now!" This was an order.

Deeply hurt, Vren left the room, left the house and without talking to the couple, entered the street. She looked up to the moon and tears came to her eyes. Christmas Eve had turned into gray nothingness.

Vren did not join her friends. She drove straight home. After a bath to warm up her shivering body she sat down next to the big window in the kitchen, poured herself a glass of wine and followed the silvery line of the tundra into the fleeting distance. The night was crystal clear and as her eyes outlined against the black sky the little white hill with the two spruce trees, that pingo she loved so much, she remembered the first poem she ever wrote, more correctly her and her father's poem. She must have been five years old or so when just three lines seemed to have created themselves in her little mind and beckoned for completion by her father.

It had become *their* poem. A few years later he took his life. *Her* linden tree had stood innocently on a hill, gently lowering its branches; the leaves of *his* linden tree started rustling in darkness, a raging storm scattered his dream and left *his* tree naked in bleak emptiness.

As a child Vren had been oblivious to her father's sadness, woven into the poem and foreshadowing his early, self-inflicted death. They had worked on this poem together and that made it an indelible memory.

With this in mind Vren finally went to bed and as she falls asleep the linden tree comes to life in full splendor:

No longer barren, its branches are covered with moonlit frost and decorated with thousands of delicate droplets of ice, which sparkle in all the rainbow colors like Christmas lights.

An Eskimo man with curly red hair rides on his snowmobile around and around the little hill with the illuminated tree on top and then takes off over the tundra towards the horizon. She has lost her left shoe somewhere in the snow. Her foot is cold and numb and she must catch up with the snowmobile. A huge thunderbird with mighty wings picks her up and drops her on the rear seat of the snowmobile. The Eskimo wears a most colorful fur parka and announces:

"I usually don't give a white woman with only one shoe a ride in the winter. But hold on to me tightly, I'll make an exception and get you safely home."

The snowmobile takes off into the air and the Eskimo shouts, "Let go, let go, you can fly!

He is transformed into a black raven and disappears into the sky. But she can't; she drops to the ground which is no longer hard and white but soft and green like the tundra during the summer, with innumerous little spring flowers between the wet tussocks.

Vren woke up with the vivid dream still blurring with her surrounding reality. She inexplicably felt reconciled and at peace with herself again.

She had distanced herself from the emotionally charged situation on Christmas Eve and considered her vulnerability as exaggerated. The embarrassment of the Eskimo man and his brusque reaction to her, a total stranger, seemed retrospectively quite understandable. He did not live in town, but came from a village somewhere in the Delta and it was unlikely she would ever see him again.

YUKON KUSKOKWIM DELTA 1981

10

It was the season of *iraluller,* the bad moon, ruling the land with hoarfrost and bitter cold. Ayuluk had come to the shore to test the conditions of the shelf ice. Even though the ice was almost too thick for hooking,' two boys had succeeded in cutting through. Pieces of string fastened to sticks with a hook dangled into the hole and they jigged their lines in anticipation of catching tomcod or smelt.

Next to a turned-over sled, covered with a blanket as protection against the wind, an older woman was squatting and spooned with a net some fish onto the frozen surface. When he squinted his eyes he easily could imagine that it was Lucy with her special little campfire stove for making tea. She had always loved ice fishing and with her great patience would often bring home a sack full of fish. Ayuluk was constantly thinking of her.

She had been buried a month and observing the activities on the ice he couldn't free himself from ruminating in self-analysis about her death which had stirred up tremendous guilt in him. How did he fail to see any signs and let her take this lonely irreversible step into the unknown?

He had mounted his snowmobile again and was slowly driving back to the village. Thirty-five years of marriage. He was fully aware how desperately he had wanted to belong somewhere after his alienation during those years of WWII in Europe. Getting married had meant to finally get settled.

They hardly had known each other, but his father and her parents considered them suitable for a solid partnership, based on practicality for survival. Because of his own introverted nature and specific background he had no experience with women and had considered the relationship with his wife as customary by Yup'ik Eskimo standard.

Back at his cabin he sat down on his desk and reached for a black and white photo in a round, golden frame. This picture of Lucy, seventeen at that time, he had taken with his very first camera, brought back from Germany. A sweet face, with brown innocent eyes, looked at him, her long black hair pulled back and held together with a barrette.

She had been a strong girl and of great help to her aging parents, who had no son. By contrast with her physical abilities, she had been shyer and more naive than most girls of her age. She easily would withdraw to her sewing skills, which she already had mastered to perfection at an early age.

He genuinely had liked her, with the secret hope that over time a deeper relationship would develop. They had helped each other, had been supportive in everyday living and were content. There was no doubt they had cared for and respected each other. His repeated attempts, however, to learn about her inner thoughts and develop more emotional closeness between them had failed.

It equally had frightened her to participate in his inner world. He remembered that day when he had asked her to attend with him a Russian Orthodox service in the little wooden chapel of Russian Mission. He was not a believer in this or any other religion —the *inua* of the spirit world of the Eskimos was much closer to his soul —but the mood of the Russian ceremony on Yup'ik land bridged his dual background and always confirmed anew the undivided wholeness of his identity. Lucy had been completely oblivious to the calling of his heart and broke into tears; she just could not do it. She belonged like her family to the Moravian Church and was very serious about it. And he had sadly accepted that they were not only vertically separated by their role assignment as man and woman, a natural division, but also horizontally by perceptiveness and sophistication .

It was on that occasion that he had decided it was wrong to want to change her. She was as much entitled to her own world as he was to his, but it had been a most disappointing insight, which only confirmed his conclusion of earlier years: an understanding on the deepest level between man and woman was not attainable in the reality of everyday life. Even Tolstoi's Constantine Levin, his hero of younger years, had to accept gracefully his disappointment to find Kitty, his beloved wife, preoccupied with the placement of the wash-stand in the corner room, while he was convinced she had sensed his yearning for sharing with her his thoughts of the meaning of life.

But why then did Lucy take her life when she had been content? And if she hadn't, why did she not respond when he reached out for her in earlier years? Who was to blame for this? The surrender to their vulnerable selves and an ongoing emotional dialogue would have meant the fulfillment of his hidden dreams.

He knew that she had wanted many children and if only one, then a daughter rather than a son. She also had once expressed admiration for the life of the nuns at St. Mary's, a curious statement, considering that she was not a Catholic but a devout Moravian.

Only retrospectively could Ayuluk interpret her wish to create a huge family or belong to a group, sharing the same convictions, as a deep-seated need for security amidst the painful disintegration of the Yup'ik people since the infiltration by outsiders.

Ayuluk was torn between self-accusations and anger and this ambivalence frustrated him, did not erase nor explain the tragedy and did not lead to any resolution. The responsibility to end her life had been hers, hers only, with no reason for him to feel guilty.

Lost in thought he had turned the frame with Lucy's picture around and away from him. It was she who had rejected him. For a split second and against his will he relives Christmas Eve, a stranger, a woman, patiently and with compassion reaching out for him and it is he, who in his embarrassment of being understood, rejects and brusquely dismisses her. No, he had no right to judge, it was not that simple. They both had to bear guilt, not because they purposely had tried to hurt each other but guilt came with living and there was no escape. However, one did not have to dwell helplessly on this predicament, instead one was free to practice tolerance, understanding and forgiveness towards each other. Surprised to see Lucy's picture facing away from him he turned it around and went to the kitchen....

Thomas would be home from school any moment, ready for supper. As he prepared some soup to go with the bread and smoked fish, he condemned his self-indulgence. Preoccupied with his own sorrow he had neglected Thomas' pain.

Since Lucy's death they had not openly talked with each other. They both had tried to act manly and deal with their grief alone. He had to help Thomas break out of his withdrawal, his desperate reaction to cope with his mother's death.

He lit two candles and was putting them on the table near the window when Thomas entered the kitchen. Ayuluk walked towards him, gently put his hands on his son's shoulders and looked him straight into the eyes:

"We do not have to carry our pain separately, Thomas. We can, we must share it."

Thomas, taken by utter surprise, started shaking.

For a second time Christmas Eve is back in Ayuluk's mind and though he is fighting the memory, he relives the unspeakable grace of being embraced. Before he is consciously aware of it, he is hugging his son, holds him until he has calmed down and can face his father again.

Neither one is hungry; they sit down on the table opposite to each other and they eat, just to do something that makes the talking easier.

"Why? Why did she do it? Why did she not trust us?" Thomas stuttered. "I feel so guilty. Did I do something wrong that caused her to do it?"

Ayuluk took his time to respond: "You rightfully ask why she did not talk to us. I do not know the answer. Part of living is openness and honesty with others and that needs strength and courage, but none of us is always strong. A relationship is an ongoing dialogue we take for granted and we assume we know all the terms."

After pausing to give Thomas time to absorb the heaviness of the shared thoughts, Ayuluk said: "You should know, Thomas, I tried, tried many times to enter her private self, but it frightened her so much and she always begged me to respect her boundaries, which I finally did. When she took her life she intentionally ended the dialogue true to her own terms and we were shocked because we had not known her terms. She left us with a dialogue unfinished and a desperate need for completion, disguised as guilt."

Ayuluk stood up and got Lucy's picture from the study. He placed the frame on the kitchen table and moved his chair over next to Thomas.

"She was a good woman, your mother, and wouldn't ever have wanted to make you feel guilty. True guilt can lead to redemption, Thomas, yet what you feel is not guilt, it's emptiness, helpless emptiness. And it will take time to experience the resilience and strength of your own self to overcome it."

Thomas was fidgeting with his mother's picture. Ayuluk's words had not really reached him. Ayuluk understood. His son's mind was in too much turmoil.

"I just can't think orderly—my mother, Roxy, Dennis. Who is next?" Thomas was leaning against Ayuluk and put his head on his father's shoulder:

"It's so scary. People say it 's the curse. I just don't want to believe it, but what *is* the explanation for all this tragedy?"

"Superstition, a neat little trick of ours to deny our very own responsibility for these frightening events and conveniently blame it on that so-called curse."

Straightening his body, Thomas said:

"I like the way you put it. To feel helpless is to be a coward. I don't want to be a coward. I want to be strong and proud of myself and help others to feel the same."

With great warmth Ayuluk smiled at Thomas. His son had his heart in the right place and he belonged here where a worthwhile task was waiting for him.....

That evening, for the first time since Lucy's death, father and son felt calm and almost peaceful. Although both were convinced their conversation with its attempt at explaining what was so hard to accept had led to it, the simple fact of their emotional closeness had been the secret magician.

11

Kanruyauciq, the coldest month of the winter, governed the northern land. Vren was the only passenger in the little bush plane. For forty minutes the colorless frozen tundra below had been gliding away, when suddenly the rising sun transformed this monotony into an enchanted landscape: thousands of ice crystals on the surface of a white blanket were quivering in iridescent colors and shades of turquoise tinted the snow. The short landing strip of the village, hardly distinguishable from the surrounding glitter of the tundra, had already come into sight. This was her first visit to Emomeguk at the Delta of the Yukon River, close to the Bering Sea.

The plane bumped along the short icy strip and came to a halt. As she stepped down she saw a young Eskimo woman coming towards her.

" I am Theresa. You must be the doctor I am expecting. Welcome to our village."

Theresa was about twenty-three and everything about her was round, her good natured face, her innocent eyes, the curves of her youthful body. Vren had been told that she just recently completed her training as a health aide.

They walked together to the end of the landing strip where a big husky in a green beaten up truck was waiting for them.

"May I introduce my dog and my truck, my most loyal companions. Wherever I go they go," Theresa laughingly explained. "And now be prepared for three and a half miles of ugly potholes and slippery patches of ice."

On the seemingly endless road, which lined up most of the little dwellings and peeling plywood houses of the village, they drove to the clinic barrack at the other end of the community.

The young woman showed Vren around in the clinic, which was not much different from the others she had visited before: a small consulting room, with a desk, several worn-out chairs and a broken bunk bed. The adjacent kitchen boasted of a double plate gas burner, a fragile- looking heater and, hidden behind a curtain, a narrow cot against the wall.

"A real telephone since January," Theresa proudly pointed out on the kitchen counter. "Most villages still have only a short wave radio. And here's your water supply for flushing." She giggled and placed two pails with water next to a good old honey bucket behind the kitchen. "The last two days we had none. All the water outside was frozen."

The charts were already pulled and piled up on the desk, documents of depression, despair and loss like in all the other villages.

"It's pretty crazy here recently, the rumor of the curse, two suicides."

"Three," Vren said. "Stuart in St. Mary's"

"Yes, he was from here," Theresa reflected, "but he didn't hang himself in the village. That makes a difference. I say there have always been suicides in the Delta. But I really don't want to think about all this right now."

Hours were creeping along, attending to the pain and agony of villagers who mourned the loss of loved ones, routinely claimed by the harsh conditions of this northern land. And as if that were not enough, people now were pushed to live between two different worlds, struggling to hold on to their roots and trying to numb their wounds in the delirium of drugs and alcohol, wounds which couldn't be healed with prescriptions.

Listening and consoling, and consoling and listening, had left her deeply humbled toward the end of the day. So many questions without answers were tearing her apart.

She didn't mind Theresa's early departure with the truck. She would finish her notes and with time enough left, walk the long road back to the runway, time she needed to compose herself again.

Before her departure she called the airline agent in Bethel, but the line was dead. On her way to the airstrip she stopped randomly at a house for a phone. An older woman came to the door:

"No telephone," she said in broken English, "but Ayuluk Zaykov, log cabin near clinic, he agent for village, has telephone," then added: "but no works perhaps."

Vren thanked her and returned to the very end of the village where she followed across a long boardwalk over the frozen tundra to the only log cabin around.

The small wooden building was surrounded by some dwarf birches and alder bushes and in this unusual setting stood out against the rest of the houses. A yellow Piper Cup was parked nearby on a short airstrip behind a storage shed.

Vren walked through the porch, filled with some rifles, an outboard motor and other paraphernalia, and knocked at the kitchen window. A tall, older teenage boy came to the door and asked her in. His narrow face was framed by shiny black hair and under a high forehead lively eyes curiously assessed her.

She introduced herself and asked whether she could use the phone to confirm her return flight to Bethel that evening.

The teenager pointed towards the poorly lit background of the kitchen, where she now recognized a man who must have entered the kitchen from inside of the house. He came closer and conspicuously said:

"No need to call, no planes tonight."

For a second she freezes, recognizes the voice, that same dark voice, and painfully remembers: *"Please leave, go now!"*

"The agent called earlier. Tomorrow at ten for sure," she hears him say.

She is rooted to the spot. He comes closer and she remembers his face as if she had contemplated it yesterday. The broad forehead, surrounded by black curly hair, slightly graying and cut short, the straight nose, the full lower lip, delicately outlined and betraying the capacity for strong emotions. Yet the eyes dominate his face, these inquisitive eyes which, like on Christmas Eve, look at her from the depth of inscrutable darkness. This face which discloses an incredible intensity and tells of an extraordinary will, this face has a name now: Ayuluk Zaykov.

And she experiences it all over again: the same strange apprehension, the throbbing of her heart, palpable in her throat. And flashbacks of the red-haired patient. She is bewildered.

They both act as though there were never a Christmas Eve. She wants to run. Before he can order her to leave, she will excuse herself.

She rushes to the door and mumbles: "Thank you for the information. That suits me fine, lots of paperwork to be done in the clinic."

He is very direct: "You don't go."

This is an order, like at Christmas Eve the order to leave, this time it is to stay. How much she wishes she had never come here.

"No more planes today," he repeats. "What's the rush? Your paperwork can wait as well as this can wait." He points at the kitchen table with pictures and newspaper clippings, strewn all over. As he shuffles them into a big envelope, she catches a fleeting glimpse of photos with air planes and headlines referring to WWII.

The teenager, sitting on the bench underneath the window, got upset: "Don't put it away. You promised we would..."

" Some other time," Ayuluk cut him off. "Not tonight, Thomas."

He put some dog salmon, seal oil for dipping and pilot bread on the table and asked his son to get the teapot from the stove.

This evening had been carefully planned in advance and her presence was quite obviously interfering. Relieved to have an excuse to return to the clinic she said to Ayuluk :

"You can keep your promise. I am leaving."

Walking back and forth in the kitchen he hadn't paid attention to her.

Thomas implored her with his eyes to stay. To secure her as an ally he made room on the bench and asked Vren to help herself to food. He then challenged his father:

"You did promise to tell me tonight —not just some other time—more about your war adventures."

Ayuluk stopped pacing :

"I would rather not talk about the war tonight, particularly not in the presence of a stranger."

Of course she is a stranger here, she is aware of that, but why then does she feel so hurt? Right in the beginning she should have followed her instinct to leave.

Nobody has touched the food. As Ayuluk begins pacing the kitchen again she senses a curious ambivalence in him. He wants and does not want to talk about the war. Had he fought in the Aleutian against the Japanese? she wonders.

Leaning against the table, halfway sitting on it, Ayuluk unexpectedly exclaimed:

"I am a Yup'ik Eskimo, maybe I am a Russian as well, yes, I am both but I am not an American. And here I fought a war I had nothing

78

to do with. But young and foolish, uncertain of myself and my goals in life, the military was the ideal escape. And I was ambitious. I should have stayed with the Territorial Guard in Alaska, but I wanted to be a pilot and needed more training in the lower Forty-Eight. Before I knew it I was assigned to a base in England, flying as a co-pilot a B 24 and bombing Berlin. It was hell."

"It was." Vren dryly said. " I did not miss a single air raid."

Before she can even think, the words have escaped her. She is startled by Ayuluk's emotional revelation. Her head is spinning. How is she to comprehend this strange serendipity, the overlapping of two worlds so apart? The Yup'ik Eskimo man from the dark arctic Bering Sea and the silence of the timeless tundra, flying over the ruins of Berlin, surrounding her, the remnants of what once had been a buzzing hustling capitol with thousands of artificial lights, illuminating the plaster and bricks of crowded buildings and paved streets.

This man at the end of the world has suddenly become part of her own past.

She couldn't sit still any longer and was standing, leaning with her back against the door. Ayuluk walked up and stopped in front of her. He looked serious like he was going to say something important, but he had changed his mind and turned away.

"The tea is getting cold. Let's all sit down and eat," Thomas suggested.

Vren was grateful for his presence and his easy way of breaking the tension . Thomas poured fresh tea for Vren and got some more fish sticks from the refrigerator.

" I guessed right. Your accent, of course, German! " He acted like a language expert. "And that coincidence! You must admit," he shot a glance at Ayuluk. "Maybe she would be willing to share her memories."

Thomas was tenacious. But Vren shook her head. Too preoccupied with the events of the evening, she wouldn't be able to leap back into the past.

"There are no coincidences," Ayuluk calmly said and fixing his gaze at Vren: "It's curious, I always wanted to meet somebody who had lived in Berlin during that time. Wasn't very likely though."

Thomas filled Vren's empty cup with more tea to encourage her to talk. "There are things which are supposed to happen and they have their way to come about! " Ayuluk's eyes, dark and insistent, are resting upon her face and forcefully challenge her.

Just seconds before not willing to comply, there is now no escape from his penetrating eyes. The past is pulling her back, a past from very long ago....

A burning Berlin, sinister black clouds turning blue days into dark nightmares. Chains of people handing pails to the rooftop, no more than little drops of water, to extinguish the fires of a burning city. She stares with others into that spectacular inferno and like Herod is perversely overwhelmed by the grandeur of the show.

With the speed of light her mind has crossed distance and time and she is the young woman, the medical student again. The kitchen walls have widened and there is no tundra, only debris of buildings and ugly smoking ruins of apartment blocks.

Night after night air raids, apartment buildings collapsing like card houses and frying people alive in the basement shelters. Hope has long been replaced by fear, fear only tolerable because of courage, daily, nightly new courage, there is no future anymore, only a horror-filled tomorrow and another horror-filled to morrow after tomorrow. There is no time to think back, there is no use to think forward.

And there is medical school. With no public transportation she daily has to walk two long hours to the university, always tired, always afraid of the sirens, seeking shelter in unfamiliar basements with total strangers. Like that woman, who in pitch darkness as the building is hit, claws in panic her fingernails into Vren's neck, screaming for help, help and consolation she herself needs as well, but nobody has to spare.

And then there is work to be done for medical school. Studying in the basement the content of iron in human milk, compared to goat milk, while listening to the artificially cheerful radio announcer or the menacing ticking of the clock: 'The American planes now overhead!' The horrifying noise of detonating bombs, one after the other, the floor trembling and everybody in the shelter room dead silent until the raid is over.

There is no energy left to hope for a future other than falling bombs, fires, dead military people hanging in the trees, content of iron in all kinds of milks, lectures in buildings without heat and without glass in the windows, with gloves, wrapped in a blanket, listening or not listening to the admirably stubborn professor in his pajamas— his house destroyed last night—explaining the biochemistry of phenylalanin.

And from the goat milk out into the street, helpless to rescue halfway buried, screaming people, back to the rooftop for useless attempts to get control of smaller fires.

Bombed out twice, rescued twice unharmed from collapsed shelter rooms. Between war and medical school she functions like a robot and not out of courage because she feels no courage anymore, or is being a robot perhaps courage? She is holding out because of medical school, because of the other brave or stubborn students, because of all those brave and stubborn role models, their teachers. There is always iron in goat milk, regardless of war or the decline of the planet.

She has moved like a rat three times already from one partially collapsed apartment building to the next and there comes the night where she cannot be a robot any longer. As the warning siren goes off panic suffocates her. Dead tired and hopelessly desperate, not finding sense in anything anymore, she runs into the open street.No more shelter rooms, no more ticking of the clock, the planes are already overhead, the first bombs are falling but she is free, so marvelously free and not trapped in a basement any longer. White search lights and green tracer bullets of the German fighter planes are illuminating the black sky, yellow flares, sent up by the American planes, decorate the night, the explosion of a plane, hitting the ground, deafens her ears; all this is more endurable than the claustrophobia underneath a building.

But people grab her and drag her back with force. The same ridiculous ordeal repeats itself for several nights until a bomb hits the half collapsed building, she is lifted off her feet and, several yards away, set on the floor again.

What was left of the building is now completely collapsed, burying them all for several days. Broken water pipes, leaking gas *pipes, dying people. She is waiting for her turn, she does not feel panic, not even fear. She is completely numb.*

And then unexpectedly they get rescued. She sees the sky again, black as ink and impenetrable from all the smoke. She stares at the flat surface. Where there had been a building just a few days before, now only clumps of melted bricks, charcoaled pieces of beams and other debris. It is all over and nothing is left to worry about. Not even a pair of slippers.

A few days later the Russians conquer Berlin. The war is over. Right or wrong makes no difference any more to anybody. They all have mothers, wives and daughters, who worried, they all lost fathers, brothers and sons. They are all human beings, tired of war, yearning for a spring day in May with a clear blue sky....

Thomas offered to pour her a new cup of hot tea, but she was still a space-time traveler. The kitchen walls had not completely enclosed her yet. Out there were still skeletons of houses against a black fuming sky and, mixed with the clatter of falling debris, she vaguely heard a deep voice:

"Two life lines, having crossed already long before Christmas Eve."

As the strong smell of more smoked salmon slowly brought her back to the present, she found herself surrounded by a weird stillness and suddenly felt vulnerable and isolated. She looked at Thomas and Ayuluk, two strangers, sitting at a table in a kitchen, a kitchen in a log cabin at the Bering Sea, and was overcome by a feeling of alienation. What was she doing here? Ayuluk's perplexing remark echoed in her mind, but had not reached her heart.

She abruptly rushed to the door and, without getting up, Ayuluk reminded her: "Tomorrow at ten, your plane," adding with a hint of a smile, "unless of course it happens to be canceled again."

In her urgency to escape all she was capable of saying was: "Thank you for having invited me."

She walked through the arctic entrance to the wooden boardwalk and, holding on to the railing, she slowly inhaled the clear winter air and shook off whatever had bewitched her this evening. She looked around and the white silence of the tundra   gently absorbed the nightmarish darkness of war....

It was cold and dark in the clinic. After she had found the switch for the pitiful light bulb, dangling from the ceiling in the middle of the kitchen, she turned the gas heater on and looked for some blankets. She should have brought her sleeping bag but had not planned to stay overnight. With all her clothes on she huddled under the cover on the narrow army cot. Unsettled and deeply stirred, she could not fall asleep. With her eyes wide open she stared at the cracks on the kitchen ceiling and tried to understand what had happened this evening. What power did this Eskimo man exert, that had forced her back into her past and made her talk so emotionally about the war? Unprepared and with no intentions of her own he had lured her inexorably into revealing her most personal feelings from thirty-five years ago, leaving her with great embarrassment.

And why again did she feel the same restlessness today that had invaded her on Christmas Eve? Yet even more perplexing was the mysterious link between this floating sensation and her memory of that incredible incident with the red-haired patient in the past. This most peculiar encounter suddenly became three dimensional and alive as if lived yesterday:

That afternoon, shortly after her divorce, she is wearing a silk dress in pastel greens and browns, the telephone rings in her office, a male voice, secure and distinct. An appointment is made for the same afternoon. He hangs up. She is used to calls from strangers for appointments, sometimes angry or hostile, or even wildly psychotic, but none of that applies. Why her tremendous anxiety?

Ten minutes before his expected arrival she gets a soda from a vending machine in the entrance hall of the medical building. Lots of people are waiting for the elevator and all at once her heart starts pounding: the tall, middle-aged man among them, with the fire red hair in the white buttoned shirt, he is the caller. Beyond any doubt she knows it, she shudders and has no explanation for that strange certainty.

A little later he sits opposite to her, separated by a round glass table with a vase full of flowers. How relieved she is that these Easter lilies obstruct part of his face for her. He hardly moves and remains silent. His hair is so remarkably red and curly; that's all she can think because of her growing uneasiness. She is unable to start a conversation without pretending to be calm, since she is not. He looks at her with a most peculiar expression in his eyes and says:

"It is cold in your office... smells like seals in here."

Silence.

"You are wearing the tundra on your skin, did you know?"

He gets up and is pacing the floor, he is now as restless as she is : "You don't belong here...either!...No, I don't think I can go through with this."

He walks to the window and stares out into the street: "Since this morning when I called you, I felt overwhelmed with anxiety. Somehow our minds have fused. I knew in advance what you would look like, even saw your dress, the tundra."

Ready to leave, he opens the door and mutters: "Remember, it's a deadly longing, the tundra...." He turns around, his eyes meet hers: "We better break this up... It's just too painful for both of us."....

Vren had never heard again from this red-haired man. Whether or not he was psychotic, it did not explain the indescribable, disturbing sensation which had stayed with her for several weeks. Textbooks talked about the disintegration of ego boundaries. Erudite words, but words only and no explanation.

Indeed, all this had been very bizarre, but it wasn't too useful to think about it right now. It would only confuse her further. The cracks on the kitchen ceiling seemed to have widened and looked so much deeper than before. She was convinced that her self-chosen isolation in the bush was beginning to play tricks on her mind. Her inexplicable apprehension since the encounter with the Eskimo elder and his son tonight was also only a distortion and derived from too vivid an imagination. Should she meet this elder again, she would guard herself and not let his powerful personality affect her.

12

The day before, an old man from Stony River had called the office, speaking in Yup'ik. Cecilia had handled his complaint. For the fourth day his young niece had refused to eat and wouldn't even come out of her sleeping bag to go to the bathroom. Afraid for the girl, he urgently needed somebody to help.

On their flight to the tiny settlement in the interior, Vren and Cecilia were the only passengers. Dense fog impeded the visibility and the pilot was forced to fly at an extremely low altitude, using the frozen Kuskokwim River for orientation.

They seemed to float through a narrow tunnel within a white opaque expanse in all directions. Suspended in a space of nothingness, Vren started daydreaming. Her visit to Ayuluk's cabin last week came vividly alive again, an event that had left her restless and unsettled.

She wondered how the death of Ayuluk's wife had affected the father-son relationship. They appeared to be close and yet there was something slightly antagonistic between them which she was not able to clearly identify. Thomas, spontaneous, outgoing and openly curious, was so different from his father and different from other Eskimo teenagers. Most of them she had met so far were taciturn and reserved. Thomas, no doubt, was burning to get out into the modern world, which somewhere was waiting for him. But Ayuluk's train of thought in this particular matter was not apparent to her. Keeping his inner world to himself, he was not easy to read. He talked very little but whatever words he used to communicate were consciously chosen and had condensed meaning.

She found herself fighting the fantasy that the war, before a gruesome memory, was perhaps a secret link between her and this enigmatic man. No, she had to curb her imagination; never again did she want to live through an emotional upheaval like Christmas Eve.

The little Cessna was frightfully close following the grayish surface of the meandering river, not more than fifty feet underneath and hardly visible.

Cecilia, slightly apprehensive, wanted reassurance from the pilot.

"Nothing to worry, my dear," he joked. "To land on the ice could be fun, providing it is still thick enough."

"Conrad would never fly under these conditions. I even think it is illegal!" Cecilia exclaimed.

"I know, I know, but we do it anyhow," the pilot laughed. "I read the Instrument Flight Rules— the IFR— as: I. Follow the River."

"Who is Conrad?" Vren asked, being uncomfortably reminded of an irresponsible adventure she had accepted on her very first day in Alaska last fall and which she had never mentioned to anybody. She had been too embarrassed, retrospectively.

"I thought you knew," Cecilia said. "We will get married, hopefully soon. He is a bush pilot, owns his own plane and, believe it or not, grew up in Texas."

In her excitement to have arrived in Anchorage Vren had fallen for the charm of a young bush pilot. Waiting for her connecting flight to Bethel she had met him in the cafeteria of the airport, where he talked her into flying with him in his private plane to Bethel.

"The only Texan who lives in Bethel," he had introduced himself, then boasting: "And no charge for an adventure with the best bush pilot ever. "

Too late had she discovered she was a fool. When she didn't respond to his bragging about easy access to drugs and alcohol, he had dived several times straight down over the Alaska Range just for provocation and obviously enjoyed seeing her truly scared. Upon their arrival in Bethel Vren was much annoyed to have so thoroughly misjudged this man.

"I think I met him." Vren regretted her statement immediately, but it was already too late.

"How? When? Do you like him? Tell me, please tell me what you think of him," Cecilia pressed her.

In a bind Vren hesitated: "I am not so sure. I think I flew with him from Anchorage to Bethel once. But let's talk about this some other time."

Cecilia looked hurt and confused: "Do you think I am not good enough for him as an Eskimo woman?"

"Oh no, Cecilia, the other way around; it is he who is not good enough for you."

"You sound like my mother. Don't try to talk me out of it. We are already engaged. He is different and I like that."

"Different from what?"

"From the village guys with no interests at all. Only bingo and snowmobiles. You just don't understand."

Not wanting to aggravate her further Vren said: "I have no right to judge him, Cecilia, I agree. It's only that I care very much about you. So let's talk about our patient in Stony River. The girl is sixteen years old, has not eaten, drunk or said a word in four days. You'll approach her first. If somebody can make her talk, it 's you."

Cecilia liked the assigned importance and stopped pouting. Vren understood this young, intelligent girl so well. Like Thomas, she was very curious about the world outside of the bush. And Conrad unfortunately meant to her the door to a more exciting life. But marrying a white man and be assimilated into a culture alien to hers was not the solution, the way Vren assessed the dilemma of Cecilia and all the other young people, so tragically caught between two lifestyles. Even though she had not lived here very long, the existing problems for this generation had already overwhelmed her; there were no easy answers.

The plane had landed on a short runway, about ten minutes from the village Aniak. They had to walk over the snow-covered frozen tundra to contact the local trooper who would fly them to Stony River, the only way of access to this isolated, small village without an airstrip.

They trod next to each other through the snow without saying much, when Cecilia suddenly pointed at Vren's boots:

" Do you really like those? I think sorrels are ugly."

" But practical. Who cares?"

"Well, you could have it both, practical and pretty. My grandmother does a funny thing. She cuts off the lower part of the sorrels, mainly for the sturdy soles, and works them into the most astonishing mukluks. Let me give her your boots; you will be surprised. A belated Christmas gift of mine."

"It's a deal, I accept your offer. They'd better be very beautiful."

Cecilia smiled and was reconciled.

They had reached the village and got in touch with the trooper who was ready for the short flight. He dropped his two passengers safely on the tundra right next to the few houses of Stony River and immediately took off again.

The fog had lifted and they first made their way to the little schoolhouse to talk to Katsoo's former schoolteacher, a missionary of the *Assembly of God.*

Katsoo, they learned, had been an extremely bright student, but dropped out several years ago, when her mother died in a plane crash. Her alcoholic father had been dead since her early childhood. Several of the eleven older siblings had died over the years, two were in prison, one brother killed a younger sister after he had raped her. Rumor went that his drowning afterwards was not an accident but had been arranged by the family as retribution and punishment.

Burdened with these depressing details they went to the uncle's house. A shriveled elderly Eskimo man asked them in. On a cot, tucked away in a corner of the kitchen between some driftwood and a dead seal to be skinned, Katsoo was hiding in a pile of quilted cotton. Even her face was covered..

Cecilia and Vren tried in vain to strike up a conversation with what appeared to be a sleeping bag, with nothing moving, breathing or emitting any sound inside. Cecilia unzipped the bag when a blood-curdling scream escaped the pile of cotton: "Don't you dare touch me! I'll sue you all!"

"Just take her with you to the hospital in Anchorage," the uncle pleaded. "I don't know anymore how to handle this girl."

How sad a situation. For a commitment, however, the village police officer was needed, which meant walking back to the schoolhouse and the only telephone in the village.

"Jack is out on a rescue mission," the contact person in Aniak announced. "A crashed private plane in the Yukon mountains. Count on several hours."

Back to Stony River and the motionless sleeping bag; back to the uncle who offered now tea, crackers and jelly to kill time, extending his hospitality also to all the relatives and neighbors who came and left after they had their tea, crackers and jelly. When the entire village had stopped by, Vren heard with relief a plane landing on the tundra next to the house.

Jack, the VPO, a young man with blond hair and blue eyes, had finally arrived. He knew Katsoo well, walked right up to the cot and approached the hidden girl with great warmth. But Katsoo did not respond. He instantly changed his tactics from a friend to a father—be a good girl—to finally a policeman with authority: "If you can't be cooperative, I won't be friendly either. I'll count to three and if you are not...."

"You don't have to shout." A disheveled, boyish-looking girl with short black hair emerged from the sleeping bag.

"Satisfied now?" she growled.

Next to a small blue pouch something shiny showed in the open sleeping bag, a machete. Jim grabbed the pouch and held up the machete, "What's that for?" He was shaking his head in disbelief. "I am your friend Jack. You know me, Katsoo. Get up and speak to me."

"Just to kill some chickens. It's nothing."

" There are only dogs and no chickens in this or any other village. You know that, girl. Cut out this nonsense and tell us."

"Nobody can force me to do anything." Katsoo had jumped up, ready to run out of the house, but Jim held her. She struggled and hit him; he handcuffed her and dragged the resisting, unhappy girl over to his plane on the tundra. The relieved uncle waved good-bye.

Vren, sick to her stomach, and Cecilia, with watery eyes, followed Jack to the plane and all four took off into the air, Katsoo sitting handcuffed next to Jack. No tears, no reaction. She had given up long, long ago when mother died, her last link to reality, staring now through the window into the nothingness of her hopeless young life.

13

It was a cold afternoon and Ayuluk kept the door to his study open, allowing some heat from the kitchen stove to warm the room. He sat at his desk, which was clustered with files and booklets, and was putting together the agenda for the next village council meeting, when Thomas entered the room. He had returned from his monthly trip to Bethel, where he attended classes to become a volunteer of the rescue team. He placed himself behind the chair and put his hands on his father's shoulders. "Guess what," he greeted him. " I met the woman doctor in the post office, invited her to the seal hunt next week." He couldn't help breaking the news about the invitation right away and was disappointed about his father's disapproval:

"Seal hunting is a men's affair, a father-son activity."

Thomas' admiration for that woman was no secret to Ayuluk. Vren represented to his son the modern outside world. He had taken a deep liking to her. Many questions regarding the war in Berlin had remained unasked during her unexpected visit in March.

It was April and *nayirciq* , the time when seals were born, had past. He knew his son well, like every year he could hardly wait to get out on the shelf ice and spot the first seal. Besides, a seal hunt! What an opportunity for Thomas to impress her.

"A total stranger to our traditions, nothing but a burden," he added, to make certain Thomas understood his decision.

Ayuluk had given her visit to his cabin a month ago a lot of thought. She had not wanted to talk about the war, but with the intuition of a Yurodivi he gently forced her into a most personal reliving of her war experience.

Vren impressed him as a timeless human being who had encountered life in all its aspects. Her age was hard to judge and in a way irrelevant. Her capacity for compassion, which he had experienced first-hand, was clearly rooted in inner strength, strength from overcoming repeated defeats and integrating trust and hope again and again. Her eyes were bright and lively, yet did not mislead him; there was unredeemed sadness deeply locked away, overcome and controlled by energy and goal-directed linear living. Two intense encounters with this woman had left him with a peculiar unsettling feeling, something he did not like to admit to himself.

Her empathy on Christmas Eve had touched him deeply, but he did not want to be touched and carried away. He was a loner by choice and considered his life in perfect balance. Besides, what had made her come to this Yup'ik Eskimo territory in the first place? She was, after all, a stranger here. He had to stop his thoughts from getting entangled with this woman doctor.

All of a sudden the seal hunt seemed to be a good occasion to have her expose weaknesses he would not accept. He could thus put her out of his mind for good.

"You already invited her, didn't you?" he said to Thomas. "Maybe we should give her a chance to prove herself."

Thomas's perplexity made him chuckle. To make his change of mind less obvious, he casually asked: "But are you really sure she wants to? Anyhow, it's you who asked her to come, it's you who must make the arrangements."

Ayuluk felt curiously excited about the plan and quickly pushed aside his calculating justification of only a few minutes ago....

A week later Ayuluk and Thomas picked Vren up at the Emomeguk clinic. She had flown to the village the evening before and stayed overnight to be ready in the morning. When she walked down the steps of the barrack Ayuluk tried to catch a glimpse of her face. Her abrupt departure from the cabin last month still puzzled him. Over a lifetime he had acquired the skill of breaking through pretense and reaching into a person's soul. Eyes never lied, if one had the power to truly *see*. But her face was hidden in the funneled hood of her parka. He suddenly was unsure of his own feelings. He would like to dismiss her as one of these Americans who come to this part of Alaska without knowledge and the deeper understanding of the true problems of these Yup'ik communities. For some reason he couldn't. What Alex had said to him, after his visit with her, proved to be right; she *was* different. Yet his decision to let her come along today had perhaps been too hasty. But whatever, he couldn't allow himself to be distracted by his ruminations any longer; he needed to get ready for the hunt.

He looked up to study the overcast sky for traces, which would indicate the distance to the edge of the ice they had to travel. Black open water reflected itself as a shadow, leaving a kind of line in the sky like in a mirror. He estimated that it wouldn't take them more than an hour, once the shore fast ice had been reached.

In gray twilight Ayuluk helped Vren into his aluminum skiff, loaded on a sled, which was tied to the snowmobile. The temperature at his house had read 20 below, and a fierce wind was howling over the white surface. Only a fool could think of taking a white woman along. A warning was in place. Before he mounted the snowmobile, he turned around and shouted:

"Long cold miles before we reach the frozen shore, many more to come on the shelf ice to the open water. It will be tough."

With Thomas on the seat behind him Ayuluk took off with a steady speed, dodging the many hardened drifts of snow, and rushed over the ice, which swayed and cracked underneath their load. A flat, sinister landscape in harsh black and white with not a trace of color surrounded them. Ayuluk wondered how Vren was holding up and coping with the cold. But there was no time to ask; he had to concentrate on his task. This was not the place to make any mistake.

They had reached the edge of the ice and after Ayuluk had unloaded the skiff he drove the sled farther back to the shore again. He only took the binoculars along. The CB radio, a little primus stove, a blanket and some food remained in the sled next to the snowmobile.

Vren followed Thomas, who had taken the 2.22 rifle and harpoon and was pulling the boat further out to the edge. She was clapping her hands and stamping her feet to get warm, when Ayuluk joined them.

"It is cold. You are not complaining?"

"Would that help? Then I will do so immediately," she sounded amused.

Ayuluk liked her response. With both hands, he lifted her head to glance at her. But her eyes did not let him in. What was she concealing? With a sudden urge to challenge Vren he asked: "What in the world made you come to this part of Alaska ? Yup'ik Eskimos and the tundra—it's all alien to you."

He felt her resistance to answer and paid her no more attention. Instead he took his binoculars to search the open water for seals. After all, Thomas was out for his first seal of the season, hunting on foot from the edge of the ice and needing his advice.

"Once you hit, I help you shove the boat into the water and you retrieve the seal with the harpoon before it sinks." Nothing filled Ayuluk's heart with more joy than to observe his son's exhilaration to keep up with the Yup'ik traditions.

He almost had forgotten about Vren. She stood there, like a child lost in the wilderness, uncertain of what was expected of her. He was going to offer her his binoculars, when he realized that she shouldn't stay with them right next to the open water. The time of breakup was too close.

"You'd better go back to the sled, it's safer, and take the blanket. You are not an Eskimo and not used to these temperatures."

Ayuluk watched her walking back to the shore. Something was not right with her, he could tell by the way she moved her body. She was not tough enough for this kind of adventure. The invitation had been a mistake. But somehow her vulnerability attracted him.

More than an hour had passed. Vren put the blanket around her body and was walking in circles around the sled and the snowmobile. Ayuluk's unexpected question, like a little stab right into her heart, had hurt her. And no, she was not an Eskimo either.

Her feelings had been in disarray ever since that evening in February in Ayuluk's cabin. She should have never responded to Thomas' suggestion at the post office the other day. To participate in a seal hunt and expose herself to Ayuluk again, how naive could one be?

Damp cold crept into her bones and she was numbed by an oppressive drowsiness. The infinite white distance in both directions along the ice diminished her own self to a nothing and the gloomy darkness of the bordering open water threatened to swallow her. Suspended in a lonely feeling of utter isolation, sadness overwhelmed her with such a force that she could hardly keep her tears back. Ayuluk had been right. What was she doing here?

She stared into the undefined dimension of timeless whiteness and discovered in the thin layer of snow that covered the ice, a delicate, windswept pattern, which endlessly repeated itself and roused a memory from long ago. As she tried to recapture it, she became aware of Ayuluk, who had come back to the sled.

94

Grateful for the presence of a human being, any human being, she couldn't hold back from sharing the image in her mind and without any explanation she burst out: "Look at this white eternity, it implicitly contains it all. I remember when I was a child that somebody showed me how to cut in a white square paper smaller squares with unlinked sides until I could pull up a pyramid, made of delicate paper lace. Our individual life, collapsing back into its white infinity when we die "

Ayuluk listened; her sadness had not escaped him. "Yes," he replied, "returning to the beginning, another way of describing life as round." And, after a pause, without any transition he declared: "A straight line can never fill a hole."

His strange remark dazzled her.

"We haven't been too successful so far," he said, ignoring their brief intimate exchange of seconds before. " Now some seals are around but still too far away to be hit with a deadly strike. An animal must be killed suddenly before it knows. It should never suffer. I'll take you back to Thomas and you can see them pop up in the distance."

She felt slightly better and was grateful for Ayuluk's presence. They cautiously trekked over the ice to the edge, where Thomas, ready with his rifle, was waiting for his lucky strike. Ayuluk handed her his binoculars and she spotted in the distance a few sleek seal heads, breaking the surface of the water. Then, unexpectedly, one showed up close enough for Thomas to fire a shot.

"Oh no!" she heard him call out, "it disappeared." Only a bloody froth on the surface was left, with no chance for him to reclaim the seal. Ayuluk encouraged his son to be patient.

"That, too, has to be learned," he remarked to Vren. "Nothing is complete without its opposite. There is no success without frustration."

Vren had hardly paid any attention. She imagined the body of the seal slowly sinking to the bottom of that black water, the instant transition from life to death, anonymous and lonely, and she shuddered.

While Ayuluk walked her back to the sled he gently touched her arm: "The seals are like all of us, part of the great chain of being, like everything alive, down to the smallest particles. And if we live right we always serve each other."

His words did not console her. The bottom of the ocean was filled with dead seals, the bottom of her heart felt empty and separated from everything alive.

"Their sacrifice and our gratitude," he said. "Their souls all return to their home in the sea to be born again and again. The bladder feast... if you are still here next December... "

Where else would she be, she thought, and a pang of sharp pain went through her chest. Yes, she knew about that celebration, when the souls of the seals, contained in their bladder, were given back to the sea through a hole in the ice. However, the mythology of reborn souls under black ice was no solace, did not help her connect with the world again.

Ayuluk had returned to the open water and she found herself alone with a sled and a snowmobile. If she could only snap out of her mood. She needed people, not sleds, not snowmobiles. And she could care less about safety—safety from what?

She decided to walk back and join Thomas and Ayuluk. The very moment she reached the edge of the ice, they were pushing the boat into the water, obviously taking off after a seal Thomas had hit.

When she tried to spot it, a strange noise, like cracking ice, intermingled with the whistling of the blowing wind, and all the black water of the open sea rushed towards her. Her eyes blurred, images doubled and seals seemed to pop up everywhere and sink again, leaving blooms of blood all over. Reality and nightmare had become indistinguishable. Some shore fast ice had broken off, sending her adrift on a floe toward the distant horizon.

The panic of her scream trembled in the air. She saw Ayuluk swing the skiff around and head toward the dislodged chunk of ice, on which she was moving fast into the open sea. He reached her, raced the outboard engine and jumped the boat right onto the float. She was shaking; he grabbed her and pulled her in. Thomas jumped out, pushed the boat back into the water and hopped in again.

Vren was in shock. She could not even cry and was overcome by an ominous sensation as if something tragic was simultaneously happening somewhere else.

Ayuluk steered the boat through the rough water back to the shore. Even though they reached the shelf ice in no time, the spray of each wave had given her a new chill. By the time they reached the shelf ice she was physically exhausted and emotionally miserable. She desperately tried to hide her embarrassment.

Nobody said a word. Ayuluk and Thomas pulled the skiff over the ice back to the snowmobile. She dragged herself behind them. Thomas immediately lit the primus stove to make hot tea and unpacked some smoked salmon fish sticks. The silence was paralyzing. She had spoiled the hunt. Sitting on the sled she shivered and couldn't control it. When she refused to take any of the offered food, Ayuluk said in his direct fashion: "You eat and drink now, this is an order." She obeyed like a child, drank the hot tea and ate a fish stick and felt as wretched as before.

The caravan with the snowmobile, sled and boat arrived at Ayuluk's cabin in late afternoon. Thomas unpacked and Ayuluk was ready to bring Vren back to the clinic, but she excused herself: "I can walk over by myself. "

Mockingly he responded: "Indeed, you already proved your independence today, when you took off all by yourself to the North Pole." An attempt at reconciliation. But all she wanted was to be left alone, go to bed and sleep.

Ayuluk pulled her toward him, took off her hood and made her look into his face with no chance for her to escape his forceful glance: "Everything happens for a reason. You have the power to choose. You can let the experience of today haunt you and make you miserable or you can allow yourself to receive its secret message with your heart and learn from it."

While he accompanied her to the clinic Ayuluk remarked: "The seals must like you. As we give their souls back to the sea, they gave your soul back to the shore ice today."

Vren remained withdrawn. She felt too apprehensive and was slightly afraid of him in spite of his good intentions. She walked ahead, up the few steps to the barrack and looked for the key underneath the mat. Ayuluk followed her. As she tried to open the door, he turned her around by the shoulders: "Let me see your eyes." But Vren's mind did not communicate with his.

"Your inner eyes are closed, " he calmly stated. "What are you hiding from me?"

"Sadness," she trembled.

"Let me reach that sadness in you," he said.

"I could not bear that."

"Yet you will—some day you will have to," he responded softly.

That very moment she dropped the key. He picked it up, put it into the keyhole, unlocked the door for her and left.

It was cold in the clinic; the heater had been turned down for the night. The 25-watt bulb in the kitchen was all the light there was. Poorly illuminated, her surrounding appeared eerie and unreal. She found an additional blanket, took her clothes off and bundled up in her sleeping bag on the cot in the kitchen.

What she had experienced today seemed more like a dream than reality. She recalled an infinite white distance, bordering a threatening black expanse of darkness, then a slowly developing sadness and frightening sensation of isolation. She faintly remembered uncertain sounds in the air and crepitating noises under the ice, when something had pulled her toward the leaden horizon away from everything alive. As she finally drifted off into sleep she left behind nothing but black straight lines in the sky and empty holes in the ice.

14

Vren leisurely poured herself another cup of coffee, enjoying the quietness of the morning. It was six o'clock. The sun hardly peeked over the horizon, but already wakened the sleeping tundra. The beginning of a beautiful winter day in April. There was time enough to write a letter before she left for work. While she had breakfast she listened to the weather station on the radio. The sky looked too blue and innocent for winds up to sixty miles per hour later this morning.

She had finished her correspondence when a hissing noise outside caught her attention. Through the window she saw some snow moving lightly over the tundra. The wind had picked up already. Here and there streamers had formed, dry blowing snow, creeping like white snakes over the surface. From minute to minute the wind grew stronger and with fascination she watched those streamers swiftly multiply. They were not creeping any longer but shooting forward rapidly. The house began to shake and the wind roared. In no time at all the tundra had turned into a fierce ocean with a gigantic surf, moving full force and without mercy toward her insignificant little shelter on the ridge.

The sky was still unperturbed and blue, but in less than one hour eight-foot snowdrifts had built up and separated her house and the car from the road. A prisoner in her own home. She called in and Ann, the secretary, who lived next to the clinic, had just walked over: "No, so far none of the staff has shown up...No, no patients either, except for one teenager from Emomeguk, flew in yesterday and wants some medicine."

Vren described her situation: "Send him over to the hospital. One of the physicians there can see him and help out. I will be in as soon as possible."

Another adventure. She would take her knapsack, climb over those white walls and walk to the main road. Hopefully a car would come by and give her a ride.

* * *

With the gun over his shoulder, Demian took off for those clustered thaw lakes, his hunting ground for waterfowl, to shoot a couple of ptarmigans for his mother. He was a slender teenager with a delicate face and nostalgic eyes who took life more seriously than other young people. The loss of his two friends, Roxy and Dennis, deeply disturbed him.

The other day he had run into Theresa from the clinic in Emomeguk and she had said: "Being sad all the time is not good for you, Demian, you must go on with your life." Then she had mentioned something about medicines that can make people cheer up. But they had to be prescribed by a physician and for that he needed to fly to Bethel.

A week ago he had forced himself to follow the advice, but due to weather conditions the doctor never came in and the suggestion of the secretary to see another physician at the hospital didn't appeal to him. By evening the windstorm had calmed down and with great relief he had flown straight back to the village.

To distract his mind he now was driving his snowmobile fast over the frozen tundra. His favorite lake, perfectly round, with a little beach on one side, would still be covered with snow .

Two suns were setting tonight, one atop of the other. He wondered for a moment, which one of the two fireballs represented the cosmic trick, the mirage. His heart was wide open to the magic of this moment, that had transformed for him the souls of his deceased friends into pure light. There was no doubt for Demian that souls were like light. He remembered his grandmother talking about life as an eternal cycle and that time itself was round, returning endlessly in transformed disguise. Nothing could ever get lost. Demian loved this concept which was deeply rooted in his culture. If time was round, there was no past to mourn, no future to fear and his two friends would never be separated from him.

Demian tortures himself with questions about the meaning of these two violent deaths. Is there something to the rumor about the curse? That he acknowledges the curse at all is disturbing, and he quickly dismisses his thoughts as superstitious. But why did Roxy do it? Didn't he have everything going for him with the opportunity to go to college?

Demian also excels in school and has the support of his teachers to continue his education at a college. However, paralyzed by his mother's possessiveness, the thought of leaving the village scares him. For the same reason he never had dared to date until recently.

His mother has been drinking ever since he can remember and rarely took care of her children. Had she consciously planned to kill them, by kneading endlessly the still flexible skulls of her newborns, as he had learned later in life from other villagers? A lonely and badly mistreated child herself, she obviously could never live up to her task as a mother. Rather than hating her, Demian feels great sadness. Her misery, her wasted life and his own incapacity to help her, it's overwhelming. The nagging guilt ,which poisons his life, seems justified.

He has arrived at his lake and hundreds of white ptarmigans are chasing each other in the afterglow of the sunset. He cannot bring himself to shoot any of them. He is contemplating his life and wishes Anna were there to share his new insights. He feels close to her, the only girlfriend he ever had. Not only has she resisted his mother's nasty and discouraging attacks, she also patiently deals with his timidness and avoidance of commitment. Yet, for the first time, she recently blamed him for not showing her his love. He does love Anna, but cannot bring himself to kiss her. It might reveal his anxiety about intimacy and he would lose her. He needs her desperately.

He is eager to get back to the village. Maybe he will talk to Anna tonight. The snowmobile is gliding over the crusty surface and the sizzling noise of breaking ice merges with the monotonous humming of the motor. In the eerie twilight of dusk the tundra suddenly appears lifeless and gray. Demian's optimism has vanished. All at once gloom hovers over him and darkens his soul.

As Demian approaches the village, the shadows of the falling night become more menacing. A sensation of unease and danger fills the air. There is no doubt, somebody is following him closely. He turns around but sees nobody. It has reached him and he hears a voice, whispering over his left shoulder to kill himself. He does not dare turn around. Instead, he speeds up, his body shaking.

He reaches the village in no time but is not relieved. He must talk to somebody to calm down. As soon as he enters the house, his mother scolds him, for he stands there empty-handed with no waterfowl. Then she mumbles something about Anna's nastiness and that she had to throw her out. Even though Demian yearns for solace himself, his mother's remark upsets him and he rushes over to Anna's house.

He finds Anna on her bed, sobbing bitterly. When Demian bends over to caress her face, she pushes him away. Her eyes are filled with angry tears. She calls him a coward who tolerates his mother's behavior. How did this woman dare to call her a whore ? Demian tries clumsily to take Anna in his arms and make her feel better. But she sarcastically advises him to live with his "mama" for the rest of his life, and storms out of the house into the dark.

A desperate Demian races his snowmobile up and down the desolate dirt road. He cannot think clearly any more. What was it that had chased him on the tundra? Being a disappointment to everybody, may be he deserved to die. Why didn't he at least shoot some birds for his mother? Tomorrow, yes, tomorrow morning, he will drive to his lake again and hunt ptarmigans to appease her. But right now, confused and bewildered, all he wants is release from his haunting conscience.

Physically and emotionally exhausted, he finally stops the snowmobile near a dumpster and cries, cries bitterly. He has no energy left and climbs into the dumpster to hide his despair from the world. He weeps and prays for salvation.

15

Last year around this time, Mary's daughter drowned. Nine-year-old Doris had played with other children on the river ice, not paying attention to those holes that were created by the current below and stayed open all winter. Her body had been swallowed, never to be found again.

For several days now the older health aide in the village had been brooding over the death of her daughter. When she threatened to take her life, Theresa had contacted Vren to ask for an emergency visit

The very next day at noon Vren found herself on the airstrip of Emomeguk. No, she did not appreciate being back in this village. Sky and tundra were ominously fused into one undefined, macabre gray without a dividing horizon and she almost lapsed into the same desolate mood that had haunted her on the shelf ice two weeks ago. Theresa had been waiting at the end of the runway. Bundled up in a colorful Eskimo parka, she and her impatient dog came toward her with a warm welcome. Without saying much they walked together over to the truck and soon rolled along the dirt road.

"It's good that you made it before we get snowed in," the young health aide said.

"The sky does look gloomy. But tell me, how is Mary doing?" Vren put her hand on Theresa's arm.

"Still the same. Confused and crying. Didn't get any sleep. I'm so glad you came."

Twenty minutes later they had arrived at a nondescript government housing unit near the slough and not far from the clinic.

"Mary has never met you," Theresa said and helped Vren climb out of the truck. "I'd better come in, too, to introduce the two of you to each other." She patted the dog who had to stay in the open truck and reached for Vren's knapsack to carry it. "Before I forget," she said, "there is a depressed teenager who needs to be seen as well. He missed you last week in Bethel. I went by his place last night to tell him you would be here today but he hadn't come home yet. His mother was rather unfriendly."

When they entered the kitchen they found Mary sitting on a table, next to a pile of drift wood and a dead seal on the floor, ready to be skinned. An old-fashioned electric wringer, right in the center of the room, took most of the space.

"Look who is here," Theresa addressed her, "the doctor from Bethel. She came all the way to see you."

Mary, a heavy woman, about forty-five years old, didn't respond and continued to stare into space. In disheveled clothes, with black, uncombed hair all over her face, she gave a pitiful appearance and looked completely forlorn. A round-faced twelve-year-old girl with bewildered eyes was squatting next to her mother on the floor.

"I'd better leave the two of you alone," Theresa patted Mary's back and winked at Vren: "See you later in the clinic."

After the young health aide had left Vren remained silent for a while before she sat down on the bench next to Mary. She began to softly stroke the rigid neck of the woman until she felt the tension subside. Mary slowly heaved herself up and walked across the kitchen where photos, arranged around a crucifix, were pinned to the wall above a television set. She motioned Vren to follow her and look at the pictures of Doris. By taking her time also to explain at length not only the pictures of Katie, Doris' sister, but all the relatives as well, she slowly grounded herself in reality again.

Nobody had paid attention to Katie, who still hovered silently on the floor. Then the girl got up and as she came over to cling to her mother, Vren followed her intuition, unfastened her own gold necklace and handed it to Mary: "For you to give to your daughter."

Mary was stunned and for a moment played with the jewelry in disbelief. She then put it carefully around Katie's neck and a smile split her face. Mother and daughter hugged each other and Vren knew she could safely leave and walk over to the clinic.

Theresa was grooming her dog when Vren joined her. "The poor thing is under the weather," she said. "But sit down and tell me, how did it go?" She filled a mug with hot tea for Vren, showing relief when she heard Mary felt better.

"Since you are already here I called a few other people in who need to be seen. By the way, our teenager, Demian, didn't show up. I may go by his home later and find out."

Except for Mary, Vren had not anticipated other patients. The afternoon dragged along with villagers trickling in for advice and refills. When the last person left, so had her scheduled plane back to Bethel. She would have to stay in the clinic overnight. Before leaving,

Theresa fixed Vren some soup, gave her two blankets and by eight o'clock she rolled home in her truck to the other end of the village.

First of all Vren needed to arrange for a plane the next morning, but, like six weeks ago, the telephone was dead, and, like six weeks ago, she had to walk over to Ayuluk's house to get to a phone. What a déjà vue. She had to do her utmost to overcome her sudden ambivalence.

She put her parka on and walked over to the log cabin. Again it was Thomas who opened the door. He was alone this time. After what happened at the shore fast ice not that long ago, he certainly had to consider her a fool, and in her embarrassment she tripped at the threshold and almost fell. Thomas did not mention the seal hunt at all.

She had made her flight arrangements over the phone and was hurrying back to the door when he asked her to stay a little. His smile brought her relief. He appeared excited to see her again. Acting as if he were going to share a secret, he led her to a small room, separated off the kitchen, an unusual arrangement of living space she never had come across in any of the villages.

The walls, made with logs of white spruce, radiated warmth and security. One side of this study was completely covered with books on wooden shelves. Against the window with a carved wooden frame and an antique samovar, there stood a narrow desk which appeared handmade. A globe and a telescope on one side, a lamp with a colorful shade on the other. Two easy chairs were arranged against a wall, which was decorated with an old lithograph of Moscow and underneath a small drawing of a little log chapel with a tin roof, dotted with Eastern crosses.

Thomas was visibly proud of this room. "Nobody around here has a study like my father," he explained. "Usually it's only a combined kitchen living area. Some villagers dislike my father. He *is* different. Even my mother was not always comfortable with his ways. She rarely ever sat in this room, but I like it in here."

He pointed at the telescope: "My father's gift when I left for boarding school."

This was Ayuluk's room. She felt like trespassing into the hidden world of his personality she had no right to enter. This was a place of bonding between a father and his son as well, and exclusively theirs.

The atmosphere in this room bore witness to how his early alienation had helped him to define himself and resolve the painful struggle of the past between his two identities. To be proud of his Russian roots did not have to interfere with his true calling as an Eskimo.

"Do you think there might be human beings on planets of other solar systems?"

Thomas' question brought her back to the present. Thanks to his spontaneity her self-doubt vanished.

Not waiting for an answer, Thomas' thoughts jumped around. He opened the lower drawer of a chest and squatted in front of it, surrounding himself with files and folders. While he was eagerly searching for something, Vren glanced at the books on the shelves. Most of them seemed to be Russian literature. Whether the two big volumes, with: 'Tolstoi' printed on the back were written in Russian or English was not obvious from the outside. She couldn't resist taking one of the books from the shelf, a book with a heavy worn cover and the German title: *"J.S.Bach und sein Zeitalter."* It looked antique and she was eager to leaf through. But Thomas asked her to sit down on the floor and view the booklet he had searched for in the drawer.

"Languages, I love them. Linguistics is what I want to study, if..." he stopped for a second, then continued with a melancholy voice, "...my father lets me." He opened the small book and took out the picture of a man with a wrinkled face and white hair.

"One of those old Russians from St. Michael." He handed her the photo and placed the small book on her knees. "His gift to my father when he brought him as a child back to Russia. One of the few authentic first books in Yup'ik in the Kuskokwim dialect, the outcome of hard work by a Russian Orthodox priest."

Vren was eager to thumb through, but Thomas didn't let her. He was determined to catch her attention by telling her in detail about his father's return to Russia and his years with the grandparents.

"My great-grandfather, imagine that, made my father read these prayers and songs every single evening to help him remember his own language."

Eager to impress her with something else, he jumped up and pointed at what looked like a framed letter on the wall. "Have you ever heard of helper Neck of the Moravian Church? He was the smartest fellow under the sun and..."

"... never went to any college." Ayuluk had entered the study. His words were directed at his son and concealed a distinct message. He had taken him by surprise. With a twinkle in his eyes he turned to Vren, still hovering on the floor: "Again canceled?"

"No, it left without me," she spurted out as if it made any difference.

"Planes, canceled or missed, the vehicles of destiny at times." Ayuluk always used words sparingly. Instead he communicated all he wanted with his eyes. Now fixing his gaze at her for a long instant, he spoke in a complex language of its own and seemed to express simultaneously the acknowledgment of the frightening event two weeks ago, and a warm reassurance of the present moment.

Thomas had not moved from the spot; he was pouting. His father's hint regarding college had irritated him, and somewhat rebelliously he announced: "College is necessary to learn more languages. I only speak two, Yup'ik and English."

"Three, if you count *maslo* and *moloko*," Ayuluk joked, referring to these Russian words for butter and milk, integrated like so many others into Yup'ik.

His father's sense of humor put Thomas at ease again. He picked up the books and folders on the floor and put them back into the drawer.

Ayuluk had settled in an easy chair and Vren was still holding the Yup'ik prayer book in her hands, when a woman entered the study.

"What's up, Sarah?" Ayuluk asked and introduced her to Vren as their neighbor and the mother of Thomas' friend.

The woman pushed her hood back. Her face showed worry and she mumbled nervously, "I came to speak with Thomas. Demian didn't come home yesterday. I guess he went hunting. He is always back the same day. Maybe you know?"

Demian ? Vren was suddenly frightened. A gloomy sense of foreboding gripped her heart—the teenager she never got to see.

Thomas did not seem to be too concerned: "I bet he is with Anna or maybe he ran out of gasoline."

"I checked with the girl; she didn't know, either," the woman said.

Ayuluk went back with her to the kitchen and Sarah sat down at the table. Thomas and Vren joined her and they all had some tea and crackers.

"Did you go by Ronny's house?" Thomas asked

"We should perhaps let the VPO know," Ayuluk suggested.

Sarah immediately cried hysterically: "You mean something has happened?"

"Oh no. I did not imply that at all. I mean we have to act rather than guess," Ayuluk said dryly.

Thomas came to the rescue: "Don't worry for nothing, Sarah. Let me hop on my snowmobile. It hasn't started to snow yet, it's easy to find him. I'll take a can of gasoline along in case. I know his favorite lake, plenty of ptarmigans there." And jokingly he added: "We'll be back in a jiffy with some of these birds and who knows, perhaps a snow fox as well."

Sarah looked slightly relieved. Ayuluk asked her to stay, but after she had another cup of tea, another fish stick and a cracker, she decided to go home.

In contrast to Thomas, Ayuluk appeared disturbed. Vren was ready to head back to the clinic when he blocked her way to the door: "Why are you always going somewhere? You just arrived." He made her sit down again and asked: "Did you ever run into Demian?"

Vren shook her head. "He never came. I was supposed to meet him today in the clinic."

Ayuluk' concern and serious misgivings were written all over his face and she decided to stay. The mood was foreboding and did not render itself to any conversation. Just to do something, Vren went back to the study to get the prayer book. Ayuluk followed her and glanced over her shoulder, glad to be distracted.

"To translate the Bible from the Russian, a written Yup'ik language had first to be invented from scratch, quite an accomplishment of these priests," he explained. "I cherish this book, even though it did not do that much for me as, I guess, Thomas wanted you to believe." Tenderness shone in his eyes and betrayed his great love for his son.

108

"I had to completely relearn my Yup'ik, when I came back from Russia. My head was too full not only with the Russian and English languages; at school in Moscow they managed to squeeze some German and French into my head as well." A whimsical smile danced over his face: "Oh, this German! Harsh and rough like spoken Yup'ik!"

Vren didn't respond. Anything said to lighten up the heaviness hanging in the room would have sounded artificial. They returned to the kitchen and drank one cup of tea after another. Time was ticking away. The waiting became unbearable. After a long silence Ayuluk startled her by asking: "What made you come to this place, so close to the end of the world?"

He had already asked her this same question on the shelf ice two weeks ago. It had upset her and she had not answered. So she would not answer today. His searching eyes studied her face. She got up to break the spell and walked to the window.

Ayuluk went to the stove for more tea, when the door was pushed open and Thomas rushed in, screaming hysterically :

"I can't bear it. Why him ? Dead, dead, dead, shot himself, six shells, his shotgun, all that blood in the snow!"

Ayuluk hurried to the door to hold Thomas and calm him, but he struggled himself free and screamed: "Nobody touches me, nobody! I want Demian to come back! Somebody tell me that he is not dead, that I am crazy."

Ayuluk tried again to restrain him, but in vain.

"Let go of me, you don't understand, I want him back. I will kill myself too! Stuck here in Emomeguk like he was."

Thomas stormed out of the door. Ayuluk dragged him back and, holding his hands in a vise-like grip, he said in a stern, almost threatening manner: "Don't you ever say that again. Calm down, son, please, calm down."

Thomas freed his wrists and again tried to escape. Becoming more aggravated, Ayuluk caught Thomas, pulled him to the floor and sat on him. "I love you, Thomas, do you hear me? Together we will get over this." He then pleaded and spoke very distinctly: "Don't fall for the curse. It's foolish talk."

But Thomas was emotionally unreachable. Humiliated by his father sitting on top of him, he tried to bite his hand. Ayuluk ignored his son's attack and in total control turned to Vren, who helplessly witnessed the dramatic scene:

"Call 6001, ask John to come over right away. Jail is the only safe place."

The terror in Alex' eyes in the prison cell flashed in her mind. No, this was no solution for Thomas. To be locked up in jail would make things worse for him. She drew close to Ayuluk, who still constrained Thomas, and said with emphasis:

" No, not jail. Give him a little time and tomorrow morning I can take him with me to the clinic in Bethel."

"I will go nowhere, do you all hear me? Nowhere!" Thomas screamed.

"Thomas does not need a hospital, only a safe place." Irritated, Ayuluk threw a piercing glance at Vren. There was no point in arguing with him. She knew him well enough by now. As ordered she made the call and then knelt down next to Thomas and stroked his back. He did not resist. He had stopped fighting and was exhausted.

Ten minutes later, John, the young village police officer, entered the kitchen. He stared in confusion at that human entanglement on the floor.

"Thomas is out of his mind," Ayuluk said. "I need your help. He just found Demian's dead body on the tundra. Lock him up in jail overnight. That will bring him back to his senses."

"Demian dead? My God, what in the world is going on here in the village! I knew this youngster well—just don't understand—and what about Thomas?"

"I said, lock him up!"

"Isn't that a little hasty? "

" I agree," Vren came to the officer's support.

"Do as I say, John." Ayuluk was adamant. He resented Vren's interference. With narrowed eyes and a harsh voice he said: "You'd better stay out of this. Thomas remains in the village."

More angry than hurt, she kept her thoughts to herself. Ayuluk rose stiffly from the floor. John bent over Thomas and put handcuffs on him. Without saying a word he left with John. He had given up.

110

Ayuluk grabbed his parka from the back of a chair and got ready to leave as well. He had to see Sarah and break the terrible news. He passed through the kitchen, intentionally ignoring Vren, and closed the door behind him, without even looking at her. Alone and upset, she held on to the table and tried to comprehend the horror of the last hour....

It was midnight and heavy snow fell from a black sky. Very slowly Vren walked back to the clinic, worrying about Thomas, alone with his despair in a pitiful little jail. Theresa had pointed it out from the truck on her first visit to Emomeguk six weeks ago. Why not visit him in his misery? She briefly entered the clinic and looked for the flashlight she always took along in her knapsack when traveling to the villages.

It was one thing to remember the exact location of that shack somewhere off the four mile dirt road; it was another to find it in total darkness and densely falling snow. How naive to even think of a flashlight as help.

Time passed and she was still stumbling through the snow. She clearly had misjudged the distance. Biting cold had crept into her tired body and she was ready to give up when a sudden wave of anger and rebellion against Ayuluk filled her with new energy. She was doubly determined to find the jail tonight. Her heart was bleeding for Thomas. His mind was quick and she understood all too well his longing for education.

At random she stopped at the door of one of the houses along the road to ask for help. After knocking a second time an old Eskimo man opened the door just a slit, eyed her suspiciously and pointed into a certain direction across the white tundra: "There, there." A woman after midnight in a blizzard, trying to find the jail. He definitely had to consider her slightly crazy.

Though sparse, the instruction had been useful. In spite of heavy flurries, shrouding the tundra, Vren miraculously spotted the run-down shack in no time. She knocked at the door but John was gone. At a loss about what to do, she stumped through the bushes around the barrack and discovered the rear wall was in disrepair. Some rotten boards were sticking out. She almost hurt herself. And then she heard somebody sobbing inside. Thomas.

She put her mouth close to the brittle wall and hollered: "Thomas, can you hear me? There is a gap here between these cracked boards. Maybe if..."

"It won't work," he shouted back.

"Come on, let's try! Push with your body against the wall, push hard. I'll pull on the boards from outside," she encouraged him. She was fully aware that her spunk to free Thomas only derived from her wish to defeat Ayuluk.

Although the shakiness of what called itself a jail was a joke, it was another matter to crack those rotten boards open and widen the gap further. And that without any tools and in a snowstorm.

"You promise to come with me and fly to Bethel tomorrow," she yelled and hoped he would hear her. She wasn't sure what he had hollered back. But she sensed rebellion and quite determined she shouted: "It's up to you, I am leaving."

The wooden planks suddenly squeaked. Thomas was throwing his weight from the inside against the wall. "I promise, I promise. Let us try." Vren could clearly hear him. He sounded desperate and she believed him.

It was the second miracle of the night—two weather-beaten, crumbly boards yielded to their combined effort. The gap, however, was still not big enough for his head, but then another damaged plank unexpectedly broke.

Thomas twisted his tense body with groaning through the widened opening, while Vren steadily pulled on his shoulders until he finally was born from the womb of the jail into the snow, bleeding from minor cuts on his hands and face. He got up on his feet and they stood next to each other like two naughty children after a successful prank.

The storm continued to sweep across the tundra. Fluffy little crystals danced wildly in the whistling wind. Vren felt exhausted and her body ached. Yet she reveled in her triumph over Ayuluk. With frozen mittens she clumsily shook the snow off on her down jacket and heavy pants, and was ready to trot with Thomas back to the clinic. But where was he? In panic she called for him, called in every direction. In panic she fought herself through the snow to the main road again, hoping to catch up with him there, but a curtain of raked snowflakes made it impossible to trace anything.

Where did Thomas go? Was he safe from himself? Devastated by fear she blamed herself for unforgivable irresponsibility. How naive had she been in her victory over Ayuluk.

Tears froze on her cheeks she stumbled back to his house. If only Thomas were there, she gladly would swallow Ayuluk's furious reaction, which she rightfully deserved. But there was no light in the house and no response to her knocking. No Thomas, no Ayuluk. Back in the clinic she also could not contact John; the line was still dead. Paralyzed by fear and desperation, she could not decide what to do next. The obligation to contact Ayuluk made her extremely anxious. She was afraid to face him and at the same time ashamed to be such a coward. How much she wished never to have come to the bush of Alaska, to be on the East Coast instead, with problems she knew how to handle.

16

Back in her office in Bethel, Vren had reached for the telephone several times to speak to John in Emomeguk and report Thomas' disappearance, but then never dialed. She had left the village this morning with the mail plane without even trying to contact Ayuluk.

She was too tense to drink the coffee Cecilia had brought her. She was too restless to see her waiting patients. She was beside herself, frightened for Thomas' life and afraid of Ayuluk's rage. She couldn't concentrate on anything.

It was around 1 p.m. when the telephone rang. She started shaking; it had to be Ayuluk. And so it was. With a rather friendly voice he told her that Thomas had escaped from the jail and had been seen at the airstrip about an hour ago, boarding the plane to Bethel.

"I notified the desk of Mark Air to keep Thomas right there but they wouldn't do that," he said. "Could you get to the airport and have him call me? He trusts you. Perhaps you were right, the handcuffing wasn't a good idea."

Unspeakably relieved she mumbled: "Anything you want me to do."

Ayuluk, of course, couldn't even guess the true circumstances. How shameful not to have presented him with the truth this morning before her departure from Emomeguk.

"Are you concealing something?" he asked. "You are ill at ease."

He had sensed her thoughts and before she could get hold of herself she blurted out: "I am afraid to tell you."

Totally matter of fact he only said: "Most likely rightfully so." And then: "Hurry, the plane is landing any minute. Have Thomas call me." Before she could respond he had hung up.

Ayuluk's remark puzzled her. Did he already assume the truth or was he only teasing? With no time to spend on this nagging question, she arranged for her patients to be seen by another staff member and asked Cecilia to go with her to the airport. The car was as good as any place to sketch for her the events of the day before.

"It's hilarious, you dragging him through a hole in the jail," Cecilia giggled.

"It's not funny. Just think what he could have done to himself."

"But he didn't. He is alive and well and probably on his way to a friend. After all, you tried to help Thomas. Forget about his father, he is an old grouch, and don't feel so guilty that you haven't told him."

By the time they arrived at the terminal the plane had already landed and most passengers were gone. The young woman at the desk of Mark Air acknowledged the earlier call by Ayuluk. By chance she remembered a young man with a patch on one eye who had inquired about the arrival time of the plane from Emomeguk. He then had left with a young passenger.

"That's Wasky from Napaskiak!" Cecilia exclaimed. "He was in a fight with another guy here in the post office the other day. I bet that's a friend of Thomas'. I know where he lives."

Napaskiak was about ten miles down the Kuskokwim River on the opposite bank. Vren had visited that village by bush plane once.

"Oh, let's go with your car; there is nothing to it." Cecilia was excited, but Vren, being a newcomer and unfamiliar with the river ice, was hesitant. She suggested a river taxi.

"To get one takes too long. If you could pull Thomas out through a hole, I swear—with me as your pilot—you can drive on the ice."

Vren was not too eager about this plan. Cecilia, however, had a point; they could not lose any time if they wanted to catch Thomas. They left the airport, drove back to town and approached the narrow spot on the bank of the Kuskokwim, where a transfer to the river ice was possible.

"Don't slow down. The overflow next to the bank is dangerous," Cecilia advised. "Get quickly across to the middle of the river, and stay right there between the tree branches and reflectors on the ice."

With no experience and hesitant in her attempt to drive through the overflow, Vren messed up. The left rear wheel of the car got immediately stuck in the slush. Two young men, loafing around and chewing tobacco, were leisurely observing the incident. One of them shouted:

"They don't teach you driving on a river in the lower Forty-Eight, do they?"

"Conrad, what are you doing here? Don't just stand there, come and help!" Cecilia hollered back.

The skinny one in the leather jacket was, indeed, Conrad, the only Conrad Vren knew, the irresponsible bush pilot, involved in her adventure last August. And he was Cecilia's boyfriend.

He sluggishly approached the car, climbed in the driver seat and raced the engine, his friend pushed and after several attempts the car jumped forward onto the solid ice of the river.

As Vren took over the steering wheel again, Cecilia leaned out of the car: "Sorry, can't see you tonight, it's an emergency. Do call me on the weekend." She rolled the window up and her face was beaming: "Isn't he a neat guy?"

Vren did not look forward to this river trip. How was she supposed to concentrate on her driving and stay on this one-lane highway of ice, when her thoughts were in turmoil? Did Ayuluk know or didn't he? Was Thomas truly safe and would they find him? Could she convince Cecilia to let go of Conrad?

Steaming green patches from the overflow of the tide, here and there a hole in the ice, snowdrifts and missing markers, oncoming cars and snowmobiles, now mixing with bloody seal heads and other remembered bits and pieces of the ill-fated seal hunt—a dangerous adventure at the wrong time. What was she doing here? Ayuluk had asked her this question twice already.

"Watch out," Cecilia suddenly screamed, "that snowmobile is trying to pass you!"

The warning, however, came too late. The car already swerved from the marked lane into a puddle of slush, hydroplaned several yards and landed on its side in a huge snowdrift.

Two guilty looking teenagers dismounted the snowmobile and came over to help them climb out of the car. Both were thoroughly shaken up but neither was hurt. In all the scary confusion, Vren heard somebody say:

"Hi, Cecilia, what a way to meet."

"I can't believe it, it's Wasky—and that must be Thomas." Cecilia was leaning against the tilted car and seemed to have recovered quickly from the shock. She found this commotion most exciting. "It's they who found us, isn't that funny?" she giggled and threw Vren a glance. "It's worth that little accident! Don't you agree?"

Wasky, with his black eye patch, looked like a pirate and Thomas, visibly contrite, made a convincing captured victim. He babbled something about being sorry and that they had to do a little shopping in Bethel for Wasky's mother, a statement that wasn't much of an explanation, but that didn't matter. After all, Thomas was well and alive.

Both boys were eager to dig the car out of the snow, turn it back on its four wheels and forget about the unfortunate incident. In a hurry Wasky hopped on his snowmobile and took off, leaving behind Thomas, who looked lost and embarrassed.

"Why don't you turn the car around and drive us back to Bethel?" Vren encouraged him.. "I bet you are more experienced on the river ice than the two of us."

Vren didn't have to ask twice. She purposely took a seat in the rear and let Cecilia settle next to him. The distance back to town now appeared so much shorter and less dangerous. The two young people were soon engaged in a lively conversation, speaking in Yup'ik. Vren heard the name Demian mentioned here and there and saw from the side tears glistening in Cecilia's eyes. Thomas' right hand was covering hers, folded in her lap. This shy and innocent tenderness in their mutual discovery, it had to mean healing for Thomas. And this was truly worth "that little accident."

Back in Bethel by late afternoon, the waiting room was empty, the secretary gone.

Thomas called his father from Vren's office. The conversation was short. As he hung up his face tightened and showed apprehension: "He insists on picking me up tonight," he said wryly. "There is no commercial flight leaving Emomeguk any more. He will fly his Piper Cub."

Thomas' trepidation about meeting his father in a few hours was evident. Vren also dreaded the arrival of Ayuluk. Wanting to be alone, she sent the two young people off to have a snack in the hospital cafeteria. She now had all the time for herself, but didn't know what to do with it. She tried to focus on some medical reports due, but her hand was shaking and she couldn't hold the pen. She made some unnecessary telephone calls, confirming appointments and checking laboratory results. She watered her flowers and dusted her desk and did anything and everything just to calm herself. She would soon have to face Ayuluk.

Two hours had dragged by. With the office door open, she saw Cecilia and Thomas coming back from the cafeteria, just as Ayuluk entered from the street. He could hardly conceal his emotions and raised both arms to greet his son. His gesture of forgiveness touched her and almost made her forget her stifling fear and uneasiness.

All four stood in the waiting room now, looking at each other. Instead of tension and uneasiness they shared a silent moment of harmony, as if an invisible thread of destiny had purposely linked them together. Ayuluk walked over to Thomas and put his arm around his shoulders. Thomas' lips twitched into a smile of relief. Father and son had bonded again. Ayuluk then turned to Vren and Cecilia, and softly said: "Thank you, thank you both. These are strange times. We all have to help each other."

He was in a great rush to get back to Emomeguk for the preparations of Demian's funeral. The taxi, which had brought him from the airport, was waiting outside. Before he and Thomas left, he shot a quick, intent glance at Vren: "Still afraid?"

Utterly perplexed she nodded. As much as she wanted to tell him what burdened her, this was neither the time nor the place for a confession.

"It's time for us, too, to go home," Cecilia said, slipping on her coat. "And, by the way, I like Thomas." She fastened her hood and put her fur mittens on. "I expected to be with Conrad tonight and now, see where I find myself? Still in your office. Grandmother was right. Never predict the future. It might change what otherwise would have happened."

17

On her way home from a coastal village on Norton Sound Vren stopped in St. Mary's, the hub of the Delta. The waiting area of the small terminal looked like an intimate living room. Worn out easy chairs and an old sofa were arranged around a small table with some outdated magazines. An old man and his two dogs had made themselves comfortable on the couch. But there was no time left to sit down. The passengers of another plane were already walking over to the single prop Cessna, ready to take off for Bethel .

She left the terminal and quickened her pace when she detected Ayuluk among those travelers. Not ready for an encounter, she instantly slowed down, trying to bypass him. She was the last one on board and ended up to sit next to the pilot.

Two weeks ago, he and Thomas had met in her office and like a sunbeam breaking through black thunderheads, their reconciliation had weakened the haunting scene of the evening before. Her role in Thomas' disappearance, however, still had been concealed from him.

They hadn't been in the air for long when the pilot encountered turbulence. The nylon webbing in the rear got loose, duffel bags and boxes tumbled and were tossed around, a child screamed.

Nobody got hurt, but there was some panic since the pilot had to land on the tundra to securely fasten the mesh again. He circled several times in the air before he came down to a bumpy stop. Everybody had to get out and Vren, as the first one, walked quickly away from the plane to avoid Ayuluk.

"Don't go too far. We will be taking off again in fifteen minutes or so," the pilot called after her.

She was heading toward a small spruce tree, the only one against the 360 degrees of wide open tundra. It was about ten o'clock in the evening and the sun behind her was almost ready to set. She reached the tree in a few minutes and her shadow, long and spooky, was cast on the skinny branches.

She began to play with her shadow by moving away from the tree to let the sun project her silhouette on the flat, still frozen tundra, stretching it even more. Suddenly a second shadow, bigger and taller, grew ghostly in the snow and began to partially fuse with hers. Before she could turn around, she felt two hands on her shoulders. Ayuluk was standing behind her.

Apprehension choked her throat, for he said nothing. She had to struggle for breath like in the night of the snowstorm, when she had stumbled in panic along the dirt road to find Thomas; like in the night of the snowstorm, when she cowardly failed to notify Ayuluk.

Vren stared at the two eerie shadows which vibrated in mute communication. Like a curious burden, she sensed Ayuluk's silent response to her thoughts, his justified reprimand. Not able to bear the growing tension any longer, she was ready to burst and finally face Ayuluk. She was to turn around when he exerted gentle force to restrain her and calmly said: "Don't. We read each other quite well without words."

Vren didn't dare to move. Without changing his position he said: "I reconciled with Thomas but I haven't changed my mind. He is going to stay in the Delta." His words were deliberate and slow: "No college...no linear living for Thomas... in spite of your support and lining up with him, that miraculous escape from jail."

At long last her wrongdoing was out in the open. But what about Thomas? She was no longer concerned about herself. Her fear of Ayuluk had vanished. She was her rebellious self again and determined to fight for Thomas.

She freed herself of his hands on her shoulders and hastened back to the plane. He walked behind her. Neither one said a word.

The other passengers had already boarded. She sat next to the pilot again, in front of Ayuluk. Before she fastened her seat belt, she turned around and said:

"Ever considered stagnation in too small a circle? What appears to be linear might be in truth slightly curved, a small section only of Thomas' much larger circle of life."

The plane rattled across the tundra, swerved a few times and was airborne. The noise of the engine hampered any conversation. Not much time had passed when Ayuluk bent forward to talk into her right ear: "You are most obstinate."

He sat back for a while, then leaned forward again and continued into her left ear: "But that's not what concerns me," he paused, "...perhaps I even like it ... no, it's your irresponsibility or is it lack of trust? You are afraid of me."

Because of the acoustics she couldn't respond and didn't want to either....

The plane had landed in Bethel. Ayuluk and Vren left the airport together and made their way to the parking area. Next to her Subaru a red truck was parked, the car of the association of village presidents and at Ayuluk's disposal when visiting Bethel.

Before they parted, Vren provocatively asked: "Why *your* lack of trust in Thomas?"

He seemed caught off guard but then sternly responded: "He is to remain a Yup'ik Eskimo, a..."

"No, not an Eskimo," Vren quickly interrupted, "an Eskimo human being in a changing world. See him with your heart, trust him and his dreams for the future."

Ayuluk got in the truck. He rolled the window down and said with a razor sharp voice : "Thomas is not *your* responsibility!" He slowly backed out of the parking space and took off.

Again he had dismissed her, like on Christmas Eve, like on the evening when Thomas had found Demian's body. All she wanted was to get home, fall asleep and forget.

18

The breakup of the Kuskokwim River was late. During the last several years the huge chunks of ice had already been squeezed out into the Bering Sea at this time. This year it was almost June when boats started popping up again on the river and the mud season, short but drastic, announced the abrupt beginning of spring.

The principal of the high school in Emomeguk had arranged a meeting for teachers, village elders and anybody concerned, to brainstorm ideas of suicide prevention. Vren had the car keys in her hand, ready to leave for the airport. She stepped out on the deck and what had been an ordinary driveway the evening before was now a brownish, mushy lake, glistening in the morning sun. Her car was sunk tire deep into slippery silt. The road had become a stream of lava with melting water from the flooded tundra that skipped and rushed through frightening gaps, digging even deeper into them.

She slogged herself through the mud to the main road and hitched a ride with an open four-wheel truck, equipped with mud tires and high clearance. Bouncing through ruts and trenches, lumps of silt were splashing and sputtering left and right, and she was covered with this special mud when she arrived at the airport. There was no choice but to clean herself up as best she could and dry off, while waiting for a later plane.

Nobody met her at the airstrip of the village and she had to trudge along the endless muddy road to the school. She dragged her feet through that slimy black silt, letting her mind hurry ahead: Certain to meet Ayuluk, she steeled herself to remain indifferent and removed. Would he still be unapproachable and distant? Would he acknowledge or ignore her?

When Vren arrived at the school she had to step over a huge round pothole, yawning at her in front of the few steps that led to the boardwalk of the building. She entered the conference room and immediately spotted Ayuluk. A tinge of amusement smoothed his face as he watched her struggle to get off those dripping mukluks that Cecilia's grandmother had created for her. She felt self-conscious and clumsily lined them up in a corner with equally sodden boots before she joined the other participants.

The meeting had started some time before. The group had agreed on special workshops for students and more community meetings with staged confrontations between parents and teenagers. As people started to leave, Vren saw Ayuluk talking with a young teacher. She joined them and was introduced to Simeon, an Eskimo of medium size, about thirty years old, with the eyes of a dreamer. Ayuluk threw her a rapid glance, but did not speak to her, no reference to the emergency landing last week, no further acknowledgment of her presence. He purposely overlooked her.

Simeon invited them both for a cup of tea in his small but comfortably furnished office. Photos of students were pinned against a wall. Three pictures, close together under a crucifix, were decorated with artificial flowers. "*Roxy—Dennis—Demian —in memoriam*" it read on a rectangular piece of cardboard underneath, nailed to the wall.

Simeon turned around from his desk on a swivel chair and joined Ayuluk and Vren, sitting at a round little table next to the wall. Without lifting his head, and stirring his tea continuously, he said: "I never thought about dying, but now...it's all so confusing... I ask myself what it's like not to be anymore."

Ayuluk was bending forward in his chair and, concentrating on the young teacher, he calmly said: "I assume, Simeon, waking up in the morning is how we really can tell that we were dreaming. I expect dying is when we one day will discover that we have been alive."

The words were resonated in the silence of the room for a long while. His face buried in his hands, Simeon said nothing. Then—more thinking to herself than speaking aloud—Vren added: "Death, a linear continuation."

Ayuluk caught her remark : "No, not linear, that would make death a point of closure and terrifying finality. Death is the gate to more consciousness, evolving toward its mysterious origin."

Simeon looked up, ready to say something, but Ayuluk continued:

"I don't know about linear living, whether one can jump a part of chronological time. In life, experienced as round—even in those so-called *much larger circles* ..." and he fixed his gaze on Vren as to bring back her remark in the parking lot of the airport, "...every section of cosmological time must be lived to be prepared for the next one."

'Every section must be lived!' The words hit her. They echoed the strong demand of an old scripture not to take one's own life—the text of an Egyptian papyrus she accidentally had discovered at a school outing to the Pergamon Museum in Berlin, a few years after her father took his life. Though still a young girl she had instantly learned by heart the part she liked best to never lose it again.

And here they poured out—almost against her will—remembered words from long ago: "*Have you lived out your life to its conclusion by ...*" In embarrassment she interrupted herself. Ayuluk's questioning eyes were resting on her but she avoided meeting his gaze.

"Go on," Ayuluk pushed swiftly, "don't stop."

Hesitantly she repeated: "*Have you lived out your life to its conclusion by extracting yourself from yourself? ...*"

"I cannot concentrate, what is meant by that?" Simeon interrupted her. He nervously played with his cup, moving it back and forth on the table. He was not in tune with Ayuluk and Vren and switched to his own agenda.

"I wonder, what's the making of a curse? One suicide, yes, but several in a row, why? Is it contagious?"

Responding to the change of topic, Vren said: "I personally did not know Roxy, but I assume it was most important that he was a positive role model. From what his suicide note explained, in his despair he believed he'd found a solution for himself. And thus the solution of the role model, the solution for his friends."

"Roxy was, indeed, a role model," Ayuluk agreed, "but there is more to it. The curse is an irrational power, a negative prayer, creating a reality of its own."

For a second Vren was carried away, saw Tony's rope vibrating on the ground, heard the little click of Linda's shiny toy gun and remembered her own fearful sensation of being chased when she fell on the tundra last fall.

"Who was this mother Shark anyhow, that woman shaman of the past?" Simeon asked.

"It does not matter," Ayuluk quietly responded. "It's our guilt we don't want to face and it's easier to project the responsibility for the suicides on that shaman of fifteen years ago."

Ayuluk pushed his chair away from the table: "What does count is that whoever believes in that curse empowers the laws of this illusion to become true."

Simeon lifted his head, his lips tight, his gaze restlessly wandering around in the room: "Something has to be done fast. This tension, this fear day and night. Who will be next?"

Simeon's growing anxiety was frightening. To soften the intense mood Vren inquired: "How do the students respond to these special workshops?"

"Not too well." The teacher sat on the edge of his chair: "Talking about their dead friends is not their thing. And discussing ...well... the curse... is impossible. The boys laugh about it, call it stupid stuff, and the girls are too afraid to even mention the word."

Simeon shoved his cup away, the tea spilled over, his hands trembled. "No workshop can undo a curse. Only a shaman can!" he exclaimed.

Ayuluk looked with fatherly concern at the young teacher: "Calm down, Simeon. I understand how you feel. It's a good suggestion. Irrationality in reverse! It does work at times."

Simeon stood up and nervously pounded with his fist on the desk. "I wish Rita were here," he erupted. "We had this terrible fight the other day. I tried to discuss the curse with her and she started laughing, called me old fashioned and superstitious. I should give up the idea with a shaman. Called me a heathen, who should convert to Jesus and..."

"Slow down, Simeon, slow down," Ayuluk said. "Your Rita does not seem to know much about shamans." The teacher plunged down on his chair again and drummed his fingers on the arm rests.

"Eskimos have lived for thousands of years with fear before Jesus. That's why the shamans were needed, specially gifted wise human beings, who had learned to transcend any reality and to experience a timeless omnipresence, where one minute, ten years and ten thousand light years count the same. Besides, if your Rita were familiar with the mythology of the first shaman she might be surprised."

"What about the first shaman?" Simeon seemed confused.

"We people don't do too well with abstractions. We can only grasp what we can see. And so the supreme being decided to let the eagle be the manifestation of the spirit. But that wasn't good enough for these early Siberian Eskimos. Only after the first innocent Eskimo maiden offered her body to carry a child from the eagle, the immaculate conception, the very first shaman was born and the people satisfied."

Simeon was too apprehensive, however, to pay much attention. He went right back to his personal concerns.

"Rita is afraid that the other teachers would ridicule my idea with the shaman," he sighed. "She considers herself modern and too sophisticated for what she calls old wives' tales. Since she knows how to run a computer she thinks she is smarter than I and that bothers the hell out of me."

"She is still a very young girl. Don't take it so seriously," Ayuluk consoled him. He poured himself another cup of tea and continued:

"The shamans of the past were exceptional and had extraordinary mental gifts, but not so today any more. Let me think about all this for a few days. Old Charlie Katchatag in Hooper Bay comes to mind, might be the right person to act like a shaman."

Simeon visibly relaxed. The tension in his face was gone. After some small talk about the weather and fish camps, they all were ready to leave.

Ayuluk and Vren slipped into their mud covered boots and walked together to the end of the boardwalk without exchanging a word. She was glad to be out in the open air with the sun still high in a radiant sky. They had reached the steps to the main road. Ayuluk stopped and, looking around, he assessed the unique scenery: "Almost no road left. What an archaic chaos. *Mariayak, mariayak* everywhere."

He suddenly laughed and his laughter not only dispelled the heaviness of the long hour before but also released the imperceptible tension between them. He turned to Vren and with a trickster jumping into his eyes he exclaimed:

"How wrong I was! Certainly, there *was* a beginning: the mud, the primordial *mariayak*, before the land was separated from the water."Vren stepped down ahead of him and remembering the big pothole, she cautioned: "Watch out for that hole."

"Negative space—only in linear living," he responded with an inscrutable tone in his voice.

Water had oozed into it and filled it to the rim. They both bent over and in a mirror of burning blue, Vren saw their heads, reflected next to each other against a cloud, crowned by a necklace of golden light. On the motionless surface a bird's feather and a little dead arctic oeneis moth, with one of its yellow wings, dipped into the water, floating over their faces.

A mud hole, a simple mud hole, holding in its perfect circle life and death, heaven and earth. And the last words of the Egyptian papyrus wanted to get out: *For above is exalted by below.*

It was then that she felt for a split second Ayuluk's presence fusing with hers. The intensity of the sensation brought her to the brink of tears. She had to fight the irresistible desire to let him enter her mind, which was flooded with the words of the ancient text. Over long years they had become the secret source of her inner strength, keeping her from trespassing into the hidden spaces of her own vulnerability. Yet she resisted the impulse and kept her feelings locked.

The image in the mud hole began to blur and got rapidly denser, transforming itself now into a solid rock, which seemed to have been there all the time. With great clarity she saw the tundra all around, the wooden boardwalk leading to the school building, and all that was left at the bottom of the steps was a big stone in an ordinary pothole.

She looked at Ayuluk, who was still standing next to her on the lower step, and she pretended indifference. His dark eyes, however, confirmed otherwise. Her conscious withdrawal had not gone unnoticed. Without disclosing his thoughts, he stepped down into the mud of the road and walked toward the village.

She had tried to protect herself, yet felt more lost than ever. The tundra had grown in its expanse, her body seemed to have shrunk and the squelching quagmire on the way to the clinic threatened to be an insurmountable obstacle. 'A straight line never fills a hole'. She remembered his statement on the shelf ice in April and it haunted her.

19

The geese had returned and so the ducks and the swans. It was the time of *Tengmiirvik*, when the villagers gathered for hunting parties on the tundra. For the last several hours, Ayuluk had watched the young people frolicking, the boys trying their skill at shooting birds, the girls searching for nests and eggs on the ground.

The mud season was over, the blanket of snow had melted and the river was free of ice for boating and fishing. Ayuluk surrendered himself with his whole being to the magic of the awakening tundra. This land was his home, the reflection of his very self. Extending to the horizon and beyond all beginnings, it meant the promise of the unbreakable continuity of life. It was the reminder of *Yuuyaraq*, the way of the human being, to live in harmony with nature and the soul of all things, their spirits. Everything around him was moist and lush again and smelled of sprouting sedge grass; everything was bright today. The air seemed to sizzle with new hope and the innocence of the day mercifully veiled the darker reality of the three recent suicides.

As Ayuluk cheerfully scanned the tundra for waterfowl, the horizon began to darken. He studied for a moment the formation of the first storm clouds, when he detected one of the young people, moving away into the distance. At a second look he recognized him: Gregory, one of Thomas' friends. He couldn't put his finger on it, but for some reason he felt slightly alarmed and decided to catch up with him. Adopted at an early age and without a father, Gregory was known as a lonely fellow. Since the suicides of his friends he had been even more withdrawn.

A few isolated rain drops were already falling and by the time he had caught up with Gregory, they had multiplied. "Hey, wait for me!" he called out.

The youngster turned around and slowly came toward him. With a warm gesture Ayulik put his arm around his shoulders, but the teenager immediately withdrew from the embrace and stepped back. His eyes were clouded, his voice hardly audible: "You don't understand. Let me go."

Ayuluk ignored Gregory's defiance and seized his arm: "With a storm exploding any second, this is not the time to sulk. We'd both better join the others and help them break up the party."

The youngster unwillingly followed him. They had reached the rest of the villagers when a hissing lightning bolt struck and a cross-shaped, black shadow thundered over them. The tundra trembled. Gregory was petrified and threw himself on the ground, whimpering fearfully: "Mercy...the curse...the evil spirit..."

Ayuluk pulled him up and firmly said: "No, Gregory, no, recover yourself. It's a plane in its final approach to the air strip."

That very moment a ghastly scream penetrated the air and Thomas came running: "Hurry, father! Katie is crazy, pointed with a rifle at herself and dropped to the ground."

Ayuluk rushed over to where the girls were gathered, to attend to Mary's daughter. By now the rain was pouring down and a sudden foreboding mood had chased away the lightheartedness of the day. Surrounded by anxious villagers, he knelt next to the girl. Her little body had stiffened and though she appeared to be unconscious, her eyes were wide open and unfocused. The rifle had not gone off. He checked her pulse and slowly, emphasizing each word, he spoke to her: "Katie, I know you can hear me. Listen carefully. Do not give in to that force which pulls on you. You are strong. We are all here to help you."

Her body began to quiver, she was breathing fast and reached with one hand for her golden necklace. She opened her eyes and looking in bewilderment at all the people around her, started to cry. Ayuluk picked her up and carried the shivering girl under the drumming downpour back to his boat on the river. He knew how scary out-of-body experiences could be, remembering his first one at the death of his mother when he, too, had only been a child.

By the time he got to the boat they were both soaking wet. He reached for a tarp to shelter her from the rain. She nestled in his arms and whispered shyly:

"I almost didn't get my soul back into my body. This saved me." She pointed at her necklace.

Ayuluk was puzzled. "Your necklace, what about it?"

"A voice told me to kill myself, but my necklace didn't let me. It's my charm! You want it? The woman doctor from Bethel gave it to me."

Vren's face, mirrored on the water surface of a pothole two weeks ago, took shape. "No Katie, no. It's yours, you keep it," he assured her in an absentminded tone. He couldn't fathom how all this had come about.

Gregory had followed him to the river. Shaken by the doomed events of the day he stood there, not knowing what to do with himself. Ayuluk helped Katie to settle in the boat and motioned Gregory to climb in as well. Both youngsters quickly huddled under the tarp. Ayuluk pull-started the outboard motor and took off into the rainstorm back to the village.

20

He had just discovered the blank spot on the wall where the framed copy of Helper Neck's writing samples usually hung. Ayuluk assumed that Thomas had taken it, but couldn't give it any further thought because Jolanda was walking in from the kitchen. She was a stout woman with a puffy face and black dull hair, cut much too short. She looked upset and the muscles of her face were incessantly twitching. For a change she was not drunk. Many times he had tried to help Gregory's mother, mainly because of her son, who all his teenage years had suffered from her violent and sometimes irrational treatment.

Gregory was not popular with the teachers at school for he was different, but he liked this young fellow with his big hands and extraordinary skill for everything, that had to do with wires and batteries. This talent had helped him many times to weather those ugly storms at home and keep to himself.

"Make yourself comfortable and take your time, Jolanda." Ayuluk offered her one of the easy chairs, but she was too anxious to sit down.

"I don't know what to do," she stammered. "Gregory has become so strange recently, acts really weird, won't pass the Catholic chapel under any circumstances..."

"The suicides of his friends... I wonder." Ayuluk recalled Gregory's disturbed mood earlier that week at the hunting party.

Jolanda did not respond. Instead she handed him a small, wrinkled piece of paper. "I found this in Gregory's sleeping bag today."

Ayuluk quickly glanced at it and repeated aloud: "Don't worry, it's all for the best. If things work out I will be back."

"How long has he been gone?" he urgently asked.

"Since this morning."

Gregory was a friend of Tony's and also knew Alex well. Both had visited the clinic in Bethel in the past and had found genuine understanding and help. Maybe they advised him to do the same and he had flown to Bethel.

He shared his assumption with Jolanda and immediately called the clinic; the line was busy, however. As he hung up for the third time, his telephone rang right away. It was Vren:

"Hard to get a hold of you. Your line is constantly busy." They had tried to reach each other at the same time. "Gregory Akuchack, from your village, I just saw him, he is extremely depressed," she said.

"He is with you, I suppose."

"Not any more. He was in a hurry to catch a plane to Anchorage and find his uncle, the only relative in his life he respects, as he put it."

"You did it again, you let him go? "Ayuluk flared up.

"I had no choice. Unless he could trust me to talk about his suicidal thoughts, and I would promise him not to get a trooper involved for transfer to the Bethel prison, he would not even enter my office."

Immense frustration mounted inside of him. Was his anger directed toward Vren or Gregory or perhaps towards his own helplessness?

"He hadn't slept for several nights, asked for just one sleeping pill. Are you familiar with his uncle?"

"Lomak Johnson left the village several years ago to find work in Anchorage. That's all I know." With a question in his mind Ayuluk looked at Jolanda. She shook her head.

" No, nobody has heard from him since."

"I have to ask you for a favor, would you..." Vren could not finish her sentence.

"Would I what?" Ayuluk cut her off.

"Never mind, I already know your answer," she stated laconically.

Ayuluk understood what she was referring to, his dismissing, harsh remark in the parking area of the airport the other day.

"No," he quickly replied, "you don't know at all—and I'm not doing you a favor either. Yet you are absolutely right: he is not your responsibility!" He paused. "I will see what I can do in Anchorage tomorrow."

"Thank you, Ayuluk," he heard her say before she hung up. Never before had she called him by his name, he was well aware of that. He suddenly felt twice as motivated to find Gregory. He put the receiver down and walked over to Jolanda, who was still standing next to the chair. To give her some reassurance, he communicated what Vren had just told him: "Gregory did go and see the doctor this morning. From what he told her he was determined to find his uncle in Anchorage."

Jolanda sighed with relief: "But how to find him in Anchorage?"

"I am not sure myself. I have to think about it."

Ayuluk left the study and walked into the kitchen to indicate that there was nothing more to discuss. Jolanda followed him. As she opened the door to leave, he reassured her:

"I'll fly to Anchorage tomorrow, will try my best to find him, Jolanda."

* * *

He had a window seat on his flight to Anchorage and was holding a piece of paper with a list of addresses, jotted down with Simeon's help the evening before, but he couldn't concentrate. He looked down at the icy blue Alaska Range, gleaming in the morning sun, and was reliving his departure from the cabin. A humming vibration in the air had alerted him: two *tegirayulik*, birds of light, serenely following their call to the rivers of the north. With ease he could make out their pointed wings and long forked tails and his delight at watching their graceful flight was still with him. Every year the late arrival of the arctic terns exulted him, the announcement of the short but intense season of light. Yet this morning, like a gray cloud briefly darkening the sun, his joy had strangely been tinged with imperceptible sadness. So long a journey and so short a stay, he pondered, from the end of the world, Antarctica, to the Alaskan tundra for only two months of breeding.

His thoughts, laced with wistfulness, moved from the birds of light to Demian's death, from Thomas to Gregory, they drifted from Katie's golden necklace to Vren in Simeon's office. He saw her slim body, her lively face and curly brown hair—he heard her voice recalling the words of a papyrus—he remembered feeling her compassion on Christmas Eve, when unprepared and vulnerable, he had turned around to look at her and for a fleeting moment found his own self reflected in her eyes. She intuitively had grasped his complexity and for this split second laid bare her own soul before him.

137

All this had been overwhelming and confusing, it had been the day his wife took her life. Ever since, an awesome, almost frightening seriousness had tied them to each other.

Except for her war experience, he knew nothing about her and didn't need to. Her compassion, her view of others, mirrored her more truthfully than any facts or conscious statements of hers could have explained. The betrayals of life were invisibly woven into the fabric of her personality, not as scars, but early seeds for her strength and tenderness, which showed in everything she did and said. Not despite, but because of her sorrows she had become who she was and that attracted him most.

Yet, he did not fool himself. His being was split into halves: one half with his timeless knowledge of things, calmly accepting their mysterious alliance, the other, fighting this inner truth; the gate to his past, his dreams and high expectations, had to remain closed. He was not young any more and had made peace long ago with life the way it was.

And it was obvious to him that she, too, did not completely trust her feelings, or was it that she had no faith in him? The latter thought irked him to such a degree that he decided to rather concentrate on the two birds of light who could not be diverted from pursuing their call. Maybe nothing could deter the irrevocable course of his and Vren's fate either. After all, their life-lines had already crossed long ago.

* * *

He looked for a room in a motel near the airport and took a taxi to 43rd Avenue off Tudor, southeast of the university campus, an address Jolanda had found at the last minute, scribbled on an old Christmas card from her brother, Lomak, three years ago. It was a good neighborhood with only one apartment building. Ayuluk felt hopeful.

He had confided his search plans to the driver and asked him to wait in the taxi. After he had tried several apartments, a woman answered the bell. She had lived for several years in this building, but to her knowledge nobody during this time ever rented a room out.

The taxi driver, an older man from Albania, knew Anchorage well and suggested a diner, a meeting place for Eskimos, on Seventh and Gambell, a downtown area of some disrepute. Knowing the owner, he went in with Ayuluk, but the woman shook her head; the name Lomak Johnson was not familiar to her.

The bar she referred them to was on Eleventh Avenue, not far off, and a waiter there suggested they come back Friday night, the traditional evening for Eskimos from the Delta to get together.

Cities were artifacts for Ayuluk. How could one live encased in these sterile boxes and daily walk the littered pavement and smell the garbage in the gutter? How could any Yup'ik Eskimo voluntarily imprison himself in holes, locked away from the wide open spaces of the tundra and the sky, bordering each other on the horizon all around? He felt justified to have been strict with Thomas; he would never let him leave for such an accumulation of synthetic insanity.

The next morning the same cab driver brought him all the way to Lake Otis Parkway, where Jerry, the son of the store owner in Emomeguk, worked as a janitor for the YMCA. He drove him to Spaniard Road, where a friend of Simeon from the neighboring village Emmonak was employed as a seamstress, but neither one could provide any clues.

And then on Friday night in the bar, one old Eskimo man remembered him: Lomak Johnson, who did not join them any longer for a drink and had no permanent address anymore. His home was the street, to be exact, Orca Street, which he shared with all the lost souls of the city.

For several days and nights Ayuluk wandered the streets near Merrill Airfield, between Gambell and Orca Street. With every hour Ayuluk's dislike for this city, for any city, for any part of any city, grew more and more into an alienating nightmare with no space to breathe, no opening to connect with cosmic time. He felt entrapped by nothing but straight lines, which were precisely intersecting with even more straight lines. Within this linear meagerness dead souls in drunk bodies were tottering around in the sterile confinement of incomplete squares, a confusing labyrinth. And he approached each one of these disheveled people, hoping for the blind chance to run into Lomak.

On his third day, around noon, something unexpected happened. He saw a young fellow, about Gregory's age, sitting at the curb, who for some reason looked familiar to him. As he came closer, the youngster started running. In spite of his leg injury Ayuluk caught up with him and grabbed him by his jacket.

"What's your name and why are you running?"

And then everything fell in place: Gus had visited Emomeguk here and there over the years to see his friends Roxy and Dennis. It was at his last visit for Demian's funeral—Ayuluk remembered now—that he had seen Gus. Adopted by an Eskimo woman in Anchorage years ago, this teenager had been homesick for the village ever since.

Gus had picked up Gregory at the airport a few days ago and had taken him home to his mother. "Yesterday," he reported, "Gregory started to act strange and...." Gus broke off abruptly.

"Take me to him right away!" Ayuluk demanded firmly, but Gus tried to escape. Ayuluk had to chase him a second time.

Out of breath the youngster stammered: "Gregory left. I don't know where he is."

"You do." Ayuluk knew the kid was lying.

Holding Gus by his jacket with one hand, he dug with the other into his pocket and waved a twenty-dollar bill: "Come on, Gus, let's go."

A few minutes later, just around the corner, in the gloomiest street of all, Ayuluk found himself face to face with Gregory. Inside of an abandoned run-down building the teenager was hovering in a stupor on the steps of a half-collapsed stairway. Gus had disappeared .

Ayuluk briefly sat down next to him, but this haunted hallway was not a place to talk....

A taxi brought them to the Earthquake Park. There was ample time now for Gregory to confide in him, before they had to catch the late plane home. On a bench, surrounded by trees, they overlooked the blue water of the Knik Arm and listened to the cackling of hundreds of geese, playfully taking off and landing again.

And on this bench, next to Ayuluk, it suddenly felt safe for Gregory to open up and let somebody enter his tortured mind.

Like Ayuluk he had cruised these desperate streets but unlike Ayuluk he had continued to hope for a miracle against his better knowledge. The collision with destiny two days ago, however, surpassed any imaginable pain: He randomly had found his uncle with

140

a whisky bottle, holding on to a telephone pole, unkempt and shoddy, a bum on skid row, who didn't recognize his own nephew.

Gregory had ceased sobbing and silently watched the geese for a while. He slowly began to talk again and allowed Ayuluk to share his menacing dreams, to enter the core of their terror:

It's night on the tundra, no moon, no stars, his friends are chasing him endlessly around the cemetery, he is out of breath, his legs are getting shorter. They tie him to a wooden cross and demand he take his life. And then that hole, deep, dark, bottomless, Roxy pushes him in and white slimy stuff, Dennis' brain, is covering him all over. He escapes to the river. Dennis becomes a headless corpse and tries to drown him, he screams for help. Strangers rescue him but bury his body in the wrong grave.

And as if these nightly repetitions of horror were not enough, strange phantasms during the day are even more frightening, because he is fully awake and not dreaming:

At times something liquid is forcefully poured into his skull and fills him up with ambiguous physical sensations. *He fears these feelings like hell, yet enjoys them with sweet lust. And then that guilt, it eats at him, he cannot pass the church any longer. At other times the evil spirit of the curse is hovering over his head and when it forms into a mask, which has in its center the devil as inua, the dark temptation of suicide tantalizes him with the promise of peace....*

Gregory fell silent. There was relief. Ayuluk had patiently listened and shared his secret burden. He was shaking himself now, trying to understand where to find himself.

In his mind Ayuluk was still walking with Gregory through endless streets, chased by the curse and confronted by dead friends. He almost physically felt the plight of the younger generation. Thomas was one of them. They all sought for solutions in these changing times. No, he was not a heartless father, when he wanted his son to remain anchored in the old traditions and save him his own pain of younger years. But maybe this could not be done, maybe... and the expressive, rebellious face of a woman took shape before him... *'Ever considered stagnation in too small a circle ?...'* Yes, trust and support...

141

A summer breeze, coming from the water, lightly brushed Ayuluk's face. Back in the present again, he moved closer to Gregory. He couldn't help noticing his big hands again, good hands and skillful ones, hands which had to be put to work and therefore needed training. No, he could no longer object to letting the young people go and get their education. The village could use a good mechanic. And Thomas, well, with his contagious enthusiasm and excellent brain he truly was entitled to follow his ambitions. There was no reason not to remain—as *she* in her anger had coined it—an 'Eskimo human being'!

The memory of her antagonism made him smile and half jokingly he said to Gregory:

"The doctor should have never let you go."

Gregory was quick in responding: "She trusted me. If it hadn't been for her, you would have never come to Anchorage to look for me."

Gregory's logic amused him and, seen from a certain angle, was quite correct. On their cab ride to the airport he remarked with a grin:

"You are right, Gregory; she and I did cooperate."

21

The desk in her office was arranged across a corner of the room between two windows with some blank wall space opposite the desk. Vren had decorated this particular area in her mind's eye with a Yup'ik dance mask she had seen several months ago in the house of an Eskimo mask maker. Last week, on her routine visit to Nunivak Island off the Bering Sea coast, she could not resist going by the house of the old man again. He only spoke Yup'ik and she had to gesticulate with her hands to express her sincere interest in this work of art. To her surprise he had immediately agreed to sell.

And this morning she was going to hang the *kegginaquq* —that thing which is like a face—on that special place where her imagination already had placed it many months ago.

She had climbed on her desk with a hammer and two hooks, when Cecilia entered the room with a flat box under her arm and started laughing:

"I swear, I have never seen a doctor on top of an office desk. Please come down. I have to show you something."

With the hammer in her hand Vren jumped to the floor. Cecilia unpacked the parcel and showed her a framed document. "I never knew of 'Uyaquq', this Moravian man and son of a shaman. Look closely: from pictographs to letters to cursive writing in only four years!" Cecilia looked happy and exited.

This arrangement of five hand-written paragraphs appeared vaguely familiar to Vren. Somewhere she had seen it and then she remembered: In Ayuluk's studio—that terrible day when Thomas found Demian's body, that day which had started so innocently with Thomas pointing at this frame, ready to explain, and Ayuluk's teasing, *Masta and Moloko*.

"How in the world did you get this?" Vren was puzzled.

Cecilia tenderly brushed with her hand over the glass and all of a sudden it dawned on Vren: The car ride on the frozen Kuskokwim River with Thomas in April, and ever since Cecilia's eager participation in that monthly training for medical emergencies.

"This Uyaquq was a real genius, Thomas says. After all, it took mankind thousands of years to develop a written language." Cecilia wrapped the frame again and said with great pride: "Thomas has so many interests."

She walked over to the wall where Vren had hung a decorative map, showing the stars of the northern hemisphere.

"He would like this. His father taught him a lot about the stars." She studied the map for a moment: " I guess these are the different constellations."

"They are phosphorescent and glow in the dark," Vren explained.

"Must look great at night. Thomas should come over one day and see this map. He even owns a telescope. His father gave it to him. Yeah, he adores him and admires his knowledge, but I think he is much too strict, rather old fashioned, won't let him go to college in the States."

" I know," Vren sighed, "know all too well."

" I told him about my father, the same story! For a year I was patiently after him, now he starts giving in a little. I am determined to go to college, not just in Anchorage."

Vren remembered Thomas' shy complaints in this matter. He definitely could learn from Cecilia's perseverance.

Cecilia looked thoughtful: "Let me tell you, his father is not easy—too stern, too outspoken, quite different from my old man, who can laugh."

"You are wrong, Cecilia, *Mariayak, mariayak* , all over," Vren wistfully remembered the muddy expanse around a pothole.

Cecilia looked baffled. Of course she couldn't understand. "Whatever. I just don't like people who can't laugh. Conrad can't either. But there is more wrong with him than that." She hesitated a little but then continued:

"I might as well tell you, he deals with drugs. Thomas has repeatedly seen him in Emomeguk. He knew. I was so shocked the other day to hear this and cried, and Thomas was so sweet to console me, without even knowing why I cried." She furtively caressed the flat parcel on the desk.

"He has also been up to Stony River, remember Katsoo? I wonder. Well, I made him promise to stop dealing with that stuff. I know he will."

"Remember, Cecilia: Never predict the future! Otherwise..." They both laughed and went to the waiting room...

It was during the noon break after the last patient of the morning had left. Vren found herself again standing with the hammer and the hooks on her desk, when the telephone rang. It was Ayuluk:

"You need to know..." he paused, "...Simeon... Simeon is dead. Hung himself. His nephew found him yesterday—I can't say more now. You understand." And he hung up.

She froze. The mask, lying on the desk, stared at her. *'The laws of the curse will obey the one who believes in them.'* Ayuluk's words six weeks ago, like a prophecy. Poor Simeon. If only she could cry. Two giant hands seemed to squeeze her entire body and yet no tears would come. She felt dry and empty.

Several more patients counted on her this afternoon and she was forced to focus her thoughts. Sixty-year-old Aga Nokapiqaq, she suffered from depression. Yes, her son had to bring her and yes, it took him every week six hours round trip by boat from Oknagamut. No, she did not understand English and no, she didn't like to take medicine. Vren could not concentrate any longer. She pushed the chair back and leapt up to get a glass of water when the telephone rang again. Theresa from Emomeguk.

"Hell got loose in the village. I don't know any more what to do. Yesterday Simeon's suicide, today his girlfriend almost dead. Rita is for sure out of her mind. Her mother left with her earlier to see you this afternoon. A sweater to strangle herself. Had to wrestle the girl to the ground. She even tried to drink a bottle of bathroom cleaner..."

Vren put the receiver down. How could the sky be so ignorantly blue, the sun so insultingly impartial today? Tears welled up finally and she could not, did not want to, suppress them. To hell with the control she would have to exert to continue the consultation with Aga Nokapiqaq and Cecilia. She excused herself and left the office, walked out of the building into the street and cried until no tear was left.

The last patient had been taken care of when Rita and her mother arrived. The slim young girl, dressed in tight blue jeans and a white turtleneck, represented the image of a modern teenager: Rita's mother looked exhausted and worn out. When Vren asked them in, Rita rebelliously stalled and cried hysterically, which made her mother extremely angry: "There is no way for me to physically control this girl.

She almost ran away at the airport. The only safe place is in prison. Whatever it takes, please put her there."

"You can't do this to me, I kill myself right here," Rita hissed back. Both women refused to sit down.

Vren took the mother back to the waiting room and left Cecilia with the girl in her office. She trusted her remarkable skill with contemporaries of her own people.

When all four got together again, mother and daughter had calmed down. Vren hated the customary involvement of troopers and the prison as the place of temporary security. She reached for Rita's hands: "We can do without the prison, Rita, but not without the hospital in Anchorage. Not because you are ill, but to give you a safe place until you are able to face the world again."

Cecilia, and not a trooper, would accompany the girl on her flight to Anchorage tonight. Rita's mother would stay with relatives in town....

She was alone now, alone with her feelings, alone with the mask. She put her head on the desk; her eyes began to swim again. It was not only Simeon's death that haunted her, but also this macabre mood which tenaciously hovered in the air. The deadly chain, which had begun with Roxy, followed by Dennis, Stuart and Demian, had not been cut off. The slow but insistent journey of the curse was arbitrarily taking one victim after the other, leaving their loved ones in agony behind.

Vren felt paralyzed by her helplessness and strangely depersonalized, like floating in a vacuum. Time did not stand still, did not pass faster, or lag behind; it just ticked away indifferently. Should she have something to eat in the hospital cafeteria or drive home, go for a walk? It did not matter, nothing made any difference.

She could call her daughter in California, who was at this time preparing supper for the children, or contact her son on the East coast, possibly just returning from a concert or a play downtown. She could try to reach her closest friends, vacationing on the Chesapeake Bay, perhaps planning right now their sailing trip for the morning. No, her world was not theirs anymore, had not been theirs for many months; they wouldn't and couldn't comprehend the shadows of her gloom.

146

She yearned for consolation, for somebody who would understand, but bravely resisted the temptation to call Ayuluk. He, too, had to feel defeated and there was no comfort she could offer him either. She lifted her head again and as she glanced at the mask, still lying on the desk, the fleeting image of the mud hole with its mirrored surface inexplicably emerged in her mind. She suddenly felt compelled to mount the mask on the wall. The curious urgency seemed to give her inner peace.

For the third time she stood on her desk and balanced, centered and secured the *kegginaquq*. She put the hammer down and dropped in the chair again, leaning back to check what had been done, when her surroundings began to blur. Slowly, very slowly, she dreamed herself toward the mask and as if some invisible force had heightened her sensitivity and intuitive understanding, she began to experience its powerful dynamic.

Harmony was flowing from the design of the universe, symbolized by the *ellanguaq*, two encircling wooden loops, and silently filled the room. Its circles calmly relayed the hidden meaning of their interaction between men and the spirits of the tundra and the sea and she sensed the importance of their mutual respect acutely.

And all the while the *ellam iinga* stared at her—the eye of awareness that heeded men and animals alike. She began to tremble, and deep compassion for everything alive kindled her heart, as sparks of the *inua,* the timeless vitality of all things, emanated powerfully from a small human face, contained in the right eye of the wolf's head in the center.

Spiritual wholeness, mysteriously signified by a mask, this was truly an *agayuliyaraput*, a way of making prayer. The mask had magically bestowed on her a widened acceptance of life as the completion of inseparable opposites, and tragedy was part of it.

As she drove home that night along the road which led from the town to her house, crossing the vast expanse, she became part of the infinite tundra and felt embraced by timeless peace again.

22

During the noon break and on her way to the post office, Vren was preoccupied with two new patients this morning—Rosie and Corine, both not even twenty, both from Emomeguk, yet so different in their outlook on life.

Rosie was a tall girl and slightly clumsy in her movements. Her eyes had looked anxious and restless and she sat passively in the chair next to Vren's desk. She had left the village a year ago to live with an aunt in Anchorage to escape the boring village life—as she phrased it—only to find a gray, alienating existence as a cleaning woman. Grief was written all over her face and homesickness had lurked between her words, which pretended success and happiness in the big city.

Her present visit with family and friends in the village, however, had been curtailed by the visitation of repeated tormenting dreams. She had wondered why Roxy and Dennis would come alive in these nightmares and urge her to commit suicide. Maybe because she had once seduced them both in the sweathouse?

And as if these frightening dreams were not enough, during the day some voice had also spookily whispered over her left shoulder to take her life. Convinced that the curse was after her as punishment, she had left the village in panic and was on her way back to Anchorage.

Rosie had complained in Vren's office about jitteriness and panic attacks. She just couldn't bear it any longer and had asked for some tranquilizing medicine.

Compared to Rosie, Corine seemed to be from a different planet. She truly represented the modern Eskimo girl. Her oval shaped, beautiful face had vibrated with enthusiasm as she talked about her plans to become a physician. After she marveled at the pieces of minerals in the copper bowl on Vren's desk, she moved her lithe body gracefully around in the office and admired the continuous undisrupted frieze of colorful prints by a contemporary Austrian artist, which Vren had mounted on all four walls to brighten up the dull office. Standing still to study the mask over the desk for a moment she said:

"The reason why I am here is to chat with you about medical school. Last month at my high school graduation an elder urged me to see you. I don't know what got into him. Ayuluk Zaykov is the most conservative of all, wouldn't let his own son go to college. But here I am, eager to talk about myself."

Corine then had babbled on about different subjects, regarding the school in the village, her devotion as the editor of the school paper and her preliminary ideas for choosing a university after college. She also had volunteered her opinion about the curse: "It's very destructive, superstitious stuff, cooked up in the brain of some old folks. I know what to do with my life and have no time to brood over rumors."

In leaving, she had stressed that all her teachers as well as her mother were supportive of her and then shrugged off an afterthought: "Only my boyfriend is adamantly against my plans, does not want me to leave, but I bet he eventually will get used to the idea."

And during all the time of their long chat, Vren hadn't been able to rid herself of the impression that the mask on the wall was alive and stood for Ayuluk's presence, that he had silently been watching them...

It started to rain on her way back to the clinic. A gray drizzle was shrouding the sky as she walked along the grotesque metallic sewage pipes which—to avoid the permafrost—were lining the houses on street level in sterile ugliness. Her thoughts were still with that cheerful girl Corine and her promising outlook on life under the benevolent supervision of the mask.

A huge raven suddenly landed on the street in front of her, a bulky piece of white bread in its beak. These ominous birds populated the streets, either sitting on these repulsive pipes or thronging in great numbers around those hideous dumpsters. When she approached the raven it dropped the loot and flew off with an eerie shriek.

A few minutes later somebody screamed: "Don't turn around!" She stopped and looked back and there was that raven again. It had picked up the spoils and was wobbling closely behind her. An old woman, who had uttered the shriek, stood rooted to the spot, her face covered with both hands.

The macabre scene in that wretched setting had plunged her spirits into a vague unease and she rushed through the drizzle back to the clinic, where she hoped to snap out of the morbid mood. Cecilia was already waiting for her with a message. A   request for a

150

consultation at the prison. Vren was mentally still involved with her uncanny little adventure and needed to share her story first.

Cecilia giggled: "Never mind, that poor woman fell for our Yup'ik saying *'Don't let a raven follow you , unless you want your death to come true.'*"

Cecilia's interpretation fitted like the missing piece into the gloomy puzzle of this early afternoon. The complete picture was even more morose when Vren had hesitantly to admit to herself that she was not completely impervious to superstition. With this insight, she went on her way to the prison.

The warden let her into a cell, which smelled of Lysol, and was bare of any furniture except for an uncovered mattress on an army cot. Squeezed against the wall, between the bed and a urinal, a shivering teenage boy was crouching on the floor. He was completely naked and his body was shaken by coughing spells. She remembered the painful encounter with Alex in this prison last fall. But she had not been prepared for this degrading, pitiful scene at all.

"Jonathan hanged himself in the village yesterday, but his mother cut him off in time," the guard coldly reported. "Had him brought here in the evening for safety reasons."

He looked with an authoritarian expression at the youngster and reproachfully proclaimed: "For this kid even prison is not safe. He threw a temper tantrum when we locked him up yesterday and tried to strangle himself with his clothes."

"You mean he stayed naked all night long?" Vren was horrified.

" Yes, Ma'm, no blanket, no clothes!"

When she asked the guard to let the boy get dressed he responded with a strict voice:

"No way, the fellow is crazy. This morning he pleaded with me to have mercy and shoot him. Said he didn't care to live anymore since his brother hanged himself last month in Emomeguk."

It took Vren a few seconds before her heart was willing to comprehend what she just heard. This fourteen-year-old teenager was Simeon's younger brother. For a brief moment all the events of the last two months superimposed each other in a kaleidoscopic design: Simeon, the high-strung, young teacher in his office, the circle of life and death in the mud hole, the trembling young Rita, the mysterious mask with the eyes of awareness and the screeching, sinister raven between those ghastly sewage pipes....

Jonathan was not to stay here another night. And was not to be shipped off to Anchorage, either, like Rita. The thought of outwitting the system almost delighted her and like magic dispersed the gloom which had oppressed her earlier. If she had managed Thomas' unique delivery from the belly of a dilapidated jail into the white trackless snow of a storm, she certainly could come up with some mischievous plot to rescue Jonathan.

Her plan was already taking shape in her mind as she walked back from the prison to the clinic. Jonathan's cough had inspired her. The physician on call had only recently joined the hospital staff of the medical ward. He was young and inexperienced; he couldn't yet be familiar with the intricate details of rules and regulations, which governed the transactions between prison and hospital. All that was needed now was Cecilia's charm and just a bit of luck.

"Are you ready to help me kidnap a young prisoner?" she gleefully greeted Cecilia.

" I would call that a mood swing, if I have ever seen one," she laughed. "What's up? No respect for jails? Not another Thomas."

"Exactly. You got it." Vren smiled maliciously and introduced Cecilia to her plan of action. Equipped with an abandoned pair of old pants and a shirt from the hospital laundry, they were to return together to visit Jonathan.

It was an hour later when the same guard let Cecilia with her billowing bag enter Jonathan's sad little cell. As a native and Yup'ik-speaking health aide, the warden welcomed her visit; he had not been able to get a single word out of this teenager, who resented him as a young white man from the lower Forty-Eight. But Cecilia's beauty topped it all. Thoroughly distracted and close to embracing her, he forgot to lock the cell behind her.

While Vren was keeping the guard hostage in his office, by diplomatically alluding to his expertise and asking endless professional questions, Cecilia and a teenager, dressed in blue jeans and a washed-out shirt, casually left the prison....

Vren had hardly returned to her office when the telephone rang and portended serious trouble. But its endless ringing had to be ignored until Jonathan could be safely admitted to the medical ward with the diagnosis of "imminent pneumonia."

He was helplessly crouching on a chair, like a true victim of abduction. Cecilia stood before him and explained the circumstances he clearly didn't comprehend:

"Come with us, Jonathan, and do as we say, "she instructed him with authority. "All you have to do is to cough, cough real hard and you won't be flown to the psychiatric hospital in Anchorage." Poor Jonathan, he was utterly confounded and felt too miserable to promise anything.

They walked over to the medical ward and Vren immediately spotted the young doctor with his blond beard in the corridor. The carefully prepared white lie came easily from her lips: "This fellow is coughing badly and is running a temperature. Should have been sent back to mama rather than being locked up in prison, after the trooper picked him up drunk in the street."

To impress the new physician and intimidate him a little, Cecilia eagerly talked in Yup'ik to Jonathan, who didn't understand a word and looked quite forlorn.

"No big deal," the innocent staff member responded. Ten minutes later Jonathan was safely tucked away in a hospital bed.

Vren's exploitation of the negligence and inexperience of two newcomers to the bush had saved the bewildered teenager from further alienation far away from home. He now could be locally counseled by her as often and as long as needed, while he was treated for his bronchitis.

Vren had carefully weighed the wrongfulness of a white lie versus the consequences for Jonathan should he have been admitted to the psychiatric hospital in Anchorage. To deal with the phenomenon of the curse was regarded there as unprofessional and, at most, worth a derogatory little smile. All the teenagers admitted after their suicide attempts during the year had been considered a burden. They always had been discharged back to the village within two days.

The warden, who forgot to lock the cell, had spared Vren the expected administrative aftermath. After all, too much attention would not do for this kind of oversight and was best overlooked by those who ran the prison.

23

It was late afternoon on one of those rare summer days that dream their way along and seem to last forever. Vren had parked her car on the waterfront of the glittering Kuskokwim and was walking to the nearby store to look for vegetables, fresh fish and a new pair of rubber boots.

The small store was well equipped and offered a unique variety of items, arranged according to a system Vren had never been able to figure out. Canned and deep frozen food was found next to a limited supply of practical clothes and boots, and fresh vegetables and apples always bordered a selection of guns, separated by lemons from colorful little packages of condoms and mosquito repellents.

The only pair of soft rubber boots in her size was on display on a high shelf, but the sales lady didn't mind taking them down. They were stuffed with crumpled newspaper to keep them straight and attractive to look at.

The store was crowded and she had to stand in line. Ready to pay, little chocolate cubes caught her attention. They were neatly displayed in a bowl on the check out counter and looked strangely familiar. At close examination she gasped. The same identical candies her father used to buy for her at their visits to the Munich zoo—the same foil of gold and red with the small print: West Germany. How did these devilish little hazelnut charms get lost in the bush of Alaska? An old-fashioned candy that had survived WWII and the first man on the moon was alive and well amidst the Bering Sea Eskimos.

An advertisement on cardboard with the word COOL written in big letters across the picture of a polar bear was mounted behind the bowl. Oh, that distinctive coldness in the mouth when they melted. She grabbed a few to add to her groceries, when somebody from behind slightly touched her the shoulder. She turned around and felt a knot in her stomach: there stood Ayuluk with a big can of motor oil, showing no surprise at all as if they ran into each other every day.

He pointed at the advertisement and out of nowhere he asked: "Can you guess where I saw my first polar bear? Indeed, it was in Munich in the zoo, right after the war, while stationed with injuries at the 98th General Hospital."

Something unspoken passed between them. He had picked up her thoughts and their separate memories had traveled together to the same place of their individual past.

She, too, had observed as a child her first polar bear right there. Yet she resisted commenting on that uncanny coincidence. His abrupt departure after the community meeting in May had not been forgotten.

Ayuluk contemplated her quizzically. Unable to escape the spell of his gaze, she pushed the candies aside. The young girl behind the counter impatiently asked:

"Do you want them or not?"

That very moment Ayuluk bent over the counter, reached for the chocolate cubes and said lightly: "I'll take them. Ring them up with the motor oil."

His gesture embarrassed her. Of course he couldn't know about her bizarre discovery and what those candies stood for. On their way out to the street she would bring up her associations and yes, talk about *her* first polar bear as well.

Ayuluk's red truck was parked in front of the store and she rushed to deliver her explanation. Since he didn't respond she felt awkward and ready to part. As he opened the door of the passenger side of his truck Vren pointed towards the waterfront : "I'll walk. My car is over there."

"It does not matter where your car is parked, you just hop in," he said dryly and took off with her towards the river.

He parked next to Vren's car, stopped the engine and sat back on the seat, his gaze lost into the colorful, motley activities along the river.

"A good spot to overlook the harbor with all those barges and their huge containers," he commented.

Vren wondered about the short ride, not even a hundred feet, and of course not for the view. Something had to be on his mind. It was August and the three long months since they had met in the office of the young teacher rapidly melted away. She, too, needed to talk and share her feelings about Simeon's death and naked Jonathan. She wanted to tell him how the curse had affected Rosie and mention Corine's referral. She sensed, however, that he was eager to speak and said nothing.

Ayuluk continued to look straight ahead and without changing his position slowly reported:

"Gregory is back in the village, partly thanks to you, you know that ... and Simeon..." he paused and turned to her, his voice slightly challenging: No, Simeon did not *live out his life to its conclusion, by extracting himself from himself...*"

He had remembered the lines of the old scripture; twice had she stalled that day to recite the whole text. He was prompting her. With a subtle change in the intensity of his presence he communicated his expectation to hear it now.

"I guess it's hard for you to reveal what lives so close to your heart," he said, his eyes not leaving her face.

Words began to swirl around in her head, words harbored inside of her for so many years that they suddenly wanted to come out. But the weird situation made her uncomfortable. Sitting next to Ayuluk in an old red truck, parked on the waterfront and pretending to watch the ships in the harbor. She tried to focus on a turgid, white cumulus cloud close over the river, her hands with splayed fingers pressed against each other in her lap, and began to recite the words when Ayuluk stopped her. He reached over, gently separated her hands and with a smile on his lips he calmly said : "The old truck isn't worth that tension."

"You are right." She liked his witty remark. "It's only a very short part anyhow that I recall from the *Rebel of the Soul,* an old Egyptian papyrus. It is his own soul that implores the rebel not to take his life, the escape from grief and despair he is so frantically seeking—like the young people in Emomeguk."

His mind had wandered off as he stared through the windshield and repeated: "Yes, the young people in Emomeguk. They have started to think linear. Rushing to die before death comes is not a shortcut to eternity."

The words were now flowing spontaneously, as she recalled aloud what had become so much a part of her:

"Listen to me!
See, it is good for man to understand
how to follow the day and overcome despair.

157

As long as you burn
you belong to life.
Have you lived out your life to its conclusion
by extracting yourself from yourself?
Only through living
can the intellect reach the heart
and beyond become the haven
for the upstream struggle;
for above is exalted by below."

"When did you learn this by heart?" he seemed puzzled.

"As a very young girl."

"Your father, did he..."

Before he could complete his question she nodded almost imperceptibly. Ayuluk didn't seem to be surprised—as if he had expected it.

She had been carried away, and in her embarrassment she decided to leave before he would want to take off and ask her to get out of the car. Ayuluk, however, jumped out of the truck and came around to open the door for her:

"Let's go for a walk."

As she hesitated he quietly said: "Why are you resisting me? If it's urgent for you to get home, say so."

Without speaking they followed the narrow bank upstream, where local fishermen were busy, selling the last salmon of the season right from their boats to steamships from Korea and Japan. Noisy motorboats made waves and crashed with delight through the water, children were playing on the beach and like the hundreds of seagulls which plunged and swayed, they all enjoyed the late blue summer day.

They soon were outside of the village all by themselves and had found a short narrow strip without vegetation, a row boat, damaged and turned over, abandoned on the brown sand. As Vren sat down on the boat something truly peculiar took place. Ayuluk was standing behind her, pressing his chin against her head and a strange sensation, as if being lifted off the ground, spread throughout her body. Like a little white cloud she seemed to be floating with the river towards the Bering Sea and a feeling of great peace filled her heart.

Ayuluk sat down next to her and as if nothing had happened, they watched the dark river, meandering away from them toward the sea.

Ayuluk got up: "The flow of the water, like our presence, constantly escaping farther and farther into the distant past."

Aware that she never before had been at such ease with Ayuluk she couldn't resist to tease him: "A pretty linear observation."

He ignored her remark and pointed up river:

"Stand next to me and do not turn around. Only listen to the sound. It's our future, always vague and uncertain, but incessantly approaching us from behind and truly unknown, until it reaches us and creates the *now*."

A rock in the river, right in front of them, was ripping the current, setting the water free to bubble and sputter with spume and spray, before it continued to flow calmly on.

"That mysterious *now,* which constantly in a split second changes the future into past and secretly holds all the power and energy of life."

Ayuluk picked up a stick, drew two slightly overlapping circles in the wet sand and pointed to the small outlined area:

"It's our joined destiny for only a short while, where the unknown will always be linked to the known, may that be a missed plane or a can of motor oil, bought at a given time at a given store. It lived itself already in the beginning, long before awareness entered our hearts."

Ayuluk threw the stick in the river and in his typical manner to change a serious subject abruptly to a witty remark, he said:

"The point of departure may have been even prior to the sighting of that conspicuous polar bear in Munich in the zoo, a very real one and not a *makkiligaarok* , like the ten-legged monster of our neighbors in Barrow."

With no desire nor need to talk, they walked back to the cars. The sudden sight of her red Subaru, parked on the waterfront, unexpectedly shocked her. A reminder of the hard run of everyday reality with no room for dreaming. She again had not guarded herself against Ayuluk's power and yet she didn't feel vulnerable this time but trusted herself. No ambivalence was tearing her heart apart.

She picked up her groceries and new boots from his truck and climbed into her car. He had followed her and was leaning with his arms crossed in the open window on her side. Aware that he was watching her, she clumsily fumbled with her key in the ignition.

"Remember, there are things which are supposed to happen and they have their way of coming about," he said. "The futility of your resistance — you finally discovered it."

She got the motor running and self-consciously waved a quick good-bye....

Home in her driveway, Vren turned the engine off and sat back, her eyes roving the vast tundra. Its translucent beauty blended with her mood, redolent of the events of this late afternoon. Overcome by a sudden desire to walk toward the horizon she rushed into the house, changed her clothes, emptied the new rubber boots of the crumpled newspaper and grabbed her mosquito head net. The August sun would linger around to ten o'clock and that gave her more than an hour to roam about.

Walking in the stillness of the late sun, she relived her encounter with Ayuluk, as perplexing and intriguing as always. The magic of his power, however, did not dissolve this time. Instead it pervaded her whole being and gently carried her. Tonight the tundra appeared to her like a reflection of Ayuluk's inner self, big, bold and challenging, mysterious and impenetrable, yet wide open and consistent.

In harmony with herself she was humming her favorite French Suite by Bach and the melody evoked the voices of the slumbering tundra. She made her way through knee high, stirring grasses and fluffy white tassels of arctic cotton, around whispering alder bushes and over squeaking lush tussocks and listened to the cries of lonely birds.

Many times she had walked over the tundra but never that consciously aware of all the treasures, hidden in the mossy ground and beckoning to be seen. She couldn't resist taking home some colorful samples of orange fungus, white and black lichen, breaking a few twigs with delicate little green and yellow leaves of miniature plants and tasting berries from dark blue and gold and fire red clusters.

After the sun had bid farewell with a gleaning red stripe along the horizon, the boundless plane was swathed in purple. She placed her collection in a small plastic bag in the pocket of her wind jacket and was heading home.

Before she could artfully arrange and mount her samples on cardboard, she had to preserve them and press each one between absorbent newspaper. For days she hadn't bought the "Tundra Drums" and had to resort to the crumpled stuffing of her new boots, pages of old newspapers, which she rescued from the garbage can in the kitchen. Flattening them, she incidentally lit upon a column of obituaries and the photo of a man, a face that instantly transported her back into the past.

"Donald Rush, 55," she read, *"freelance writer of Arlington, Va., died April 7, 1981, in a fatal plane crash just off the coast of Nunivak Island."*—The red-haired patient from several years ago! Astounded and with a mixture of shock and incredulity she read on:

"Pilot Negmar Johnson, resident of Mekoryuk and owner of the Piper Cub, was also killed. Donald was a long time friend of his. The bodies have not been retrieved yet. Mark Chemugok and his family from Emomeguk will also remember him from his many visits to the Delta within the last ten years. There are no immediate survivors. Memorial service will be held in the Covenant Church of Mekoryuk"....

Vren's head was spinning and words she never had forgotten resounded with clarity: *"...You are wearing the tundra on your skin..... the tundra, a deadly longing..."*

Her mind was too stirred to concentrate on the collected samples. How much she wished to share her bewilderment with somebody, no, not really somebody, to be precise, with Ayuluk. Had he by any chance known this man?

Donald Rush had crashed on April 7. The date swirled in her head. With a strange premonition, she rushed to find her pocket calendar: It was that Tuesday Ayuluk and Thomas had taken her along to the seal hunt.

After a restless night with bits and pieces of bizarre dreams Vren carefully folded the ominous page of the old newspaper and put it in her jacket. It was wishful thinking to hope for the serendipity of running into Ayuluk. Several months might go by before they would see each other again. The times they had met were secretly linked to each other by an invisible law which defied ordinary logic. She could not just call him, as she would have done with anybody else....

Several weeks had passed. She was driving through town when a red truck passed her, a truck with a bent running board on the right side, like the corporation truck Ayuluk drove when in town. She felt her heart throbbing in excitement and followed the car, lost it temporarily but then saw it parked in front of the library.

With great expectations and the paper clipping of the obituary in her jacket she entered the building. It took only a minute to realize that Ayuluk had not been the driver.

As she was leaving, one of the few visitors to the library followed her to the car, a tall American man in his thirties, with glasses and a little black mustache. "Excuse me," he said. "In case you are driving in the direction of the hospital, could you give me a ride ? A physician advertised a Honda for sale."

"No problem, that's where I'm going too."

The young man was a newly employed high school teacher in Emomeguk. He had been hired a few months before the summer vacation started and enjoyed talking about his first impressions of village life. He had known Demian, was around when Simeon took his life, and was appalled by these two suicides.

"It's pure stupidity of these people to believe in a curse, a question of lacking intelligence."

"You haven't lived in the bush long enough to understand. It's more complex than that—not a question of intelligence."

"I don't agree...by the way, my name is Richard Bonner ..." They were walking into the hospital when he took the word again: "...and I can prove it. I had this exceptionally bright female student in her last year who plans to go to medical school. You should have heard her declare the curse as ridiculous. She is the best supporter of my opinion."

" Corine by any chance ?" Vren was quite certain.

"You know her ?"

"I agree, she is not only bright, she is determined and charming, too. Met her just recently." Vren was ready to part and get to her office but the teacher was all fired up to continue this conversation:

"You haven't introduced yourself. A physician, I assume? Well, I would be interested to hear what you think about the curse."

"Sorry, you are right,"she said and introduced herself. "Let's talk about this some other time. It's too important an issue, quite a complicated one with no easy answers."

"I am looking forward to following this up sometime, but believe me, it's the simple question of education and intelligence." A man who did not easily give up.

24

The scheduled bush plane to Russian Mission was leaving at noon. It would take two hours to reach this village that stretched itself along the west bank of the mighty Yukon river in the interior of the Delta. It was Saturday and Vren planned to stay over the weekend as a guest of Nelly, who had invited her for the Sunday morning service in their church of the Elevation of the Holy Cross. The occasion was a celebration in remembrance of the translation of Monk Herman, the first of the two Saints of Alaska.

Nellie eagerly waved when she picked her up at the air strip that afternoon. She was a stout Eskimo woman over fifty, solid in body and mind, and quite experienced as the health aide of that small Yup'ik settlement. Like almost all of the 175 villagers, she could boast of being a devout Russian Orthodox parishioner. During her monthly telephone consultations with her, Nellie had succeeded in relaying her religious enthusiasm long distance and Vren was well prepared.

On Sunday morning, under a clear blue sky, Vren hopped on Nellie's shiny red four wheeler and over rugged and bumpy territory they drove up to the little plywood church, high on the bluff above the village.

People, approaching from all directions, by foot or on ATVs, were called together by the fierce ringing of a mighty bell within a wooden scaffold outside of the church and operated by a heavy rope which led through a hole in the wall into the interior. The service had not started yet.

Through a very small narthex with plain white walls they entered the nave.

Forgetting for a moment to be in the subarctic, Vren was taken aback by the plentiful use of artificial flowers, but in the light of hundreds of candles, reflected in the abundance of golden tinsel, they had come to life. Their imperceptible breath fused with the benumbing incense and rose with the ardent prayers of worship up to the cupola. A moment of enchantment.

It was the first Russian Orthodox service she had attended. She watched Nellie light a candle and place it in a central chandelier, which an acolyte had lowered from the ceiling. She admired the ecclesiastical vestment of the Eskimo priest, Gabriel Gabriellof, as he passed by and then, among a few people not far from the North Deacon Door, she recognized Ayuluk.

She had not expected him here— and yet she was not surprised. The Russian who stood there against the wall with a black short tunic over his blue jeans, his glance fixed towards a distance beyond the open Royal Doors and the Sanctuary, beyond the altar, beyond the horizon of the tundra, the Russian, who perhaps was musing about years gone by, his childhood in Moscow and long lost secret dreams.

As the two-hour service progressed, the older people sat down in between but Ayuluk, the loner, remained standing. In her excitement to share this special place and time with him she secretly watched his every move. He was humming along with the congressional singing of the St. John Chrysostom Liturgy. Here and there he joined in with one of the hymns, all orderly sung in Yup'ik, Slovanik and English. But he did not participate by crossing himself when the Trinity was invoked nor would he prostrate or kiss an icon like the rest of the Eskimos.

Nellie had noticed that Vren was observing Ayuluk and she whispered: "An elder from Emomeguk, comes here once in a while. He never truly joins in—quite a self-reliant and demanding character."

It was then that Vren recalled her ambivalent feelings upon entering Ayuluk's study in March, as if trespassing what was only his, and she understood his distancing himself from the parish as an expression of his vital sense of self-definition. It was his way to maintain his independent integrity of being both an Eskimo and a Russian.

The long, stern service had come to an end and the mood abruptly changed to a noisy social event. Children laughed and giggled, parishioners kissed each other elaborately on both cheeks and Vren was not excluded. As she struggled to separate herself from the crowd she saw Ayuluk coming toward her. His stride was composed, his face serene, only the flicker of an eyelid betrayed his unspoken reaction to their surprise encounter.

Nellie wanted to introduce Vren and Ayuluk to each other, but he cut her off: "Not necessary, we know each other..." He sought Vren's eyes and added: "...know each other already for a long time."

The health aide looked puzzled, her eyes wandered back and forth between them, until she gave up trying to understand. As she offered

Vren a ride back to the village Ayuluk took over and said: "Why don't you go ahead, Nelly. Let me show her the remnants of the old log chapel first. To walk down later will be good for her."

Different from the bare tundra in the lower Delta, the bluff was covered with spruce trees which protectively surrounded the little church. Near the entrance an old, overturned metal garbage can, covered with moss, offered itself as a bench with a nostalgic view over the river, which loyally bordered the village.

"The place where I was born," Ayuluk said. "'Ikogmiut,' as my father always referred to 'The People of the Point.' He disliked the name Russian Mission like everything which reminded him of Russia. 'Ikogmiut on the Kvikhpak, the mighty river,' he used to say, this full-blooded Russian, who so desperately wanted to be a Yup'ik Eskimo."

Never before had Ayuluk shown that much eagerness to talk about himself. He who hardly ever disclosed his feelings and limited his words to an absolute minimum. Ayuluk pointed to a hill across the ravine, where something distinctly stood out like a wooden ruin. "The leftovers from 1851 of the first Russian Orthodox log chapel in the interior of Alaska. They call this old, but it really isn't, considering my mother's ancestors, who found this bluff as the only dry ground at the head of the Delta and used to live here for thousands of years. My mother, whom I hardly knew, didn't go to any church. In the olden days it was the shamans who took care of the people's needs, but today it's the Church and there are no authentic healers around any more."

Ayuluk had opened up and she cherished any bit of what he shared with her.

"When I was a child, they had already replaced that chapel with a truly beautiful cathedral, of course primitive compared to the Archangel Cathedral in Moscow, which is magnificent. But no services were held while I lived there because of the Communist regime; the building served only as a museum." Ayuluk paused for a moment. "But that was then and there. What counts is not the visible exterior of things and not the ritual, but the invisible, the spirit, the fervor, the devotion within the soul of people."

Vren glanced down on the tundra. The river was reflecting the sun of high noon and kept arriving from the Yukon mountains, had done so long before his ancestors settled here as the people of the point. Next to Ayuluk, past and present merged to a timeless space with only the moment to live, his memories and compassion for his people.

His mind was still dwelling in the past: "My father didn't care much about the Russian Orthodoxy. His rebellious soul was captured by the hard, adventurous life of the Yup'ik Eskimos and by the wide open expanse, the tundra, which never relinquished its spell on him."

'...*the tundra—a deadly longing...*'

Ayuluk's description of his father's dreams reminded her of the red-haired patient and his last words. Here was the unforeseen opportunity to show Ayuluk the announcement of the obituary, the paper clipping she had been carrying along in her jacket all these days. She hastily reached for the pocket, but no, she should not interrupt Ayuluk

"What is it?" he asked.

"Nothing really, something just came to my mind. It can wait."

"Wouldn't have popped up like that, if it could wait. It wants to be unearthed right now."

Embarrassed to have distracted him, she was putting it back into her pocket when he bent over to reach for the folded piece of paper and unfurled it on his knees. After only a flash at it, he quietly remarked: "Oh, I know, his last flight to Nunivak Island. A straying emperor goose --entangled in the propeller, they say."

"So you knew him!" Vren exclaimed.

"Used to come to Emomeguk every spring to go seal hunting with Mark Chemugok. Was a kind of clairvoyant, always correctly smelling where the seals were. The last few years he flew to Nunivak Island and stayed with Negmar Johnson in Mekoryuk. ....By the way, when did I see him the last time? Oh yeah, I think three years ago in spring, when Thomas came back from Edgecombe for his last year of high school in the village."

There was silence. And awkwardness for Vren. She suddenly couldn't bring herself to talk about her encounter with Donald Rush.

"Why did you cut this out?" Ayuluk was curious.

His elbows resting on his knees, head between two fists, Ayuluk was now bending the full weight of his attention to the details of her bizarre story. He did not immediately respond. He absentmindedly grabbed a small rock from the ground: "When exactly did you meet him?"

Vren did not have to think twice, it had been the year of her divorce. "Sometime in 1978."

"When precisely?" Ayuluk pushed.

Vren wasn't sure. Had it been afterwards? Yes, she remembered now, the city all in cherry blossoms. "In May," she said.

"That's when I talked to him for the last time.... He must have...."

Ayuluk interrupted himself, as though watching the many ravens circling over the village, and then with a peculiar expression in his voice he stated: "Psychotic or not, he did sense something your unconscious was only vaguely aware of. What better proof than your strange apprehension at that time. The invisible touching the visible."

"Like Christmas Eve,' she wanted to say, but didn't. She shuddered. She tried to recall how and when the far-fetched idea of her exotic travel plans had taken hold of her. During those weeks after her mysterious encounter with Donald Rush the word 'tundra' had assumed a magic meaning, mysteriously linked to the almost frightening intensity and suddenness of her intention to travel alone through Alaska that summer. And then the northern lights near the Brook Range and the particular poem of Robert Service with its hidden message, calling her two years later back to Alaska again.

"The blurred boundary of two realities... " Ayuluk's hands toyed with the rock,"...just a brief exposure to an alternate pattern and we are aghast... "

Everything around her suddenly changed, the contrast of dark and light in the landscape had melted away, a dull sun turned black shadows into gray, white coldness crept into her body. Transported to a different place and time, she shivered. A plane, plunging into the dark Bering Sea....

With the obituary in his hand Ayuluk stood up. His eyes came right on her, forcing Vren back to the presence: "Certainly, I remember..." his finger pointed at the date of the crash,"...you on the ice float taking off..." And without the slightest puzzlement he said: "His death on that day within a pattern of destiny we don't understand, a hint of fate. It defies logic and linear thinking—but not intuition."

Rattling and sputtering, two three-wheelers were coming up from the village and stopped conspicuously in front of them. The two older Eskimo men got off their vehicles and approached Ayuluk. They were elders on the board of the corporation and she remembered them well, remembered their adamant opposition to hiring her, a woman and outsider. She always had outlasted these hostile meetings. She fully accepted the validity of their opinion; outsiders *were* ignorant of the severe problems in the Delta. But she was learning daily and felt dedicated to her chosen work.

The two men seemed to confront Ayuluk with some matter she knew had to do with her employment. They talked in Yup'ik, their voices angry and irritated, one of them pointed twice at her. Continuing their hectic discussion Ayuluk walked away with them, leaving her like a scolded child behind. Rather than waiting for him, she returned to the church to give the Icon screen a closer look. A unique work of art, Nellie had said, preserved from the former cathedral.

She was about to enter when Ayuluk emerged from the distance and caught up with her. "I need to leave, only have a moment. You will make it back to the village in no time."

He moved closer and in a low voice he said: "And try not to think linear, to break down with questions the round of the whole, the mystery. It's more than all its parts. Don't puzzle about the few revealed to you. Separately they have no meaning."

The hostile interlude with the two elders and Ayuluk's abrupt departure brought her without mercy straight back to what he called her linear reality. She pulled herself together and from a sunlit summer day she entered the church, its interior without burning candles colorless and dull. The Nave, a few hours ago a place of devotion, had turned into a gloomy cave, the perpetual votive lamp into an inimically lurking eye of evil. The peeling plywood walls, in need of paint, disgusted her. The tinsel all over looked cheap, the dusty artificial flowers grotesque. A tenacious, moldy smell made her nauseated.

This was reality, the reality, like it or not, she had to live. Not the dream of blissful timelessness with Ayuluk. Not the illusion of the mysterious liminal twilight of synchronicity. What a painful transition.

Her constant hope to see Ayuluk again was nothing but wishful thinking, a dream too brittle to touch. With bitterness she wondered:

Would a next time be randomly on the river, ice fishing during deep winter, or perhaps not before next spring, when May with its mud streams would impede again her entrance to some community hall to join the antagonistic assembly of village elders?

An old, shriveled Eskimo man had entered the church. He rattled with his keys to lock the door and motioned her to leave. As she walked out into the open clouds cloaked the sun and darkened the horizon, foreboding a fierce thunderstorm.

She never saw the icon screen in detail.

25

Richard Bonner was looking forward to the beginning of the new school year next week. He was excited about the change in his life, from conventional Boston to an Eskimo village near the coast of the Bering Sea; instead of students "New England style," now seal-hunting Yup'ik Eskimo teenagers.

He had started his new position right after Christmas, the middle of the school year, because of the unforeseen resignation of an older teacher. Although it was an unusual situation for his senior students, Bonner had been able to lead them successfully to their graduation in spring.

He lived in a run-down bungalow, small and dark, provided by the school system and free of rent. Only the kitchen could boast of a window. He used its table as his desk and the cracked narrow desk in his sleeping quarter as a shelf for his clothes in lack of a closet.

He had been visiting other teachers all Sunday long and it was midnight now. Yet he felt no fatigue. He sat down at the kitchen table, sorting some teaching material for the next semester, when a sudden gust of wind rattled the open window. He looked up but was not surprised— the onset of one of those storms, most likely. It was fall, after all. Some old school newspapers caught his attention and he began to browse through them. His eye fell on the report of the graduation party in May and some citations of joking forecasts for the graduates. He randomly read what had been said about Corine, one of his favorite students: '...she who wants to become a wild scientist will be one of them to disappear and never again to be seen on the face of the earth!...'

The statement didn't strike him as funny at all. What was the background of a prediction like this.? Possibly the general preoccupation with that curse. Yes, thorough education was the only remedy for superstitions and beliefs in shamans. This primitive belief system had to stop.

That very second a sizzling lightning bolt exploded with crackling thunder and illuminated the tundra with a ghostly greenish light. Richard Bonner was startled. The walls of his bungalow squeaked. In the distance the pitifully howling of frightened dogs.

A second lightning and instant thunder clap followed. The kitchen turned dark. The power line of the village generator had been knocked out. Richard Bonner dropped the paper and, searching for a candle on a shelf overhead, he accidentally knocked over a glass, which instantly broke and cut his finger. He felt blood running down his hand.

A third lightning and another violent gale, the door to the bedroom burst open and he bumped against it. The teacher shuddered. What an ominous night.

A working television, any distraction would have been welcomed, this night just didn't render itself any longer for theoretical contemplations about the relationship between education and a shaman's curse.

* * *

"... And then... that green lightning flash and deafening thunder clap at once... the curse? ... the community hall dark... Was her mother not home?... and Andrew..." Cecilia choked on her incoherent words and broke into tears.

It was the Thursday after Vren's visit to Russian Mission. Cecilia sat in the patient chair of her office next to the desk. Her face was pale and she stared into the lap of her colorful *qaspeq*, crying. She had not returned on Monday as expected from an invitation to Emomeguk. 'Stayed for a funeral.' The secretary had taken the telephone message.

How fragile she looked, this girl of inexhaustible vitality!

"Stay with me, please. I need to talk." Cecilia reached for the little copper bowl on Vren's desk. She picked a sparkling piece of fool's gold and a blood stone, a polished, black hematite with a metallic luster. The two minerals moved back and forth from one hand to the other, until she put the pyrite back. She closed her right hand tight around the blood stone and it is Saturday evening for her again.

She is surrounded by the young people of the village, a party in the community hall. There is laughter and joking and good food. And after eleven their secret dreams for the future take shape, dancing wildly along with the crowd. One girl is already a famous doctor. Andrew, her boyfriend, is irritated. He teases Corine again and again, can't stop poking fun at her. What a brag-mouth she is. Nobody comes to her rescue. She says nothing and leaves. The party goes on without her. And then Andrew leaves too...

By now Vren knows with certainty what she does not want to know and she prays: Oh, God, let me be wrong, no, not her!

With shaky hands Cecilia reached for another blood stone and continued: "I suddenly felt weird and terribly afraid, something was really wrong." She once more turned inward: *I rush outside to find Corine, and then that howling wind, lashing the alder bushes, the tundra in wait for a thunderstorm to explode. It's pitch dark and I cannot see her. I call her name. No answer. I walk on, almost all the way to her house and faintly hear her holler: 'For heaven's sake, go back to the party.' I come closer, all the windows dark. I wait, I see the light come on. She must be home with her mother. I am relieved. Suddenly thunder and lightening all at once. I hear a shot and another one. In terror I stagger back tot eh community hall. I am wet to the skin. And then another flash, the electricity gone, the community hall dark, a foreboding silence. 'The curse!' somebody yells...All my friends disappear, sneak home....*

Cecilia's eyes were moist and her voice hardly audible, when she continued: "That night in my friend's house I couldn't sleep at all. And the next morning—the next morning—I knew it even before we were told. Corine had shot herself. Her mother found her in a puddle of blood outside the house."

Cecilia put the two black stones back into the copper bowl, got up and stood next to Vren's chair. Her voice trembled: " She missed the first time, it tore her arm apart and then... then ..."

Cecilia crumbled, unable to speak the words that were on her tongue, and wept. Vren pushed her chair away, got up to hold the shaking girl and gently helped her to sit down again.

Cecilia got a hold of herself and wiped her eyes. "How could she, in so much pain with only one arm, anchor a sixteen-gauge shotgun between her feet to shoot herself in the chest? And why? Why? Happy as she always was...No. I don't believe in the curse, I really don't and yet ..." She nervously shifted in her seat and mumbled: "Something scary is going on in that village, I tell you. At the funeral Andrew took a picture of Corine in the coffin, fainted and fell over the casket."

Cecilia started crying again, tears running down her cheeks And then a whisper: "He too,—the following night—he, too—shot himself." ....

175

That evening Vren took Cecilia home with her. Cecilia needed her and she needed Cecilia. Their company meant sheltering consolation for both. They were driving along the road when out of a subdued mood Cecilia broke the silence: "I can't comprehend that Corine isn't any more. I don't understand death. I am a Christian, but I don't believe in an afterlife. Maybe our souls return to something abstract without consciousness. I can't accept that either. When I die I want to remain Cecilia."

"Maybe you do."

"I don't believe in little angels."

"Neither do I, Cecilia. Yet, did you ever sing in a choir?"

"In my last high school year and I loved it, why?"

"What about the quality of the performance if you one night would have been absent?"

"No difference. It was an excellent choir."

"And all the times you did join in, did you cease to be Cecilia?"

"Never! "

"And you singing a solo wouldn't have been a choir."

There was a long pause before Cecilia responded: "I like the way you put it. I have to think about that."

As night descended and kindled thousands of lights high up above the sleeping tundra, they stood outside on the deck of Vren's house. Holding hands they wistfully sifted the star-lit sky for a reason. "Why, oh God, why?" Cecilia murmured.

And Vren found herself repeating Ayuluk's words: "It's only a separate part of Corine's destiny. Let us accept it and not question the mystery of the whole; it is more than its parts."

That moment a meteorite burned up in the atmosphere and slowly signed the nocturnal sky, its luminous tail blazing for a few seconds. Corine's soul had agreed and answered.

26

The chartered Cessna 182 was due to leave for Emomeguk in ten minutes. The airport, a small wooden building, complete with coffee shop and gift store, was buzzing with life. The majority of coming and going passengers were Eskimo who over the weekend had indulged in buying sprees in town. They were loaded with parcels, boxes and shopping nets full of fresh produce, heading home to any of the sixty villages spread over northwest Alaska.

Vren threaded herself through the crowd to the flight desk to meet the pilot and make sure he wasn't drunk. She had learned fast in the bush to be responsible for her own safety. An intoxicated pilot—it had happened twice since her arrival a year ago. Both times, a miserable situation. Should the one today not be sober, she just wouldn't fly. As always she carried in her knapsack her personal emergency locator transmitter, a device that would help rescue workers to find her if the plane crashed.

She hadn't reached the desk when somebody tapped her on the shoulder and a jeering voice asked: "Do I have the honor to be your pilot to Emomeguk?"

She turned around. No, this man was not drunk, but he was Conrad, the last pilot she wanted to fly with. She stared into his face: "I hope I'm not the only passenger."

"You are. Let's go," he said and dragged her by the arm to the runway.

If it hadn't been for the community meeting of several villages in reaction to the self-inflicted death of Corine and Andrew two weeks ago, she would have canceled her flight. Her absence, however, would have been misunderstood. Her input in the discussions was expected. Besides, her heart demanded to pay tribute to these two tragedies. There was also another motive, hiding like a frightened bird behind her reasoning, the chance to run into Ayuluk sooner than she had dared to hope. She needed to see him, hear his voice and disentangle her nagging feelings of ambivalence.

Conrad turned the propeller to prime the engine and helped her into the passenger seat. He took his jacket off, dumped it on the two only seats behind them and inquired: "How is Cecilia these days? Since you appeared in the bush I don't get to see much of her anymore."

Good news after all. She cared for Cecilia, for Thomas, and watched over them almost like a mother. They fastened their belts and within seconds were lifted off into the air.

The morning was too spectacular to waste any more thoughts on Conrad. The land had dropped below them, endless miles of tundra, dotted with hundreds of lakes, sparkling like golden coins, guiding her to Ayuluk.

Conrad flew at a low altitude, following the Yukon River towards the Bering Sea. Without binoculars she had spotted grazing moose and leaned hard at the window to see better when the door creaked and slowly opened.

"Conrad, the door!" she screamed.

"Good God, you scared me!" he shouted. "Control yourself! What's the big deal? Your seat belt is fastened. Pull the door in, please. It's an old plane, nothing to get exited about."

Her mistrust in Conrad instantly flared up again. She stiffened and swept her body to the left, not daring to move any more. Why did the flight take so long today? Emomeguk should have popped up already in the distance. She was counting the minutes when the engine started to sound rough and something splashed all over the windshield.

"Dammit, a fuel leak!" Conrad yelled, "I have to land right here and fix it."

The plane abruptly dropped, leveled out about fifty feet above the tundra and hardly cleared some spruce trees, the wings hopping and jerking. Conrad steered towards a lake and with only a few feet to spare, he swung around and settled to a bouncing landing.

Without any further explanation he climbed out, spit in his handkerchief and wiped the windshield clean. Vren followed him within seconds. Solid ground underneath her feet, what a wonderful, secure feeling. She had no desire to get back into the plane.

After some twenty minutes of futile attempts to fix whatever had to be fixed under the cowling, Conrad gave up.

"Get ready for a brisk walk, lady, just five miles or so to the village. I will even be a gentleman and carry your knapsack and sleeping bag."

Without rubber boots or head-nets they stumbled behind each other for more than two hours without a single word. It had rained during the night, the tundra was soaked, the hiking slow. They dragged themselves over the wobbly tussocks, their shoes sucked into the slimy bog, their feet blistered, muddy and wet, their faces swollen from the attacks of ferocious mosquitoes. The tundra had lost its charm, had turned into her enemy....

Vren was late and her appearance disheveled, her itching face sweaty, her shoes slushy and wet. Everybody looked up when she entered the community hall. Self-conscious and preoccupied with her physical appearance, she almost felt relieved rather than disappointed that Ayuluk was missing.

About twenty people, elders, native representatives of the corporation and health aides, were sitting around a long table, their discussions held in Yup'ik. They were preparing for the official meeting with the community, to begin the following day. Vren was supposed to report about her monthly overnight workshops in Bethel for suicide attempters from villages in the Delta. She pulled a chair up to join the group, but was purposely ignored . After a while somebody handed her a sheet, typed in English and signed by A. Z. The listed programs, like teleconferences, video showings, school workshops and regular meetings for parents, had all been initiated by Ayuluk.

Early afternoon several Americans arrived, two frumpy woman missionaries representing the *Assembly of God,* and a peevish looking gentleman, an official of the local government in Bethel. The dialogue had to change to a bilingual mode. The latent hostility of the assembly gradually came to the open. "...Her coming here is embarrassing..." somebody said, topped by another voice: "...Americans don't really understand, they only take our values away..."

There had always been different opinions, but never before had she been confronted by so much overt antagonism. She was not given a chance to contribute her recommendations or report about her work. And that was as well; today she was not going to force herself on anybody.

People were discussing now the two latest suicides. Two groups had formed and were fiercely arguing the nature of Corine's death. Did she perhaps not commit suicide at all and was murdered by her boyfriend, Andrew, who was jealous of her future career plans?

179

Somebody claimed to have seen her flirting repeatedly with a cousin of Andrew's and suspected unfaithfulness. May be she killed herself out of guilt?

Vren couldn't bear to hear any more speculations about the gruesome tragedy. Her feet were aching, her body tired and now this feeling of isolation. An unwanted outsider. She abruptly got up and departed. She walked over to the clinic, hoping to have left behind the gory details of Corine's death. But like evil little spirits they viciously kept flickering in her mind and obsessed her. The closure under a starry sky two weeks ago had been an illusion....

The office in the clinic was crowded with people. Vren went straight to the kitchen, where Theresa and a handsome little boy were playing with the husky.

"Welcome back to Emomeguk," the health aide greeted her. "You made it after all. How about the meeting, already over?"

" No, I just couldn't take any more."

"I like to play outside; can I?" the child interrupted.

"That's Andy from Kotlik, my sister's boy. I am baby-sitting today. Yes, Andy, go ahead." She handed the boy his wind jacket and turned to Vren, laughing: "What for heaven's sake happened to your face? Have a cup of tea and tell me."

"Nothing, just mosquitoes. But what's going on in the office? All these people?"

"Well, we had a busy day, too."

Vren had taken off her muddy shoes and sat down at the kitchen table opposite Theresa, slowly drinking her tea.

"There was a boating accident this morning," Theresa reported. "Two young guys from Emmonak disappeared. Several boats went out, but no luck. The elder Ayuluk flew up and down the coast and detected them from the air at a beach near Cape Romanof. These kids nowadays. Capsized and luckily made it ashore."

Vren pricked her ears. That was the reason for his absence at the community center this afternoon. "Thank heavens! No more tragedies," she sighed, still flooded with the horror of Corine's death, and haunted by a lovely face, distorted by agonizing pain, and an arm torn off and soaked in blood.

180

"They are all in there with Mary," Theresa pointed out. "The boys drenched, hypothermia. Will be okay."

The mother of one of the teenagers entered the kitchen and asked for tea. Theresa got up and poured her a cup, when out of nowhere a deep voice asked: "Can I have some too? "

Ayuluk stood in the door frame. Theresa helped him to a mug of fresh tea and made him sit with them on the table. Vren was still caught in her ruminations about Corine. He cocked his head at her and after a moment of eye contact he said: "You look sad. Is it Corine who is on your mind?"

His peculiar ability to instantly tune in with her thoughts had taken her by surprise. Avoiding his eyes she bent her head and nodded.

"We considered her safe; we both were wrong." he calmly said.

"You sent her to me. I feel guilty. Could I have prevented this tragedy?" she faltered.

"It's not guilt, it's helplessness you feel," he corrected her. "Acknowledge that, but don't dwell on it."

Vren was embarrassed.

"Lift your head and look at me," he forcefully demanded. "You need to let go of it and return to the here and now."

That moment Andy stormed in and took refuge between Theresa's knees. He stared at Ayuluk and asked: "Who are you?"

Briefly fixing his gaze at Vren, he responded: *"I am an Eskimo human being"*

"And who is she?" Andy pointed at Vren.

"A white woman human being!" Ayuluk teased the child. He walked over to Theresa, grabbed the boy and gently threw him into the air.

"And now you tell me who you are, little fellow."

"A little Eskimo human being!" the child giggled.

His hidden message, so characteristic for Ayuluk, worked wonders for her mood. He had not forgotten her hectic defense of Thomas after their emergency landing in spring.

Mary and the parents of the rescued teenagers came over to the kitchen. Ayuluk let Andy down and signaled Vren: "It's getting crowded in here. Let's make room for all these people. I'd like to show you where I learned to *see.*"

Vren didn't know what he meant, but she eagerly got up. Nothing could have healed her soul and body faster than this invitation. Ayuluk quietly observed her slip into what no longer could be recognized as walking shoes. Crusted by lumps of dry bog they looked like parts of the tundra itself. "*Mariayak, mariayak!* " he smiled. "You must have come by foot all the way from Bethel over the marshy tundra."

"Almost," Vren said, and told him cheerfully about her adventure with Conrad.

"Another few miles after that are nothing!" he joked.

Vren wouldn't even have minded the five miles back to the stranded plane.

"Let's go by my cabin first; an old pair of rubber boots will do. And a head net. Enough is enough—your face already had its share."

All her fatigue was gone. The short periods of time they had spent together since Christmas Eve suddenly didn't appear disconnected any longer. She felt light and happy.

27

They had left his cabin and were carefully choosing their way across the open rugged plane toward a sandy ridge in the distance. Not before frost turned the plants into a resistant crust would one walk over the tundra with ease again.

The community meeting was to begin the next morning, three days of tears and heartbreaking discussions, and it was good to get some detachment from it all for a few hours. The sky was deep blue and myriads of ice crystals had formed feathery cirrus clouds that were gradually growing into a delicate web. Vren was slowly sloshing along next to Ayuluk. He understood. She had to be exhausted after that torturous walk with the pilot this morning.

"Despite two pairs of socks, Thomas' boots are still plenty big for you." Her outfit amused him. She agreed and laughed. They were in total harmony with each other.

He liked her self-discipline and lack of complaints. Yet she was not impassive. He remembered her on the shelf ice in spring. And in the kitchen today he had immediately sensed her intense reaction to the fate of Corine. Toughness, a sign of strength, and sensitivity were no contradictions in her. The curious combination intrigued him. He repeatedly had caught himself in his desire to expose her vulnerability and have her trust him for protection.

They struggled over the uneven ground without talking, came to the ridge and climbed up to the top. Except for a few low brushes the place was barren and free of mosquitoes. Without their head nets they could freely see in all directions, even as far as the Bering Sea, which lined the western horizon like a glinting band. He had never shown this particular spot to anybody. Only Thomas knew about this favorite place of his childhood.

"This ridge," he said, "was my secret sanctuary before I was sent to Russia. It was here, where I was taught to *see*." Sitting on the ground next to her, he sifted the soft sand through his fingers and remembered aloud:

"My uncle, Agapick, used to say: 'As long as this means sand to you, you are only looking. Once you have learned to truly *see*, it will be a multitude of grains and each grain will show itself as unique and different.' Sometimes I had to look at an alder bush in the distance or at a pebble in his hand, until whatever it was would reveal its *inua* and speak to me."

Ayuluk wanted Vren to comprehend this with her heart. And so he shared with her the tale of the boy who lived with a bearded seal and taught him how it judged a hunter by his gaze. A gaze, endowed with this secret power, would make it quake under the force of his eyes. The boy could obtain this supernatural gift by learning to *see,* yet would lose it if he haphazardly wasted his sight on everything or looked at people indiscriminately.

"*Seeing* means more than to use the eyes; it means to focus the full attention of your whole being at something or somebody."

While he was talking, he watched her eyes follow the cirrus clouds on the sky slowly drifting apart. She now looked at him and said: "... and that forces us to live exclusively in the moment—is what you were going to say."

"That's all we are granted. Remember the rock in the river. But with our rational mind we tenaciously cling to this illusion of time."

" I don't agree." She vigorously shook her head. "Without time there would be no justification for hope."

Ayuluk recalled the occasions they had to part and her great vulnerability to separation. She still lived so linearly, measured importance by length and frequency and needed assurance of continuity. She didn't trust the simple fact that anything meaningful that ever happened was forever.

"...and there could not be any music either..." she interrupted his musing, "...that constant promise of something to come." The expression in her eyes was passionate, her voice full of challenge. "There is music everywhere, one only has to listen. When I am walking by myself, I hear the voices of the tundra like polyphonic melodies and it is always Johann Sebastian Bach who comes to life for me."

Her unexpected mention of Bach evoked the image of a woman in him, his grandmother in Moscow, who like Vren, had once associated the tundra with his music. Yes, those tender little musical games she had invented to help him overcome his homesickness for the Alaskan tundra!

But also bittersweet recollections were stirred by Vren's remark, recollections he purposely had never dwelt on. When his great expectations at his return from Russia were not met and he had felt disillusioned and lost, he would sit on this ridge, yearning to hear these preludes and fugues from the *Well Tempered Piano* again, to still the longing for his grandparents. He later came to resent this music, wanted to forget it forever. It had betrayed him, had not kept its promise to begin with and had tricked him a second time, by reversing his longing back to Russia. Ever since, music had meant seeking for something one could not have and therefore meant missing living in the moment. But that was then. Next to Vren suddenly all those melodies and rhythms clearly resounded in his ears; he could hear this music again, heard it without resentment all over the tundra, heard it for the first time pure and without longing. Her presence meant wordless validation of his entire being. She was music and movement and brought forth memories from long ago, memories of high expectations he had believed to be buried forever.

Their shadows had grown long and darkened the sand, when the most unusual sight unfolded: three huge suns, the center one surrounded by a large prismatic ring, were floating in unison along the horizon.

"The wonder of refraction," Ayuluk exclaimed as they were standing up, spellbound by this enchantment.

"Only once before in my life have I witnessed such a perfect parhelion," he reflected and now vividly recalled for Vren how he had been traveling as a child with his uncle to a neighborhood village. Agapick had suddenly stopped the dog sled, calling out to him:

'Ayuluk, see!' Three bleeding suns were slowly sinking from a wintry sky into a field of snow.

"A miracle—I absolutely was convinced—the spell of my uncle, the shaman." Ayuluk reminisced and with amusement he resumed: "I remember that I hesitantly asked whether this was the mysterious *qaumanec* I had heard about. And then my indescribable disappointment, when my uncle laughingly replied: 'I have nothing to do with the radiance of the three suns; this is nature's artwork, not mine, enjoy it. And forget about the *qaumanec*.'"

"A *qaumaneq*?" Vren asked.

He should not have mentioned that word and didn't understand why he did. "I'll tell you some other time," he said briskly. This had to suffice.

The phenomenon slowly dissolved and they decided to return to the village. The sun had sunk below the horizon and clouds, painted from underneath with purple and red, were bouncing off the filtered light, transforming the tundra into a golden, luminous plane.

As they stumbled down the ridge Ayuluk ceased talking. He still dwelled in his past. He appreciated Vren's ease with silence and that she asked no more questions, allowing him to remain immersed in his memories.

Yes, he later had asked his uncle once more to reveal the meaning of *a qaumaneq* to him. Ignoring his request the old man had only casually remarked that it was known all the way from the Yakoot Eskimos in Siberia to the Iglulirmiut in the Arctic. A child wouldn't be able to comprehend its significance.

His uncle then had gone into details about shamans, human beings, who had worked hard to free themselves at will from the prison of everyday life. An explanation he couldn't grasp at the time. Yet in his long life he had come to understand it because of his own experience and unrelenting mental toil. The *qaumaneq*, however, could also be an act of grace and he had been blessed to experience it once and unexpectedly in his deeply felt gratitude at the birth of Thomas. This event had changed his whole outlook on life.....

They had reached the dirt road and when they came to the wooden boardwalk which led to his cabin, he stopped and turned to Vren. Her question was still hanging in the air. He was overcome by the desire to take both her hands into his and initiate her into the nature of the *qaumaneq*. Instead he only looked into her eyes and his answer was short: "The *qaumaneq,* you asked, a mysterium tremendum."

Words would only amount to a hollow description of a phenomenon that defied explanations, for it was sacred and had to be personally lived to be understood.

And without words, like times before, they parted.

28

The Boeing 747 had left the Munich airport at 8:10 pm and was on its way to the United States. Restless in her window seat, she was trying in vain to fall asleep. She had attended a week-long international medical meeting and the highlights of sessions on existentialism and psychiatry were still swirling around in her mind.

Vren looked out of the window, attempting to make out the surface of the Atlantic, but thirty-two thousand feet above the planet homogeneous grayness had suspended the plane in a vacuum without any points of reference to time or place. If she were standing in the aisle with her eyes closed and not touching a seat, she wouldn't even have been able to tell the direction the plane was moving. Every single second she was somewhere else in this nowhere.

Observing the other passengers as they were reading, watching a movie, enjoying a glass of wine or dozing, she became aware of the many ways one could escape the puzzling insight of this extraordinary situation. Even a visit to the restroom helped reestablish a concrete, yet trivial, reality.

Many times in her life she had flown from continent to continent but this was the first time she consciously resisted those available distractions that kept the self safely attached to its surroundings. She was willing to let go and experience this distinctly existential loneliness.

Like a depression, this state of mind was frightening but also presented an opportunity to look at her own life from the outside while listening only to her inner self. Out of nowhere, the lonesome night in the foothills of the Brook Range several years ago suddenly came to life, that night when she had known with great clarity that she had to return to Alaska.

The tundra was her destiny and so was Ayuluk. How to explain to anybody the nature of this relationship, which was a mystery even to herself?

She slowly had learned to overcome her constant doubts and rely on that unshakable certainty deep in her heart, that certainty of Ayuluk's existence, regardless of where he was, and with no urgency to be physically close to him. But she wasn't a saint either and his abruptness had left her many times vulnerable beyond words.

After long hours, suspended in this self-chosen isolation, she increasingly grew disturbed. When she tried to recall her last visit to Emomeguk and what they had talked about, her memories were rather blurred. That mysteriously beautiful word that Ayuluk had avoided explaining to her had also slipped her mind. She found it difficult to project her self back into the reality of the bush and that scared her. The trip had begun to turn into an ordeal. She had lost all sense of time and place What she had purposely brought about, a sensation of floating in nothingness, had become a threat. She desperately needed to be anchored again, stand still on one spot and know where she was, to belong and smell the tundra, to look up and see thousands of stars flicker over her house. She finally drifted off into sleep. It was the announcement through the intercom that the plane was on its final descent that woke her up.

The miniature airport of Bethel had already fallen asleep. The ticket counters were abandoned and the coffee shop closed. Vren and the few other passengers of the late commuter plane from Anchorage grabbed their luggage at the conveyer belt and left the building. After twenty-two hours of travel she felt fatigue and that slight disorientation which comes with a time shift of ten hours.

She had been looking forward to her return so much but, oddly enough, it did not feel like being back at all. As if from high above she saw herself sleepwalking toward a red car and suddenly she knew herself to be only a visitor to an arbitrary reality. Slightly bewildered, she wondered how at the same time one could be the observer and the observed as well. This was not a new experience, it had happened before, but never so intense. Already as a child she would come home from a vacation and her bed, the toys, the kitchen, everything in her environment appeared different and only vaguely familiar.

By the time she had found her car she still felt confused, the strange illusion had hardly faded. She put her travel bag on the rear seat and was ready to drive home when she decided not to take the short cut on the dirt road across the tundra but to go by the clinic. She was curious to look through her mail, which Cecilia had offered to collect and leave on her desk.

188

Close to midnight the dry little town without bars and no movie theater was dark and dead. All public activities had ceased several hours ago. The barking of a lonely dog remained the only sign of life.

As she approached the clinic a faint flickering of light showed in the windows of her office. Curious rather than alarmed Vren rushed into the building and pushed the unlocked office door open. There was Cecilia, squatting in the dark on the floor, underneath the astronomy map on the wall, her left arm in a cast, a flashlight in her right hand, pointing at Vren. Cecilia was embarrassed: "To come here in the middle of the night." She clumsily got up. "I didn't expect you before tomorrow. You surely scared me."

"And you being here in the middle of the night. Who scared whom? I wonder." Vren chuckled and turned on the dim ceiling light.

"What's going on here, Cecilia? And what about your arm? "

"Just to see the star constellations glow in the dark."

Vren helped Cecilia to a chair. The young woman beamed:

" I am so happy, so extremely happy."

"Your arm, I don't get it. Too much input for me at once."

"It's broken, no big deal."

There was no doubt, Cecilia was elated. Vren got two Cokes from the vending machine in the hall, took her coat off and made herself comfortable in her chair. The comical aspect of this situation had temporarily centered her again and though extremely tired she had to hear Cecilia's story first, before she would leave for home: "What happened? Tell me, I can't even guess."

"Because of the arm it's all out into the open. No more Conrad." And without any transition Cecilia added: "I need to know where to get such a map!"

"Wait. I first want to hear the whole story."

Having finished her Coke, Cecilia positioned her cast on the arm rest again and sat back: "It was in mid-air, returning from Tununak, when Conrad asked me to marry him." She now sputtered out the dramatic events of last week in chronological order.

"...After a few days at home with my mother Conrad picked me up with his plane as a special favor. Hardly in the air, we immediately started fighting. His dealing with drugs, it irks me. I had to confront him, he got mad, terribly mad: 'You know nothing about those blue little bags, nothing, I dare you! Don't you ever talk to anybody about it."

Cecilia moved and shifted around in the chair to find a more comfortable position for her arm in the cast. "Blue bags," she continued. "I first was puzzled but then—don't you remember Stony River and that blue little something in Katsoo's sleeping bag? I got furious. Just before Bethel, I threatened him; he hit me. I tried to hit him back and fell over the wheel, he lost control or whatever, the engine started thudding, the plane trembled, was dragged down and there we were, a crash landing on the tundra, just a mile or so from the airport. His leg got hurt badly and so my arm, but I didn't feel anything, was in total shock. All I wanted was to get a hold of the emergency transmitter of the plane and contact the airport." Cecilia took a deep breath: "And then, yes, the rescue squad found us and I couldn't believe it, there was Thomas, more shaken up than I. Dragged me out of the plane, accompanied me to the hospital and... well, the broken arm was worth it to find out that I love him..."

"You were lucky, Cecilia, very lucky!"

"Yes, I am." With a grin they both acknowledged that they referred to something entirely different. Cecilia had nothing to say anymore. And Vren's fatigue was catching up with her again. They were ready to go home.

After Cecilia was gone one wall of the office yawned at Vren in emptiness. With no difficulty in guessing what Cecilia's interest in the astronomy map was all about, Vren had rolled it up to gently squeeze it under Cecilia's right arm while leaving.

A pile of mail on her desk waited to be sorted, but Vren was too tired. As she tried to stuff it all in her briefcase to take it home, she dropped some of the letters. The room was but dimly illuminated. She tried the switch for the ceiling light once more, when the only working bulb blew out with a click. Fortunately Cecilia had forgotten to take her flashlight along.

Vren randomly lit upon a purple envelope without a stamp, lying on the floor, which caught her attention. She sat down again and opened it. The handwriting, showing originality and depth, struck her as most remarkable. She quickly scanned the note:

"....was disappointed to have missed you. So I must have the courage to do it alone, to admit myself to the psychiatric hospital in Anchorage. I can't heal myself here in Emomeguk. With my father around, the escaped parts of myself won't come back. Sincerely, Leslie Oletuk."

Must be an unusual young girl, who admits herself, Vren thought and yawned. Purple stationary from Emomeguk. And myself sitting at midnight in a dark office with a flashlight in my hand. What a weird situation.

She put the flashlight down when its beam accidentally struck the mask and mute shadows began to quiver over her desk. There was something very different and uncanny about this mask tonight. Did her fatigue or possibly the meager light play tricks on her, that made the mask appear much closer, with every detail more outspoken? And the color of the mask, an iridescent purple, the color of sacredness. Why had she never been aware of that before?

—*You only looked, you never did see.*—The inua in the right eye of the wolf is fixed upon her with hypnotic intensity and is breathing, or is this her own breath?

—*I am mysterious.*—

Vren is sleepy and in a daze: "Mysterious? Like the word Ayuluk never explained?"

—*Step back and see me as I am longing to be seen. Now you are beginning to see, learning to see, like Ayuluk as a child on the ridge.*-

"You are talking to me."

—*I always did, but you never noticed.*—

Utterly mystified by what was going on and wondering whether she was really there, she again glanced at the mask, which now appeared so strikingly round: "You are round, perfectly round like the mud hole in Emomeguk."

—*Like time, like life itself, mysteriously round, holding in my circle life and death, heaven and earth.*—

"You are shifting. Why are you two circles now?"

—*To help you see, how destinies of human beings overlap and intersect.*—

"But your ellanguak are all bones, broken bones."

191

—Shaman bones of course. No break through without being broken first.—

"And that luminous brightness in your center."

—I am a window for the spirit to shine through.—

"Like Stuart's little window; I remember his diary."

—Small or large it does not matter, as long as the light shines through...—

The beam of the flashlight glared right into her face as she found herself with her head resting on her arms on the desk. For a split second she was confused. Was she still in Munich and had fallen asleep at the meeting and this was an usher's flashlight?

Bewitched by the dream still hanging over her, she rubbed her eyes and cautiously looked up, looked up to a timeless mask that no longer was involved with her. Dead tired, she reached for her briefcase and coat and left the office.

29

The colors of autumn had lasted into late September this year. Taking advantage of the good weather more older non-English speaking villagers than usual had come to the clinic and Cecilia's absence impeded the flow of the afternoon hours. She was volunteering in the town hall as an interpreter between state representatives and some village elder presidents. In addition the telephone had been ringing since noon. At Vren's request, Trooper Peter Lammert kept her informed about the search for two missing children. Volunteers in their private planes and a trooper were skimming the tundra around the town and the nearby village Kweethluk. The day before, twelve-year-old Alexa and her younger sister had left home without permission to go berry-picking and had not returned by evening. There was fear that they might have drowned in the river.

Late afternoon the last patient had left and Vren got ready to go home. Tonight she would visit her favorite hill on the tundra again and shake off all her disturbing feelings.

Ever since her return from Munich she experienced her environment as different and only slightly familiar. And now the two lost girls worried her. But what distressed her most was the paling of a memory. Had it been only several weeks ago that she witnessed with Ayuluk the three delirious suns, hovering over the horizon? The more she tried to pinpoint the details the more evanescent the memory became, like an elusive dream from long ago, hiding in the shadows of flickering lights and noisy sounds of the impressions she had brought back from abroad.

On her way to the car she saw two girls with a *yaaruin,* a story knife, carved out of driftwood. They were squatting on the ground and sketching their story into a flattened area of dried mud. She stopped to watch this old Yup'ik tradition for a moment and overheard the one girl telling her tale: "... and then the woman found herself on the road between the old house in town and the new one on the tundra but she had forgotten where she belonged..."

This was her, was how she felt. Strangely affected, Vren moved closer when the other girl stood up and started rapidly spinning around, exclaiming out of breath: "That's what she should do, try to make herself dizzy and by magic she will find herself on the tundra!"

Amused and wondering whether she should give it a try she walked up to her car and drove home. She entered the house and was immediately overcome by claustrophobia. The walls were closing in on her, the ceiling so low, she felt helplessly imprisoned. She had to get out into the open again. In a rush she tucked her wind jacket under the arm, put the rubber boots on and took off for that special little hill in the distance.

As so many times before, the two small spruce trees welcomed her to sit down between them. With all her might she longed to be part of the tundra again, let the place happen to her, but only menacing indifference emerged from the surrounding land that appeared colorless and dead.

The sudden purring noise of a plane interrupted the strangling silence around her. Relieved, she got up and saw two Piper Cubs approaching, flying low overhead. One swung around, banked and swooped down to land, now bumping along between the hummocks.

Convinced that she had been taken as one of the missing children, she made her way to the plane. The pilot had stepped out and was cutting through the tundra toward her. Little was she prepared for the surprise of discovering it was Ayuluk. Her heartbeat was suddenly throbbing in her ears. They exchanged rapid glances and he winked at her. "From the air, a dreamer on a pingo—I was curious,"

She was dazzled, didn't know how to respond and rather than saying nothing she asked: "What about the children, were they found?"

While walking back with Vren to the pingo he said: "They are safe—were safe with a bad conscience all through the night, hiding in somebody's empty house in Kweethluk."

They sat down on top of the hill and with that familiar stern scrutiny he looked into her eyes. "You are not really here—where can I find you?"

Vren was still struggling with that eerie illusion of being suspended in nothingness, observing her life from above. She wasn't sure herself where to be found at this moment.

"It's weird, between realities!" she responded and shared with him how she had purposely detached her self from the surrounding reality on the transatlantic flight.

194

"A difficult place to be," he agreed. "A strange solitude to experience one's true self which *does,* indeed, reside outside of all possible realities."

" It's lonely out there," she whispered.

"It is. To be that *alone,* to be this separated self and be *all one,* unattached to any reality."

"I desperately want to be back."

His eyes lit with momentary amusement: "So I sensed it right from the air: a lonely dreamer, who needs help to dream herself back to the here and now."

As he spoke he moved closer and without being touched she felt his embrace, an embrace of pure presence and so intense that she trembled. The sensation of aimlessly drifting through gray space rapidly ebbed away. She suddenly saw the light of autumn colors dancing along the horizon. She absorbed the last warmth of a late sun and smelled already in the air the early frost to come. The tundra was singing. Ayuluk had brought her back, she belonged again.

At peace at long last, Vren sat with Ayuluk in silence. The evening wind whispered through the needles of the spruce trees and the stunted birch, already barren, was swaying in melancholy.

"The last one." Vren pointed at the only leaf left at its branches. Luminous and transparent in its frail splendor it was still holding on to life, twisting and twirling on its delicate stem, its final dance with the wistful wind.

"It's waiting to be taken," Ayuluk mused, "that it may return to the earth completing its circle. It is *waiting* to be taken..."

A little leaf unexpectedly the reminder of senseless tragedies, a little leaf touching them in its vigilance to die.

Ayuluk was absentmindedly combing with his hand the sedge grasses around him. He suddenly focused on something and picked one stem. He critically examined it and handed Vren a long, slim blade that had curved itself 180 degrees and grown back into the stem:

"The secret of the eternal circle," he said."The twist, when the inside imperceptibly becomes the outside and the outside simultaneously turns in. The enigmatic transition from life to that other reality we call death."

A convoluted blade of grass embodying the mystery of the *Moebius strip*, the conundrum of death.

It had been death that brought them together in their stormy encounter at Christmas Eve and ever since had remained the silent participant in the unfolding of their destiny, their ride on a wave of life, demanding and inexorable in its stern beauty .

"Christmas Eve—you went home," Ayuluk suddenly said. An avowal, statement and question in one. The golden little leaf, how could it not have conjured up the same memories for them?

"I did..." she paused.

"And?..."

"... Sat at the kitchen window and looked at this pingo, moonlit and far away, remembering a little poem from long ago." And without hesitancy she told him about her lonely linden tree and the dark dreams of her father's.

"Let me hear that poem."

"It's in German."

"I like to hear it in German!"

With Ayuluk's encouragement the German words came to life and two Christmas Eves, though fifty years apart, melted into one memory:

Dort droben auf dem Berge
da steht ein Lindenbaum,
er neiget seine Zweige
and saeuselt wie im Traum.

Leis geht ein dunkles Rauschen
durch seine Blaetter hin.
Mir ist als muesst' ich lauschen
dem tief verborgnen Sinn.

Wenn wieder Stuerme toben
und oede Feld und Wald,

dann ist der Traum zerstoben.
der mir dort droben galt.*

After pondering for a while Ayuluk said: "I sense great sadness in those lines, the same—is it *Traurigkeit?*—you so early locked away in yourself, but that later gave you your strength and..." he smiled, "your courage to rebel— and quite successfully so at times."

The expression of serious attention had yielded to that familiar whimsical twinkle in his eyes: "No more danger of *stagnated circles.* Yes, Thomas will apply this spring to several universities and none of them is near Emomeguk."

He named several colleges and went to great length to point out to her with surprising details their advantages and shortcomings, an expansive way of talking, which wasn't his style at all. More than a tribute to her relentless support of Thomas, it was a clumsy attempt to send her a message from his heart.

When Ayuluk got up, Vren accompanied him the short distance to the Piper Cub. Just as they reached the plane, he stopped and bent down. Something had caught his attention. More talking to himself, he remarked softly: "The arctic terns—long gone already—back to Antarctica."

He turned the propeller and before he climbed into the cockpit, he met her eyes once more:

---

* On top of that blue mountain
there grows a linden tree,
caught in its swaying branches
an ancient melody.

And dark, mysterious voices
as if from far away
are begging me to listen
to what they have to say.

When storms again are raging
and battering the tree
my dreams like dead leaves scattered
will deeply sadden me.

"Open your hands," he said and dropped a white, immaculate little feather. "So small and precious. A bird of light rarely ever loses a feather in flight."

A purple cloud had split the setting sun into rays, diverging starlike against the fading blue of the sky. Holding the fragile treasure in her hand, she suddenly could recall the magic word again: *qaumaneq*! And she received it to remember it forever.

Ayuluk had taken off and she followed his plane, until it disappeared as a silvery speck in the radiant display of the sun.

30

The dead bird was a young raven. Vren was looking out of the window and recognized the black spot on the white snow on this gray November day. A young woman came up the steps to the clinic, stopped, lifted the bird up and placed it on the ground next to the stairs. Vren had to stretch her neck to see better what was happening. The woman looked around for something, then piled a few rocks on top of the bird and covered the little grave with snow. With that tender scene still on her mind she returned to her desk and finished the paperwork of today. All her morning consultations had been taken care of without Cecilia, who wouldn't be back from her advanced training course in Seattle before the end of the month.

Vren was ready for her noon break, when there was a knock at the door. The secretary announced the arrival of another patient, a new one from Emomeguk, and through the door walked the woman who just had buried a raven.

She appeared older than twenty, was tall and stunningly beautiful. Shiny black hair framed her pale face and dark, inquisitive eyes were scrutinizing Vren. She just had met Leslie Oletuk.

Leslie sat down next to Vren's desk and with great ease started talking: "I missed you when I came by here six weeks ago. But you got my note I left, I assume."

How articulate she was and how mature. Vren was impressed. Leslie was after all only seventeen years old.

"Actually I have no reason anymore to see you. It was Mary in Emomeguk who urged me to get a check up and a new prescription. But I have never taken any medicine."

Vren was puzzled and Leslie immediately picked it up:

"It must sound confusing to you. Let me explain. From my letter you know that I admitted myself to the hospital in Anchorage, while you were gone. They were good to me and I liked it there, but the medicine I was supposed to take, I always flushed down the toilet right away."

Before Vren could ask any question Leslie eagerly stated:

"To understand you would need to hear my whole story and that would take too long."

The young girl looked around in the room, and discovering the mask on the wall, quickly stood up and stared at it. "From Nunivak Island, isn't it?"

Vren nodded.

"Oh, I hated the legend about this island as a child. And still do. What kind of father forces his daughter to marry a dog, a dog, however, who had more heart than the old man, and swam with the girl on his back to the island. And their puppies, dogs, became the first inhabitants of Nunivak. What an ugly story."

Leslie's eyes were moist: "My father is even worse." She sat down again and cried softly.

"Tell me your whole story," Vren coaxed her. "We have all the time it needs."

Grateful for the encouragement the bright young girl guided Vren's mind back to Emomeguk. Vren sees the endless dirt road, has already entered the run-down shack, where Leslie lives, and hears thirteen younger siblings crying, those siblings Leslie has to take care of day and night. She feels the coldness of her mother, a harsh woman, full of hatred for her daughter, full of envy since she cannot compete with her daughter's intelligence and beauty, her unusual strength and wisdom at such a young age. Vren smells the cloud of alcohol hanging around the father, that choleric man who hollers orders all day long at every family member and guards an ugly secret of the past: Leslie was only a child, will she ever be able to forgive him?

Attending school is her legitimate daily escape from the parents and the challenge of school her only solace. As homework becomes more time-consuming with the years, her mother forces her to quit school and destroys her daughter's dream for the future. After all, there are thirteen little children to look after. And Leslie silently yields to the task.

But then one day, not that long ago, there are only eleven siblings left to care for. Lola, the very young step-aunt, whose mind is living in the twilight of insanity, has set fire to the house of Leslie's family next door and two little sisters burn to death in the flames of that macabre night.

Her soul is paralyzed and a few days later hardly registers another one of Lola's tantrums, the futile attempt to attack her with a knife.

Leslie cannot bear any more horror and feels with relief the most painful parts of her self splitting off. For weeks to come they keep calling her from far away, she can clearly hear their voices day and night. But she is numb, so numb, it does not even require courage, to grab one evening the whisky bottle from her father at supper time to prevent him from drinking. He gets violent and pushes her on the floor.

'Give me that bottle, you bitch,' he roars, 'or I will cut your head off and throw it to the dogs.' And Leslie offers him her table knife to do it. Nothing matters anymore.

How much she envies other youngsters in the village, particularly Thomas, a former classmate, whose father cares. What is left of her self collapses and an irresistible temptation fills her confused mind. Is this perhaps what the curse had whispered into the ears of all her friends, who took their lives? As the distant voices of her fractured self continue to haunt her she comes close to sacrificing herself....

Leslie was leaning back in her chair and after she had paused for a long while, she said simply: "But deep down I wanted to live and it was then that I reached out for help."

Tears ran down her cheeks. She slowly caught herself and reached for the copper bowl, taking one rock out after the other and arranging them in a circle on the desk.

"Is this real gold?" she asked, holding up a small piece of a glittering metallic mineral.

" No, not really; it's pyrite, called fool's gold."

Leslie mused: "Like the pills in the hospital I was supposed to take. But I was not a fool. I knew it was I who had to call all my parts back some day. No medicine could do this for me."

She put the minerals back into the bowl and her gaze turned inward: "If it hadn't been for Nora, who knows how long it would have taken me to get whole again."

She now told Vren about a girl three years younger than herself and from a village in the interior of the Delta.

"I saw Nora one day in the corridor of the hospital ward, one arm and one leg in a cast and so pale, no blood left after she miscarried. Her drunk boyfriend had beaten her up, hit her with a crowbar on the abdomen. Kept her locked in a room for three days and then shot himself in remorse to join his dead baby. Neighbors had to break the

door open and found her soaked in blood underneath his dead body."
Leslie shook herself as if to get rid of this image of horror.

"That evening after Nora had talked to me, I saw through the
window of my hospital room several geese circling in the sky, ready to
land any moment on one of the lawns in the city. I had learned from a
nurse that they are permanent residents of Anchorage and don't
migrate."

Leslie opened her folded hands, leaned back in the chair and
totally self-absorbed continued: "Strangely enough that thought had
made me happy and I vividly imagined that the geese were returning all
the parts of my self I had split off in my pain. I was ready to reclaim
them, every single one of them, because suddenly I knew I had a
mission in life to help others, to help Nora in her despair. What I felt
that night, how can I best describe it? Yes, I know, a 'happy
depression.'

Only with silence could Vren express her admiration for Leslie's
emotional bravery and strength. The young girl seemed to read Vren's
thoughts. A melancholy smile danced across her face: "You admire my
strength but I am weak too. I have to confess I am still jealous of
Thomas, who accompanied his father to Russia last week..."

"Russia?" Vren didn't want to believe her ears.

"Sorry, you couldn't know that." Leslie explained. "His father is
half Russian. There were problems with the transfer of an old
inheritance. I guess the money comes in handy for Thomas' college
plans."

For more than one hour Vren had relived with Leslie her painful
past, had inhabited Nora's life, when this unexpected mention of
Ayukuk's travel sent her reeling and transported her back with might
into her own life. Was she more angry than disappointed, that he hadn't
let her know? Utterly numb, she was shrinking into herself.

"Did I say something wrong?" Leslie asked.

Vren ignored the remark and quickly gathered herself. As she lit
upon a piece of fool's gold, left on the desk, she bent over to Leslie and
slipped it into her hand.

"A reminder of your next appointment in two weeks. No
medicine, I promise."

"I won't forget." Leslie was pleased, got up and waved good bye.

Alone in the office Vren took another piece of fool's gold from the bowl. She squeezed it hard until her hand was hurting and tears blurred her eyes. Ayuluk had gone to Russia without a word to her. It felt as if she would never see him again.

31

The hospital cafeteria had only one table for two and this was their favorite one. They were munching on their standard hamburger with French fries and onion rings and Cecilia, back from her workshop in Seattle, was bubbling over with excitement. She had never been outside of Alaska and was describing her impressions of the city and the courses and the new friends all at once.

Vren paid little attention. She was only burning to ask her one question, the one question she harbored in her mind since her encounter with Leslie.

When Cecilia came back from the counter with more French fries Vren made an effort to sound casual: "By the way, have you heard from Thomas? I understand he is in Russia."

She hardly had mentioned his name, when Cecilia's chin dropped: "I completely forgot. I was supposed to give you a little parcel from him, before he left. But the fellowship, you know, and the trip and everything, I just forgot."

She jokingly knelt down as if asking for forgiveness and mimicked contrition: "Mea culpa. I'll get it to you today."

Later that afternoon and between patients, Cecilia handed Vren what looked like a small book, neatly wrapped in blue paper. Vren couldn't even guess what it was. As she unpacked it, her heart started pounding. Bound in leather, worn by the years, she was holding Ayuluk's prayer book in her hands, the book that had accompanied him to Russia and later Thomas to boarding school. She hastily leafed through this collection of psalms and prayers when a few lines on the first page, handwritten in Yup'ik and signed with Ayuluk, caught her eyes.

Cecilia made no effort to hide her curiosity: "What did Thomas give you ?"

No, she wouldn't tell Cecilia that it was not from Thomas. She so much wished to be alone at this moment. Though she could not read the inscription she at least could have savored Ayuluk's handwriting and signature, she had never seen them before.

"I always wanted to borrow this prayer book from Thomas," she said. "It's written in Yup'ik; he knows my interest. Remember the framed handwriting samples of Helper Neck he gave you once?"

Cecilia looked perplexed. She couldn't make sense of that answer. How easy it would have been for Vren to ask her right now for a translation of Ayuluk's personal note. Her heart, however, told her differently. With pretended nonchalance and without any mention of Ayuluk, she asked: "When will Thomas be back?"

"He wasn't sure. His father had mentioned something to him about possibly having to stay over Christmas but that wouldn't bother me..."

More than once had they not seen each other for several months, but at least she always knew Ayuluk to be somewhere within the Delta, at the most two hours away by plane. But Russia was like another planet.

"Come to think of it, that would suit me fine," Cecilia said. "Remember Irma, the nurse from Arizona? She invited me for the holidays to Tucson. I really get to see the world now."

Cecilia had opened the door to the waiting room. Five more patients before she could study Ayuluk's writing.

It was already dark, when the last patient left. Vren opened the door to the waiting room and saw the secretary, putting her coat on to go home.

"Wait," Vren hollered and took the prayer book out of her briefcase. She quickly copied on a note pad the first two lines of what Ayuluk had written. Nobody would get to see and translate the whole text at once. The inscription was for her, for her only. She rushed out of the office and held the sheet under Ann's face: "Please, translate this for me."

"*Alussistuaq* stands for 'Christmas' and *taillruten* means: 'You came.' Doesn't make much sense to me." With this the Yupik lady buttoned her coat and was gone.

Back in her office Vren closed the door. She finally was alone. She moved the desk lamp closer, placed the book on her lap and opened it with great care to examine Ayuluk's penmanship in detail. The free floating rhythm and his energetic vertical stroke were beautiful to look at and his harmonious signature was the emblem of his personality par excellence. Headed by a large capital A the letters were natural and well balanced and expressed self-contained independence, a script within itself.

With more leisure she now looked through the whole book and discovered single Russian words, here and there even short sentences in English, scribbled all over in a child's handwriting. The signs of an eager young boy, studying those prayers for the sake of the Yup'ik language. Evidence of a lonely boy, dreaming of the Alaskan tundra on the Bering Sea.

She returned to the first page once more and let her fingers again and again move over his inscription, as if caressing his writing and being caressed by it at the same time. And it struck her, that she was holding a priceless treasure in her hands, witness to Ayuluk the child and the man.

But why would he give her this living memory of his Russian childhood? All kinds of doubt suddenly sprang up. What Leslie had coined a 'happy depression,' how accurate a description of her own emotions at this moment. May be he had found his trip to Moscow a good opportunity for a farewell note. By trying to decipher what he had written, she perhaps only fooled herself with false expectations.

Her morbid thoughts were interrupted, when somebody entered without knocking. The janitor wanted to empty the wastepaper basket. "Sorry, if I scared you, thought everybody was gone for today."

"You didn't. You came just in time to help me out." This was her opportunity for a translation of the third line!

While the Eskimo was putting a new lining into the basket she copied the words: *Elpet kenkengavnga* on a scrap of paper, handed it to him and asked for the meaning.

"No problem, it says: 'You cared.' Anything else?"

"No, that's all. Yup'ik is such a difficult language."

"Not for me," he laughed and left with the full plastic bag.

Vren felt slightly better, but the fact still remained that Ayuluk wouldn't be back by Christmas. Nor would Cecilia. And she remembered the dark, cold room of last year's Christmas Eve. Perhaps she should leave as well.

The more she considered a visit back to the East Coast the less city life appealed to her. Images emerged in her mind of anonymous crowds, filling shopping malls and populating subway stations, crowds, consisting of human beings, who would hide from each other and from themselves. With different hairdos, beards, make up, jewelry and clothes, by owning expensive cars or living in pretentious houses, they all did wear their individual masks to either conceal their true selves or pretend to be somebody else.

A sudden sensation, as if not being alone in the room, made her look up to the Yup'ik mask, which seemed to talk to her, conveying timeless truth to be perceived with one glance all at once and it struck her, that rather than disguising, a *"keggginaquq"* revealed itself.

And she knew she would not travel over Christmas. She would stay where she had chosen to belong, in the solitude of the wide open tundra. At peace with herself again, she decided to drive home, fix herself supper and learn Ayuluk's inscription by heart. Since she couldn't translate it all, she at least would be able to repeat it aloud in Yup'ik.

Not far from the hospital she noticed that she was low on gas. She stopped at Joe's Gas Station and the owner, a middle-aged Eskimo man, came out to help her. He was known for his almost flawless mastery of the English language. She would have him translate the fourth line of the text. While he was filling the tank of her car she read and repeated the words several times to herself.

"*Elpet agtullruarpenga*—what does that mean, Joe?" She asked as she paid.

"Are you learning Yup'ik or what?" He was amused.

"I try to translate a poem."

"You have touched me!" Joe giggled. "But actually you didn't. Why didn't you? Well, show me the whole poem. The words may be taken out of context and mean something else."

"No, no, they fit, it's all right. Thank you."

She swiftly drove off and right around the corner she stopped the car again. She couldn't wait until home to put together what she had learned: 'Christmas. You came. You cared. You have touched me...' And she imagined hearing Ayuluk's dark voice gently saying these words to her.

The two last lines were still untranslated and by the time she entered her house, she had decided to learn them first. She wasn't hungry at all, only eager to get command of these last words. She stood on the window and looked out into the silence of a bottomless night, repeating: "*Nepailnguq assiikaqa —Wangkugni*" over and over again.

The longer she listened to the words, the more they took on a life of their own. She could stretch them and they became the whistling winter wind, gently bend them and they sparkled like stars on the firmament. They sounded like sadness and joy all at once and stood for the secret bond between her and Ayuluk. No, she would not ever want them to be translated. They were to remain her secret treasure, like the part of a poem by Robert Service, which once in the Brook Range had emerged from the depth of the night.

Before she went to bed she took from a small, wooden box a little white feather, glued it next to Ayuluk's signature on the first page and named it 'qaumaneq.'

With the prayer book underneath her pillow, she was falling asleep, and the two last lines she just had learned were still on her lips, when the letters of the words began to separate and dance. They regrouped in her dream in endless new patterns and colorful designs around a center and became the mask in her office.

The words had created a three-dimensional masterpiece, that contained the hidden meaning of the two last lines. The magical mask and those impenetrable words had become each other and were all one.

32

The longest night of the year had passed; the tired sun of the shortest day, gleaming in murky red, was glued to the horizon and soon would sink behind the rim again. Christmas Eve in three more days, to be celebrated with friends and their children in her little red house. The traditional goose had already been ordered from Anchorage. A spruce tree in her living room was waiting to be decorated.

Early memories kept emerging like long forgotten fairy tales. The official festive opening of the door, ostentatiously locked for several days before, and then all at once the overwhelming splendor of innumerable burning candles, associated forever with the strong fragrance of a mighty spruce tree and the familiar melodies of Christmas songs, conjured up by her father on the piano.

And then those rare oranges. Imported and only available during the winter months, dangling from the branches of the tree, each one neatly wrapped in silk paper with an exotic picture of an Italian landscape. Vren remembered the impressive glittering star on the top and that delicate blown-glass strawberry, to her the two most precious of the old fashioned ornaments, handed down for several generations. Before she would open any of the gifts she always had looked as a child for this strawberry, usually concealed in the thicket of the lower branches. like a hidden promise of life secretly to be discovered....

Vren walked through the waiting room to her office, her mind preoccupied with preparations for Christmas Eve. She was late this morning because of some early telephone calls, made from home.

"What took you so long?" Ann was annoyed. She was sitting at her secretarial desk, shuffled away into a corner of the waiting room, and needed to express her disapproval. "Theresa from Emomeguk called, to be precise, three times already. Wants you to call back immediately."

Vren ignored Ann's grouchy mood and got to the phone. Three days before Christmas, it had to be an emergency. Ten minutes later she felt sick to her stomach. Henderson, a much younger brother of Mary, the older health aide, had shot himself. She had raised him like a mother for a few years before he left for Anchorage to study political science with the ambitious goal of becoming a senator one day.

"He happened to be visiting last fall, when Dennis blew his brains out. That's what actually finished him," Theresa said. "He never got over the sight of his friend's demolished face after the accident and hasn't come back to Emomeguk ever since. Mary is terribly upset and is asking for you. She trusts you so much since Doris died."

Theresa had brought her back to a merciless, harsh reality. Poor Mary, first her little daughter, who drowned last year and now Henderson. Could she truly be of any help to her? In any case she would fly up to the Bering Sea tomorrow with what little she had to offer.

* * *

"A day before Christmas Eve, bad timing for asking you to come." Theresa apologetically greeted her the next morning on the airstrip outside the village.

"And then that horrible weather drawing up." She pointed at the black horizon.

They walked up to the truck and soon were rattling along the main road with its perennial potholes and uneven cover of snow and ice. There wasn't much conversation going on between them. Only Aniu was barking here and there to chase some ravens off the road.

Theresa, usually quite talkative, didn't say much and Vren didn't want to press her. Henderson's suicide gave enough reason for her silence.

As Theresa stopped the truck in front of the clinic she said: "I'm embarrassed. You came actually for nothing. Mary is so unpredictable. She left already this morning for Anchorage to see her dead brother one more time before the funeral. I learned it too late to let you know."

Before Vren could respond Theresa exclaimed: "But there are several patients in the village I can call right away, who could benefit from your visit. Refills, you know, encouraging little chats and..."

"... so on and so on." Vren cut her off and laughed. "Don't feel responsible for Mary. She did the right thing."

Her hope to fly back that afternoon did not come true. More patients than expected showed up for consultation and it wasn't before evening that Vren and Theresa got a chance to talk with each other.

The wind was howling outside and it felt cozy to sit together at the kitchen table and drink hot tea. Theresa had brought some pita bread and smoked dog salmon, Vren contributed two apples and a chocolate bar.

While dipping a piece of salmon into seal oil Vren asked: "You knew Henderson?"

"Not very well. He was quite a bright youngster. According to Mary he lost interest in studying after Dennis' death. And then in June Simeon..."

"Simeon was also close to him ?"

"Was his best friend. Henderson must have felt completely destroyed, that's why he didn't come to the funeral and that's why he didn't attend classes any longer, Mary says. Three days ago he cried for help over the phone. His brother Tommy flew the same day to Anchorage to comfort him."

"And came too late?"

"No, it was the alcohol. Tommy called Mary from Anchorage yesterday and admitted that they had been drinking to cheer each other up before Henderson shot himself in the bathroom."

" It all started with Roxy," Vren sighed. "Eight young people from the same village and in such a short time, the victims of this obscure compulsion."

"No, nine, you forgot Terry."

"Who is Terry?"

"See! You, too, didn't know about her. After two years of boarding school she strangled herself this spring with her own hands behind the house of her parents ."

Vren had to put the piece of salmon back on her plate. She was not hungry anymore.

Outside the wind had gotten stronger and rattled the shutters. The light in the bulb was flickering, the barrack shaking. The windows were groaning in their hinges and some old boards of the building seemed to moan. The dark potency of the curse filled the room.

As the wind temporarily calmed down, Theresa continued: "Everybody in the village acted at that time as if Terry had never existed..."

"But why?"

The letter did it, found next to her body. Complaints and accusations."

"Accusations of what?"

"Lack of understanding among the older people of what it is like for a young person to be torn between two ways of living. But worst of all she mentioned the power of the curse, which she blamed for her urge to choke herself to death."

Vren felt numb and had nothing to say. To see in her mind the confused young girl kill herself in that gruesome way, rocked her to the core. All her dreaming memories of Christmas were silted under and suddenly so deep and far away.

Theresa's thoughts flowed on: "Because of guilt or fear or both, only a few people attended her funeral. The elder Ayuluk was one of them. It wasn't only the way she died that got him but the similarity with Roxy's situation. Both students ignored by the entire village, when they came home from college. He called in a meeting the next day and read that letter three times aloud, to shake up every last member of the community, a letter so similar to Roxy's note a year ago."

Theresa got up to pour them another cup of tea. She was leaning on the counter next to the burner when she stated with a voice of authority: "You met Ayuluk, I am aware of that, but you don't know him. He violently stands up for the truth and really gave it to the villagers this time. Being so outrageously direct isn't necessarily what he is liked for."

She sat down again, playfully reached for an apple and said with a sweet smile: "But I am fond of him. He, indeed, is different and has ideas of his own. Two years ago he came to the clinic to pick up some medicine for his wife and accidentally overheard Mary advising me to get married and find happiness. 'Happiness is not what marriage is about, Theresa,' he said. 'Marriage is only an invention of practicality.'"

Theresa chuckled. She reached for the chocolate bar and now, in a more relaxed mood, talked about his wife: "She was perfect, any Yup'ik man had to envy him for her. She made the best mukluks in the lower Delta and was famous for her fur decorated parkas of caribou hide. She was good at everything, skinning seals, smoking salmon, hunting for ptarmigan eggs, picking berries, you name it."

While she munched on her chocolate she mused: "But he must have sought something else in a woman, I suppose. Maybe because of his Russian blood. Too bad that she suffered from depressed moods. Tomorrow it will be a year that she took her life. Must be lonely for him now. But then again he was always a loner."

"Even as a child," Vren almost said, but didn't. Theresa had stirred her feelings, she hardly could bear it. Irrational fears for his life sneaked into her thinking, her helplessness to protect him overwhelmed her. By preparing for her party at Christmas Eve she been convinced to have all her emotions under control and now she wasn't so sure any more.

Theresa had walked over to the window: "It 's snowing hard. I better take off. You need your sleep too. And don't count on a plane tomorrow, it looks real bad out there."

Theresa woke Aniu, who had fallen asleep under the table, then put her boots on and slipped into her parka. She needed Vren's help to get out of the barrack for a relentless wind was assaulting the clinic from outside. Together they leaned against the door with all their might and succeeded in opening it just enough for Theresa and Aniu to quickly squeeze themselves through. Theresa and the dog immediately disappeared in the fierce snow squall. Vren couldn't even see them take off in the truck.

Vren's heart was in turmoil when she retired on the small cot in the kitchen. The wind was shouting over the tundra and whistling around the barrack. The dim, shaky kitchen light threw eerie shadows against the wall. She suddenly felt very alone. Thoughts, questions and images were hurtling by in a chaotic flood.

The horrid picture of a young girl, choking herself to death, glared in her mind again. What had Ayuluk called the curse, a negative prayer? Oh, yes, the Yup'ik prayer book with Ayuluk's inscription, did she take it along in her knapsack? And was it only a year ago that Christmas Eve, when she studied his beautiful parka in detail, as he lay over the table, that parka of white caribou hide, his skillful wife had made for him and he was certainly wearing right now in Moscow? And then his wife who took her life that day like her own father, the day the blown- glass strawberry was accidentally dropped and shattered into pieces, as if aware of what was to come: no tree to decorate, no

Christmas Eve. No, there would be no strawberry on her little tree tomorrow night at the party, a party which was unlikely to be, because of the weather and no plane to bring her home in time. How easily unexpected obstacles could interfere with one's plans and more so if one was far away in a foreign country like Ayuluk.

Vren had cuddled up in her sleeping bag and stared at the same old cracks in the ceiling she had studied after her first visit to Ayuluk's cabin in March. To escape the torture of her splintered thoughts she compulsively tried with her eyes to disentangle those crooked lines and make sense of them. Everything was better than thinking about the curse and Ayuluk in Russia.

Overtired and emotionally exhausted, all her worries slowly floated away. Only one fear threatened not to be quiet and caused her a restless sleep: What if something did happen to Ayuluk in Russia?....

It was pitch dark when she woke up the next morning and she needed her flashlight to decipher the time on her wristwatch. It was not quite six o'clock and not before noon would it get light. She looked out of the window; it was still snowing. Rolling up her sleeping bag as if it mattered, she wondered how she ever would get home. She felt irritated and disappointed, knowing that no plane would come this morning. She was hardly dressed and just putting on one boot when she heard Theresa and Aniu enter the clinic.

"Hope you got some sleep. What a night! And the storm still going." Theresa was busy shaking off the snow from her head and shoulders and Aniu ran in circles around and around in the kitchen.

"Look at that nutty dog. Aniu is crazy about snow, that's why he got that name, means snow in Yup'ik. I'd better let him out."

She opened the door for him, when he snatched Vren's other boot and was gone. Theresa went right after him and returned five minutes later, covered with snow again, but without the shoe. "Don't be concerned, I know Aniu, he will be back with your sorrel."

Vren had already surrendered to her lot. There was nothing anybody could do about the weather. And her boot, well, she had to trust Theresa's optimism.

The health aide had taken off her coat and opened a bag she had brought. "Look what my mother gave me. It's for you, cookies she

216

baked for the holidays. Let's have some with a cup of coffee for a change rather than tea."

Vren hopped up to the counter and was sitting next to the electric coffee pot, dangling with her feet. One dressed in a white wool sock, the other hiding in a strange hybrid boot, half sorrel, half mukluk.

Theresa was pouring hot coffee into the mugs, when somebody pushed the door open to the clinic and Vren hears a familiar, oh so familiar voice holler:

"Guess what I found !"

With his snow-covered parka Ayuluk stands already in the kitchen, the missing boot, dripping wet, in his hand. His eyes stay on Vren's face. In total disbelief she shudders.

"I thought you were in Russia!" Theresa exclaimed

"Indeed, I was. Back now for two days already. Everything worked out faster than expected."

Theresa reached for a third mug on the cupboard and whispered into Vren's ear: "Don't mention Henderson. He will learn soon enough." She filled the mug and gave it to him. He put it down on the table,

" That strange boot, how could I not have recognized it on the spot." Ayuluk took his parka off and shook it. "The big husky raced me on my way to check the conditions of the airstrip and dropped it right in front of the snowmobile."

Vren hops down from the counter. He walks toward her and hands her the boot:

"To make you symmetrical again," he laughs.

They stand close to each other. The words he really wants to say and would never say aloud, are leaping into his eyes and gently caress her.

She burns to ask and tell him so many things at once, but most of all she wants to thank him for the prayer book. She is ready to put into words how much his inscription means to her, when he says:

"Don't!" His eyes don't leave her face: *"Nepailnguq assikaqa — wangkugni."*

Moving her lips, she has whispered the words with him, the words of these two lines she has repeated so many times. His intuitive reading of her has rendered ordinary words between them unnecessary.

Theresa motioned them over to the kitchen table. She was too upset to offer Ayuluk her mother's cookies. "What do you mean: '*I like the quiet between us.*' You are a strange man, Ayuluk."

Here it was, the translation Vren didn't want to know and didn't need to, for what they conveyed had lived already deep in her heart and stood mysteriously for their secret relationship.

"Love your own quietness as much as you desire." Theresa voice was agitated, "but this woman needs to be talked to. She urgently must get back to Bethel, has already wasted one day here, is stuck now for the second day."

"Nothing she does is ever wasted and she isn't stuck for a second day either!" Ayuluk dryly remarked. "Planes are flying from St. Mary's according to schedule."

He gave Vren a signal and said: "Canceled planes, part of destiny, there are things which are supposed to happen and they have their way to come about. I just returned in time."

"In time for what?" Theresa was irritated.

"To give her a ride to St. Mary's."

"You are out of your mind," Theresa's irritation was growing. "Only two days home and then a five-hour snowmobile ride in a storm like this. You'd better think it over."

Vren could predict his reaction: There was nothing to think over for Ayuluk. In his decisive way he was determined to carry out his plan. He needed nobody's approval, nor would have any disapproval derailed him from his intention. He hadn't even asked Vren. She knew that he knew how she felt. A snowmobile ride with Ayuluk early in the morning, the day of Christmas Eve, her very first snowmobile ride ever. Whether she would catch the plane at St. Mary's and be in time home for the party, was of no importance any longer.

"The worst may be over," he said with a relaxed voice. "According to the radio the weather will clear up later."

Theresa pushed the cookies over to Vren: "You'd better stay here another day. You don't know what it's like on a snowmobile in such a storm and with him, who is tougher than seal skin."

"She is to go home, Theresa." Simple words, which affected her strangely the way he had put them.

Ayuluk finished his coffee and got up. "To catch the flight at noon we have to take off now. But put on your lost boot. I don't give a woman with only one boot a ride in the winter."

Had she lived this moment before, riding on a snowmobile with only one shoe? The sudden image is too elusive and she can't hold it. Disoriented for a brief instant she is only vaguely aware of what Ayuluk is saying:

"Wait here, I'll drive over to my cabin and get you one of Thomas' parkas. One can never be dressed too warmly on a snowmobile."

33

Ayuluk had returned from his cabin with Thomas' heavy sealskin parka. They bid farewell to Theresa, who stood in the open door, shaking her head, while he helped Vren get on the back seat of the snowmobile.

The wind had ceased temporarily and amidst big, lazy snowflakes Ayuluk cut across the dirt road onto the tundra toward the Yukon River. The storm appeared to have calmed down. As soon as the village was out of sight he turned halfway around to Vren:

"We will cut the bend of the river and follow the land trail for a while until we reach the river again."

Vren was dressed warmly. She felt comfortable and the block of blackness before her, Ayuluk's body, conveyed concentrated force, meant utter security. They were gliding silently over the frozen darkness of the tundra, the crunch of trackless snow underneath the only sound. How much she hoped with her innermost being to miss the plane, to miss any plane, and timelessly ride on forever behind Ayuluk, this man with whom she shared that secret bond of destiny.

With great resolve he picked his way between alder bushes, covered with hoarfrost, around and across frozen little thaw lakes, trusting the beam of the snowmobile lamp to guide him. He drove on with a steady speed until he had reached the river again. As he traversed the ice to get to the center, there was a sudden squall and the snowmobile started shaking. A blustering flurry had changed everything around them into an indistinguishable whiteness. Flakes were stinging Vren's face; she turned and twisted on her seat and tried to lower her head. Her eyes were swimming, tears frozen and crusting her skin. Gusts of wind from the north lashed her back.

Ayuluk stopped the engine. He got off the snowmobile, struggled back and was standing behind Vren. Ignoring the new onset of the storm he took her hood down; snow fell on her face and the ferocious wind, hissing sharply in two tones, pulled and disheveled her hair. While pressing his chin onto her head, Ayuluk's hands moved slowly down her shoulders and their touch spread throughout her body. His power had taken possession of her.

The river ice suddenly glared in purple light and thousands of iridescent snowflakes tossed around in a fury. Ayuluk bent over; she trembled trying to comprehend what was happening and heard his hypnotic voice whispering into her ear:

"Wind whistling in two tones, snowflakes glowing in the dark! A special time for legend let loose. Hear the beat of his wings above that of your own heart. *Negaqvaq* in command. The Spirit of the Northwind, testing your endurance. Don't resist!"

He fastened her hood again, climbed back on the snowmobile and as if impassive to the frenzy of the storm, beat his way southward, following the frozen river.

The power of his spoken words evoked the somber suggestion. Eerie noises filled the darkness. A deafening roar overhead. The moaning and shrieking of the river ice underneath.

Cold shivers ran through Vren's body, snaked into her limbs, stiffened them and numbed her brain. She couldn't think clearly anymore. Her endurance, why was it tested? And why was she not to resist? No, he couldn't have meant to give up, to give in; acceptance, was what his words had signified. But acceptance of what?

The treacherous wind, charged with heavy blowing snow, impeded the visibility. Yet Ayuluk rushed on over the ice that swayed and cracked under the snowmobile. Whenever he had to detour around one of the huge hardened drifts, his driving became unsteady and archaic icy critters jumped up from the frozen ground, whipping her trembling body without mercy. What was she fated for?

Ayuluk had slowed down and was driving close to the bank, trying to find his way back onto the tundra between the overflow of ice. He turned around, and fighting a fresh gale, he shouted:

"Another serpentine bend of the river we will abridge. Very rough territory! Put your hands into the side pockets of my parka and tightly hold on to me."

The ride had become very bumpy. In trying to avoid unexpected obstacles, Ayuluk constantly changed direction. She couldn't tell any more where they were going. Lumps of ice had formed beneath the soles of her mukluks. Her head was buzzing from the cold and with Ayuluk's frequent turns the relentless blowing of the wind attacked her from all sides.

She had lost all sense of time. Had they been traveling for several hours or a whole night? Where were they going?

"Back to the beginning, always only home."

Did her heart whisper these words or was it Ayuluk's voice reverberating in the air?

Branches of alder bushes, tossing wildly around, tore off her hood and brushed her cheeks. The biting cold shredded her face to ribbons. She suddenly felt most vulnerable and like a child she was holding on to him, he who bore the brunt of the storm and had to defy its onslaught.

Ayuluk had returned to a section of the river that the violent wind had swept free of snow. On black ice with twirling streamers moving fast ahead of the snowmobile, they seemed to be flying over the polished surface.

Has she not been sitting once before behind the back of an Eskimo, taking off straight into the racing wind? The unyielding assault of the elements has altered her perceptions, has melded dream and reality; her memory is obscure and broken into a multitude of images. The rumbling of rhythmic clatter, the flapping of wings in the air—she unsuspecting and vulnerable—suddenly present a creature of legend, *Negaqvaq*, he who has dropped her on this seat of a snowmobile and chases her with a vengeance.

Startled ravens are shrieking: let go, let go! He dives—no, do not dare— she is tottering on her seat and stoops her head—he plunges and bites into her neck. Her world is disintegrating. In utmost terror she screams but no one hears her, the body in front no longer means permanence and protection, is just the shadow of an impervious rock, her heart feels like a stone. Utterly lonely and numb she will have to ride forever through grayness, biting cold and blistering winds. A long, long journey from delight through horror to nothingness. With no resistance left she is yielding to whatever awaits her.

Ayuluk has dismounted the snowmobile and is standing next to her. It is still dark but the storm has abated. The wind has changed the direction, black clouds are scudding frantically across the sky and here and there a timid star reluctantly peeks through. Benumbed and disoriented she is awakening from a nightmare .

"The weather is clearing up, we are almost there." The words come from far away. Ayuluk smoothly moves her to the front of the seat to protect her with his body from the wind behind. He reaches into an inside pocket of his parka, unwraps the foil of two chocolate cubes and gently slips one between her lips. On the brink of tears, incapable to form a sentence, she scrapes for words: "The grocery store, Munich, these candies!"

With tenderness Ayuluk crosses her arms against her chest and covering them with his arms, he tightly holds her onto his body. Sheltered by his embrace she breaks into tears, crying bitterly, releasing the pent-up emotions from the gruesome ordeal of the blizzard and reclaiming the sadness she so proudly had banished from her entire life.

The wind has died and white silence fallen around them. The sun still hides behind the rim and yet, one gleaming beam has zealously escaped. It vertically pierces the twilight of the early sky and intersects with the horizontal section of a partial parhelion. With both hands Ayuluk ever so gently lifts her chin and points to the horizon. A miracle is born: In dreamlike translucence the *Arctic Cross* radiantly hovers over rose-colored snow, elusive, holy, unspeakably rare. Oh, remembrance of young lives, sacrificed and lost. Oh, all encompassing glory, the vibrance of the golden glow attesting to her unspoken communion with Ayuluk. Her entire self is shaken, she hardly dares to breathe. In the bliss of pure existence all the moments they inhabited together during this year, all her times alone on the tundra, have fused and are inseparably intertwined with the joy and sorrow of all mankind, the mysterious unity of life. He is still holding her and she knows her circle is completed, she has returned to a point Ayuluk never left. At long last she is home....

Ayuluk switched to the front of the seat again to drive the remaining distance from the river to St. Marie's runway. The plane to Bethel was leaving in half an hour and he had to rush. So many times they had been together in silence but never on a snowmobile. She had not put her hands back into the pockets of his parka but he felt her arms holding on to his body. He wouldn't mind to travel on for ever. A temptation briefly sneaked into his mind to slow down and purposely miss her flight. But things had to happen by themselves, couldn't be forced, had to happen naturally, like last year's Christmas Eve and this early morning ride through a relentless storm, two events that now appeared to him superimposed and simultaneous. Past and present had merged into one. He had those sensations before, that all life happens at once, and was convinced that time was an illusion, coming about in the attempt to grasp at the world with the rational mind.

They had found each other not as a Yup'ik Eskimo man with Russian ancestry and a German woman who had become a psychiatrist, but, stripped of all layers, as nothing other than simply two human beings, regardless of heritage and environment. This year, a year of invisible inner completion, was standing out against the rest of his entire life. And the insight struck him that he had always been waiting. In the world they lived in, a world of appearance, where nothing had permanence, a timeless presence, more powerful than love, had silently linked their solitudes....

St. Mary's was already in sight and it irritated him that he would have to wait for serendipity to meet her again. He caught himself thinking linearly, like a white man, and that annoyed him, but he couldn't help it. And again he puzzled what it was that had led her to the tundra on the Bering Sea, this distant place, only known to few.

It was noon when they arrived. He passed the little terminal and drove right up to the plane on the runway, which was ready to take off any minute. Helping Vren to get off the snowmobile he said:

"No need to check in at the desk, step right in, the pilot can take care of it. It's a Super Caravan with plenty of room, twelve seats and usually only a few taken."

She dismounted the snowmobile and opened her knapsack, looking for something. He saw her with one foot on the running board and, using her knee as support, scribbling on a piece of paper. She put the ballpoint into a pocket of Thomas' parka and said: "You get his parka back next time, when I come to Emomeguk and pick mine up in the clinic."

Ayuluk had walked around to the other side of the snowmobile to check how much gasoline was left, when she announced: "I still owe you an answer to a question of yours."

He, too, had pondered that question just a little while ago and marveled at her intuition.

" Indeed, I asked you twice and each time you did something outrageous afterwards. Remember?" He chuckled. In his mind's eye he saw her drifting away on an ice float and pictured her dragging Thomas' body through a widened gap in the rotten wall of a jail.

She innocently shrugged her shoulders, but the corners of her mouth were curling and betrayed her. Coming around the snowmobile, she handed him what she had written: "So that you won't forget!"

He could not lose any time by looking at it. The pilot had already signaled her to board. Wanting to hold her and never let her go again, he walked her to the plane. She stepped up the ladder and turned around. Her inner eyes were wide open and let him in. For no apparent reason a sudden disturbing unrest befell him and he quickly tried to brush it aside. Before the door to the cabin closed, she smiled and this radiant smile of hers set his mind at rest again.

What she had given him, he now came to recognize as a prescription pad with maybe fifty sheets, all with a printed Rx on it. He lit upon her writing on the top sheet and the back of his hand didn't wipe his eyes fast enough, two big tears had already wet her message: "*...since His loneliness is calling and He knows I must obey...*Robert Service." The only two letters H, capital letters, had been crossed out and replaced by the small letter h. And it felt to him as if these two lines had been written on every single one of the many.

He vaguely could make out her face behind one of the small windows and lifted both his arms, as the plane started taxiing along the runway for take off. With the prescription pad in his hand he slowly went back to his snowmobile. He did not turn around. He did not want to see the plane rise into the sky and take her away from him.

Getting ready for his return trip he stowed the pad away and found one chocolate cube accidentally left in that pocket. With a warm smile he imagined giving it to Vren next time they would meet. His eyes caressed the gleaming gold foil that wrapped the candy, and a little girl came to life, who peered through iron bars to watch a polar bear, while munching away at those candies her father had bought for her in the Munich zoo.

He put the little cube back into the pocket and took off into the white undulating plain, brimming with rime. The unique scene of Vren as a child was lingering on and he enjoyed it, when all of a sudden it began to blur and wrinkle like a mirrored reflection on the surface of water disturbed by a willfully thrown rock. A hidden force twirled everything around and sucked him into a delirious vertigo. In trying to regain the image, a powerful, alarming sensation took hold of him and for a few moments the essence of his being escaped his body....

The sputtering of the engine called him back and required his immediate attention. Disoriented and shaken, he looked around to see where he was and took possession of himself again. He stopped, got off the snowmobile and filled the tank from the reserve can.

For a second he fixed his gaze at the distant horizon and then checked his belongings. When he wistfully reached in the pocket that had harbored the candy, and found it empty, his dark premonition was confirmed. He knew with certainty now, what before he had only dreaded to comprehend. But human beings came with different callings to complete their own destiny, they bear within. There were things that had to happen and they had their way to come about.

Numbed by nameless grief he sat on the snowmobile and did not move; sat motionless for a long time, until his body suddenly jerked. He abruptly straightened up and looked at his wristwatch. He would not allow himself to be detached any longer from that reality, which had to be lived. The sky was clear. In less than five hours he could make it back to Emomeguk, where Thomas was waiting for him.

34

The plane had six seats on each side. After having her ticket checked by the pilot Vren took the last one on the right. She was hardly aware of the two other passengers for she was preoccupied with reliving the last few minutes with Ayuluk.

Before entering the plane she had turned around in the open door, had met his eyes, these eyes that always told her more than any words, and had detected in them a hidden concern she didn't know how to interpret.

From her seat she saw him raise both his arms and it struck her that she only once before had witnessed this gesture: that evening in April in her office when he met Thomas again, grateful that his son was alive. After acknowledging her note on the prescription pad, Ayuluk immediately had walked back to his snowmobile.

The plane now taxied along the runway, then stopped and turned around, which was unusual. For some reason the departure was delayed.

A lively little boy, about six years of age, with a fire red woolen cap, was sitting in front of her, his father had taken the seat across the aisle next to him. From what she could gather from their conversation, they were returning from a visit with the boy's grandmother and, loaded with gifts and food, they looked forward to be back in time to celebrate Christmas at home in Bethel.

The child had opened his seat belt and stood in the aisle, staring at her. "Look at me, Ma'am, look!" He demonstratively showed her his hands, "I don't wear gloves, I am tough. I never wear gloves! Why do you?" He made her laugh. According to him she was obviously a spoiled American, who was not used to the cold.

"Be quiet, Enok," the father said and motioned him to get back into his seat. The boy just could not sit still. When the pilot came out of the cockpit to apologize for the delay, he jumped up again and exclaimed: "But that's a woman, where is the pilot?"

"Sit down and fasten your seat belt, son." The father was annoyed.

Enok did as he was told but now started wiggling in his seat, shaking his head rapidly from left to right and fumbling with his arms in the air.

The plane taxied into the wind for a second time. Vren sat back and was relieved that they finally took off. Faster than ever it seemed to her that they were high up in the air when a terrible vibration seized the plane and shook it violently. She instantly understood the danger. Fear pierced her heart. The child screamed, his father threw up. Something pushed her with a tremendous impact back into her seat and she could not move. Everything around her faded away; close to fainting, she could not think straight anymore. Maybe she was not in a plane at all, she perhaps was just dreaming and the harsh encounter with the back of her seat was only a misconception. Whatever she leaned on was actually soft and warm and no longer a seat in an airplane but a human body. She was going to turn around, when a sound like the breathing of a rising wind filled the cabin and a deep, distinct voice instructed her:

"Don't! You wouldn't see me. Just trust."

She was utterly perplexed and didn't dare to look back. She fixed her gaze on Enok's cap which appeared alarmingly red. But how could she see his cap? He was only a child and the back of his seat so high. In fact it was not his cap at all. Utterly confused and disoriented she decided it was a traffic light and that frightened her. Did the pilot see it, too, and would she stop in time?

"Fear not!"

The same dark voice had addressed her again with great determination. She could not possibly be in a plane. There was no seat in back of her and yet somebody talked to her from behind. Now she understood, of course she was sitting on the snowmobile with Ayuluk behind her.

"Ayuluk?" she hesitantly asked. There was no answer. She had to turn around to find out and was shocked to see only nylon webbing securing the luggage. She was convinced she had lost her mind. Where was she, what had happened to her? It almost meant relief to see in front of her the red light again. As it got bigger and brighter it filled the whole interior of the plane and indescribably panic engulfed her.

"That light, that light," she stammered.

Two arms reached out from behind and a piece of chocolate began to melt in her mouth. She was firmly embraced as two strong hands folded with hers across her chest giving her assurance.

"Ayuluk?" Her voice trembled.

"You questioned it?"

She shuddered. Feeling his body behind her, she heard him calmly announce:

"Qaumaneq, qaumaneq, the light inside of you."

That very moment a lightning flash struck her and ignited the innermost core of her being. She had become light and it was radiating from her head and entire body. Outside of all times and limiting spaces, she could see, not only with her eyes but with her entire body, through the walls of the plane and in all directions, over endless miles of her beloved tundra, over spruce forests sprinkled with frozen lakes and ponds, over peopleless valleys and nameless mountains, to the cities of this world, as if the earth were one great plane. Reality had revealed itself as an ephemeral illusion in perpetual transition.

As she could see beyond the horizon she experienced her soul as part of the oneness that pervades all creation and her awareness expanded into being the newborn splendor of the white tundra, the tumbling mirth of summer clouds. She was the hardness of rocks and became the tears of Demian, the laughter of Cecilia. She lived in Ayuluk and Thomas and all the people who had touched her.

And yet she had remained the woman who was sitting in the last seat on the right side of a plane, that had taken off too steeply and would crash any moment.

With full force she suddenly was sharply slammed into the seat in front of her. She felt a chin gently pressed against her head and her body began to ascend higher and higher into the sky. Free of all fear in silent exuberance her heart was filled with illimitable peace and joy; she knew Ayuluk to be lifting her up to the stars.

The End